I COULD BE YOURS

NEW YORK TIMES BESTSELLING AUTHOR
HELENA HUNTING

I COULD BE YOURS CAST

NATHAN STILES
BEST MAN
MIDDLE BROTHER TO TRISTAN STILES (THE GROOM)

SIBLINGS
BRODY & TRISTAN
YOUNGER BROTHER   GROOM—OLDER BROTHER

PARENTS
GIDEON STILES

FRIENDS OF THE GROOM

FLIP MADDEN
FRIEND & TERROR TEAMMATE
BROTHER OF THE BRIDE

DALLAS BRIGHT
FRIEND & TERROR TEAMMATE
ENGAGED TO HEMI

ASHISH PALANIAPPA
FRIEND & TERROR TEAMMATE
HUSBAND TO SHILPA (TEAM LAWYER)

ROMAN FORREST-HAMMER
FRIEND & FORMER TERROR TEAMMATE
HUSBAND TO LEXI

CONNOR GRACE
FRIEND & TERROR TEAMMATE

HOLLIS HENDRIX
FRIEND &
FORMER TERROR TEAMMATE

ESSIE LOVELOCK
MAID OF HONOUR
BEST FRIEND TO RIX MADDEN (THE BRIDE)

SIBLINGS
CAMMIE

PARENTS
ATHENA & DEMETRIUS

BADASS BABE BRIGADE

BEATRIX MADDEN
(RIX, BEX)
ESSIE'S BESTIE
ENGAGED TO TRISTAN STILES
SISTER TO FLIP MADDEN

PEGGY AURORA HAMMERSTEIN
(PEGGY, AURORA, HAMMER, PRINCESS)
DAUGHTER TO ROMAN HAMMERSTEIN,
GIRLFRIEND TO HOLLIS HENDRIX

HEMI REDDI-GRINST
(HEMI, WILLS, HONEY)
BEST FRIEND TO SHILPA
ENGAGED TO DALLAS BRIGHT

TALLULAH VANDER ZEE
(TALLY/TALLS)
DAUGHTER OF TERROR COACH

SHILPA PALANIAPPA
(SHILPS)
BEST FRIEND TO HEMI
MARRIED TO ASHISH PALANIAPPA

MILDRED REFORMER
(DRED)
FRIEND TO ESSIE
PLATONIC FRIEND OF FLIP'S

ALEXANDRIA FORREST-HAMMER
(LEXI, ANGEL)
FRIEND TO ESSIE
PLATONIC FRIEND OF FLIP'S

ACKNOWLEDGMENTS

Husband and kidlet, I adore you. You inspire me every day and I'm so grateful for your love.

Deb, how have we been at this for so long? Thank you for always coming along for the ride.

Becca, thank you for making this journey such a joy.

Kimberly, thank you for finding an amazing home for the audio at Dreamscape.

Sarah, your organizational skills are legendary and I'm so grateful for you.

Victoria, thank you for sharing your creative energy with me, and for always sending the reminder texts.

Alpha-Betas your feedback is so greatly appreciated, thank you for being on my team.

BBB, thank you for sharing your creativity with me!

Catherine, Natasha, and Tricia, your kindness and wonderful energy are such a source of inspiration, thank you for your friendship.

Jessica, Erica, Amanda, Julia, and Sarah, thank you so much for working on this project with me. I couldn't do this without you.

Kate and Rae, thank you for being graphic gurus. Your incredible talent never ceases to amaze me.

Beavers, thank you for giving me a safe place to land, and for always being excited about what's next.

Kat & Krystin, your friendship means the world to me. Thank you for pulling me away from the keyboard to live life.

Readers, bloggers, bookstagrammers and booktokers, thank you for sharing your love of romance and happily ever afters.

For all fairytale lovers, the lovers of love, the hopeless romantics, and the underestimated.

CHAPTER 1

ESSIE

I snap several pictures, but the mirror doesn't allow me to fully capture the miles of poofy satin, tulle, and lace that make up this wildly ostentatious dress. My best friend, Rix, the bride-to-be, should be here any minute, and I want to give her a reason to smile. She's been stressing over every wedding detail lately. Tonight, we're having dinner to tick all the boxes on the upcoming bridal shower and the stag and doe. Rix is determined everything go smoothly, which is why I'm here ahead of her, checking on the dresses. I take my role of maid of honor seriously—most of the time anyway—but when I saw this dress, I couldn't resist trying it on.

The chime of the door signals her arrival. "Trixie Rixie, I have something amazing to show you!" I singsong as I grab a suit jacket from the rack. Me and my makeshift groom twirl into the viewing area, belting out the lyrics to our favorite slow-dance song from high school.

Except my best friend is not standing in the middle of the store. It's her soon-to-be brother-in-law, Nate Stiles. Looking wildly uncomfortable. And ungodly gorgeous. And also horrified and unimpressed. How someone can wear so many feelings at the same time is an absolute wonder.

1

His delightfully dark brows pull together, chocolate eyes narrowing, full lips pulling down. "What in the actual fuck?"

"What are you doing here?" I attempt to backtrack, but this dress has more yards of material than freaking Fabricland. I step on the train and topple backwards, landing on the floor with an oof. My makeshift suit-jacket groom goes flying. The hoop skirt flips up, and I raise my arm just in time to prevent it from smacking me in the face.

I feel like a flipped-over beetle as I struggle to right myself.

Uma, the sales associate who has been our go-to for all wedding-dress-related issues, rushes over. "Oh my goodness! Are you okay?"

Nate's stupidly pretty, displeased face appears above me, and he extends a hand. "That's a loaded question."

I ignore his offer of assistance and try, again, to right myself, but the freaking hoop is a menace. Nate's face is a telling shade of red. I am ten thousand percent sure my underwear is show-ing, and probably ninety percent of my ass since it's a thong. My mortification doubles.

Nate disappears, and two strong hands slide under my arms. A moment later I'm on my feet. I fight the goose bumps that skitter across my skin. The hoop skirt somehow flips up again, but this time I'm not fast enough to keep it from hitting me in the face. I jerk my head back and connect with his chin.

Nate grunts and releases me. I wobble perilously before settling, still on my feet thankfully.

"Are you okay?" Uma asks again.

"I'm fine. Just peachy. Thanks so much. I'm very sorry." I can't die of embarrassment today, not when Rix is counting on me.

I spin, and the excessively poofy skirt flares, returning to the appropriate location. I bet it looks so cool. But I can't confirm this because Nate is glaring at me, his thick, defined forearms crossed over his equally thick, defined chest. The Stileses have excellent genes. All three brothers are ridiculously good looking. But Nate has that tall-dark blond-and-grumpy thing going, and I'm such a fan.

I shouldn't be, based on our history, but I tend to be attracted to the wrong men—including the one standing in front of me, looking displeased.

My face is on fire as I try to give him a wide berth, but the expansive skirt makes it impossible.

"Is this Rix's dress?" His gaze moves over me, expression reflecting judgment, skepticism, and several other feelings I'm too busy being mortified and offended by to identify.

"Of course not! I was just..." *Good Lord, what was I doing?* Anyway, Rix is getting married on a beach. She would sweat to death in this number. Besides, she's about simplicity. "Why are you even here?"

"Rix had some kind of emergency, so I've been sent to collect you."

They might as well have asked him to clean up roadkill, based on how unhappy he looks.

"Is everything okay? Why didn't she call me?"

"Probably because you're here managing shit already, and I was available." He consults his wristwatch. "You need to change out of that. It's a twenty-minute drive, and we're already cutting it close."

"Yes, sir!" I salute him and click my heels together, then cross to the fitting room and attempt to get the hoop skirt through the door without flashing anyone, again.

Once inside, I realize the zipper is stuck. Which means I need help.

I poke my head out. Nate's back is to me, phone in hand, forearms flexing as he thumb-types. Probably telling Tristan, his older brother and Rix's fiancé, that we'll be late thanks to me. I search for Uma, but she's helping another customer.

Nate turns as if sensing my presence, his exasperation clear. "Why are you still wearing that? Hoping your fairy godmother shows up so you can be next in the ball-and-chain parade?"

It's no secret that Nate is anti-marriage. Hell, he's anti-relationship. According to Rix, he hasn't so much as gone on a date since his girlfriend Lisa broke up with him a year and a half ago. After cheating. I ignore the dig at my very different views on love. "The zipper is stuck."

"Well, unstuck it."

"Like I haven't tried." I roll my eyes. "I have many talents, but rotating my head and dislocating my arms are not among them."

His look of disapproval deepens.

"Why are you always such a grumpy old man?"

"Why are you always trying to be a fairy tale princess?"

"Why are you such a storm cloud?"

I try to pass him so I can ask Uma for help, but he steps in front of me and crosses his arms. "Because I enjoy raining on your parade, obviously."

"Obviously." I really wish I couldn't and didn't appreciate how nice his forearms are.

He unfolds them and points to the fitting room. "In."

"I need help!"

"Oh, I know."

I flip up a middle finger and blow him a kiss with it. His eyes drop to my mouth and darken.

I hope like hell he's remembering how my lips feel. It's been six years. I should not have any feelings about that one stupid kiss. But even now, when I'm faced with his surly, black-cloud-of-doom attitude—which is the version of Nate I'm *always* graced with—my entire body remembers that kiss in technicolor detail. Every perfect, toe-curling moment of it. It was the best kiss of my life. Still is. Which is endlessly frustrating.

The elusive, brilliant, untouchable Nathan Stiles had been interested in *me*. I'd been so flattered, so enamored—which admittedly was not uncommon for me. But Nate ruined it by being a giant dick after the fact. Unfortunately, that wasn't a unique experience for me, either, especially during my serial-dater high school days. But it sucked to have him join the ranks of the hot guys who'd just wanted to taste the forbidden fruit.

We've never addressed the aftermath. I assumed the best kiss of my life was entirely forgettable for him, that he never messaged because I wasn't on his radar. Nate has made it clear that he's about as partial to me as a case of food poisoning.

Not that it matters. I'm not interested in him anyway. He might be hot, and wildly intelligent, and delightfully broody, but he's a jerk. Besides, he's off-limits. He's my best friend's fiancé's brother. The best man to my maid of honor. Also, and most importantly, I've sworn off men for the foreseeable future. Especially men who are bad for me. I've had my heart broken too many times by guys who didn't deserve it in the first place.

I head for the fitting room because this stare down with Nate is making me sweaty.

I pull the hoop up so I can get through the door. Again. I turn to pull it closed, but Nate is on my heels. "What are you doing?"

"Helping you so we're not half an hour late for dinner. Unless you'd like to go dressed like this."

It's hard to argue with that logic.

He pulls the door closed and makes a turnaround motion. I do as he wordlessly instructs, because facing him means I have to continue to look at his irritated, pretty face. Turning around isn't much better. In front of me is a three-sided mirror meant to provide a multi-angled view of the dress I'm wearing. It also means I'm looking at three versions of Nate.

He has on black dress pants, a black button-down, a blue tie, and, in a bold move, shoes to match. He's taller than me by at least a head. And broad. He takes up way more space than he has any right to. Even worse, he smells phenomenal.

I pull my hair over my shoulder to expose the zipper and tip my head forward to make it easier. The sooner he unzips me, the sooner I'll be alone in this space, and the easier it will be to breathe again.

5

I grit my teeth and steel myself as his warm fingers skim between my shoulders.

"The lace is caught in the zipper," he explains.

"Don't tear it. I can't afford to pay for this dress."

"Why were you trying it on in the first place?" He tugs but the zipper doesn't budge.

"I wanted to make Rix laugh," I grumble.

"You in this dress is a horror show, not a comedy reel." His fingers slide into the back of the dress, knuckles pressing against my spine.

"Thanks," I reply sarcastically.

"It's too much. It overwhelms you." He continues to work the lace free from the teeth.

This time the zipper comes down, but I'm not prepared. Too busy processing his last comment, perhaps? I grab for the bodice a moment too late. It slides down my torso, stopping at my hips.

I'm not wearing a bra. Nate freezes. My eyes lift as his drop. His nostrils flare. His fists clench.

His hot gaze flashes back to mine. "I'll be in the car."

He spins around and leaves me in the fitting room with perky pierced nipples and a whole lot of embarrassment.

I sigh. "Dinner should be fun."

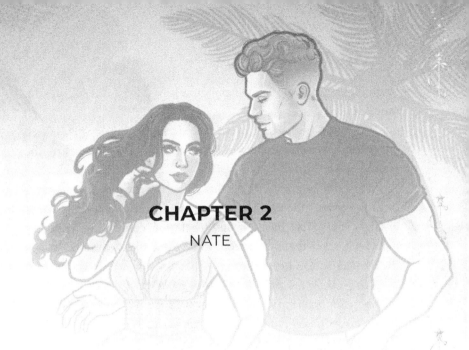

CHAPTER 2
NATE

I give my crotch an annoyed look as I shift around in the driver's seat, waiting for Essie. The next several weeks are going to be long AF.

Spending all this pre-wedding time in proximity to Essie has been bad enough. She's frustratingly beautiful—irrationally stunning in a way that makes my palms damp and my heart rate spike every fucking time I look at her. She's also an eternal optimist. Her zeal for romance and falling in love is a barely tolerable irritant. She's the glorious ray of sunshine peeking through my rain clouds to create a rainbow.

But the real kick in the balls, and the thing that takes up an unreasonable amount of my mental bandwidth, is that I know exactly how her lips feel and taste.

It's been six years. That kiss should be like a photograph left in the sun too long. Faded. Barely a memory.

But it's not.

That kiss is as vivid as a sunrise. Every time I look at her soft mouth, I'm reminded of her cotton-candy-flavored lip gloss and the feel of her curves pressed against me.

And now. *Now* I have a new memory to add to the one I wish I could erase. Essie's pierced nipples are forever burned into my brain. Etched in stone. Permanent. Irascible. And so fucking fantastic.

Tiny buds framed by heart shields with pink jewels. It's so laughably, perfectly Essie. And based on the reaction below the waist, I like it.

My phone buzzes with a call. I'm happy for this distraction—until I register the number. Then my heart rate spikes and sweat breaks across the back of my neck for completely different reasons. I send the call to voicemail. And like an idiot, I check the message once it registers.

"Hi, Nathan. It's your mother. This is the fourth time I've tried to call you with no answer. I understand that you're upset with me, but we can't work things out if you don't talk to me. Please call me back."

I swallow past the tightness in my chest and erase the message so I don't listen to it again. I don't want to dissect it, to read into her pleading tone, to give in and call her back. I haven't seen her since the morning she walked out on our family more than a decade and a half ago. I haven't heard her voice in more than ten years. I don't want to miss what I never had, what she robbed me and my brothers and my father of when she abandoned us.

My phone pings again, this time with a text message. Thankfully, it's my older brother.

TRISTAN

We'll be at the restaurant in 15. You get Ess okay?

According to my GPS, it will take us nineteen minutes to get to the restaurant if we leave immediately.

NATE

We're a few minutes behind you, but we'll see you soon.

TRISTAN
Cool. Thanks for picking her up. We appreciate
it.

Another call comes through. This time it's Essie. My stomach
pitches with equal parts relief and anxiety.

"Please tell me you're not still in the store," I bark.

There's a beat of silence. "I don't know where you're
parked."

Of course she doesn't. Because I didn't tell her, and I couldn't
get out of the dressing room fast enough. "Turn right out of the
store. I'm half a block down."

She ends the call without another word. Less than a minute
later, Essie passes my car. I honk and she startles, dropping her
purse. Shit scatters on the sidewalk. I fight with my body to stay
in my seat and let her handle it. But all I've done so far is be a
dick to her. It's not her fault I'm guilt riddled, or that I'm not
over the kiss we shared all those years ago, or how apathetic she
seems in my presence. She acts like it never happened, like it
was insignificant, and I'm over here obsessing and hating myself
for not being able to be a normal person around her.

I cut the engine and hop out of the driver's seat. Essie scram-
bles to reclaim the items all over the ground while I round the
hood.

I nab one of her lip balms before it can roll into a sewer grate.
She frantically jams things back in her purse as I crouch protec-
tively in front of her to help.

"Sorry, sorry," she says. "I know we're already late."

I barely resist the urge to pocket one of her lip balms. Instead,
I scoop up a handful of pens—she has many—and hand them
over. A man on his phone kicks a tube of lip gloss down the sidewalk. It ricochets off a woman's foot and ping-pongs into traffic,
then promptly gets run over by a taxi.

We stand at the same time, and I move toward my car,
opening the passenger door for her.

"Thanks." She slides in, face red, eyes anywhere but on me.

I round the hood and steel myself. Back in high school she wore some kind of perfume or lotion that I attributed only to her. Something sweet and lightly fruity. That hasn't changed, and it never fails to trigger the memory of that kiss.

So many emotions are tangled up in that memory. Ones I don't like to deal with. My shame over the way I handled things still makes me uncomfortable and embarrassed. But we were kids, just out of high school. And I was all kinds of fucked up. I still am. Probably more than I was then. Definitely more fucked up. I saved us both a world of heartache by doing what I did, even if it was shitty.

I take my spot behind the wheel and grit my teeth as I close the door, trapping us in the confined space together.

"I'm sorry about my nipples," she blurts.

I fasten my seat belt aggressively as heat rushes through me and the hard-on that had disappeared returns. "Never mention them again."

"Never again," she whispers.

Why can't I stop being a jerk? I should do better. Be *nicer*. It's not her fault that everything about my brother's wedding is a fucking trigger. I should be over the breakup with Lisa. It's been more than a year since she left me for someone more emotionally available—*before* she actually broke things off. We obviously weren't right for each other, yet I still have a lot of inconvenient feelings tied to the breakup. But just because I can't make someone happy doesn't mean all relationships are doomed to the same fate as mine. Apart from any of that, though, Essie's positive-Petunia attitude about love irks me endlessly. Maybe I'm envious. Maybe I'm just a jaded asshole. Who fucking knows?

"How's your day going?" Essie asks.

"I've had better." Still scoring zero on the being-nicer front.

"Would you like to talk about it? It's not good to hold your feelings inside, Nathan," she says sweetly.

I *hate* when she says my full name, because I *love* when she says my full name. "Anything that comes out of my mouth will likely hurt your precious feelings, so it's better if I keep those thoughts in my head." At least I'm being honest. I don't need more things to feel bad about.

"My feelings aren't precious."

I side-eye her.

"Seriously, say whatever you need to say, Nate. I'm sure you'd love to get whatever is eating at you off your chest."

"You. You're eating at me," I blurt before I can find the self-restraint necessary to bite my idiot tongue. "You and your sunshine-and-roses perspective on everything. Love sucks. All it does is make you vulnerable, and then people leave." Without a word. Without an explanation. Or they find someone better.

Essie shifts in her seat. I almost expect her to call me out, to force me to deal with the assholery I've carried from the past into the present. But she doesn't. Likely because she's not thinking about *us*, about me being a hypocrite. She's thinking about her best friend and my brother. "You don't think Tristan and Rix will last?"

The steering wheel groans under my hands. I need to calm the hell down. My blood pressure is rising along with my fucking guilt. "I'm not discussing this with you."

She doesn't let it go. "Tristan has grown so much. He worships the ground Rix walks on. And Rix loves him just as much."

But she could still leave him. I keep that thought to myself. I adore Rix. She's always been part of our lives in one facet or another. When we were kids, she and I would often get tossed together because we're the same age. I thought of her like a sister. And soon that's the title and role she'll have in my life. I want that. But I'm nervous to have it and lose it.

My brother is my best friend. But he's a surly fucker. And while Essie is right, and he's made huge strides since he and Rix became a thing, I still worry about the future. For him. But also

11

for me. What if it all falls apart? People leave. *Women* leave. My mother left. Lisa left. I have no faith in love. No faith that it can endure, because in my experience, it doesn't.

And then there's Essie, who falls in love over and over. It doesn't seem to matter that she's been broken up with countless times; she still somehow believes that love conquers all. I can't decide if I should envy her or pity her.

The rest of the ride to the restaurant is silent, and Essie practically launches herself out of the car as soon as I put it in park. She's already at the door when I'm still crossing the lot. By the time I make it inside, she's at the host stand, flashing her megawatt smile, making him splutter and stumble over his words.

He doesn't tear his eyes away from Essie as he mumbles, "I'll be right with you," vaguely in my direction.

Essie glances over her shoulder. "Oh, he's with me."

Disappointment flashes across his face, but he plasters on a smile. "Of course. Follow me."

He guides us to the table where Tristan, Rix, and Flip, my roommate, who is Rix's older brother and Tristan's good friend and teammate, are already seated.

Rix gets up to hug me. "Thanks for picking up Ess."

"No problem," I lie.

"I could have picked up Essie," Flip says.

"You were with me on a beverage run. You wouldn't have had time." Tristan stands to give me a brotherly back pat as he pulls me in close and whispers, "Everything okay?"

"All good. Just hit traffic." I slide into the seat next to Essie, which is the only one available.

The server stops at the table and takes our drink order.

"Did you sort everything out?" Essie asks Rix. "Nate said you had some kind of emergency. Was it wedding related? You know you can always offload stuff to me. I'm here to help."

"It was work related," Rix explains. "It's fine now."

Tristan stretches his arm across the back of her seat. "If it's too much, you can always reduce your hours, Bea."

Her full name is Beatrix, and he's the only one who shortens it to this.

She smiles up at him. "I know. I have it under control."

He purses his lips. Tristan would love for Rix to quit her job. He and Flip are pro hockey players with the Toronto Terror, our local team, and both have multimillion-dollar contracts. But Rix and Flip grew up in a house where it was tough to make ends meet. Rix is used to taking care of herself financially, and she wants the autonomy, which I can respect, even if it means she's spread a little thin right now.

She kisses the edge of his jaw. "Put your serious face away. We're planning all the fun stuff tonight."

His expression softens. "I can't wait until you're my wife."

"I can't wait until you're my husband."

"You two are so cute!" Essie takes a picture.

"Almost as cute as me, right, Ess?" Flip winks.

Essie laughs and holds her fingers a hairsbreadth apart. "They're this much cuter than you."

I try not to let my feelings show, but for some stupid reason, I seriously want to punch Flip in the face.

The server returns with my vodka and soda and Essie's Aperol spritz.

"We already put in an order for all of our favorites," Rix informs us.

It's a tapas-style restaurant, and everything is made for sharing.

Essie's eyes light up. "Did you get the tempura cauliflower?"

"Of course." Rix smiles.

"I'm so excited." Essie does some weird thing with her hands and bumps my arm. Her fingers brush my wrist. "Sorry." She snatches her hand away. "Okay, should we get down to business?"

"I would get down to business with you any day," Flip quips.

"Oh my God, stop flirting with my best friend." Rix flicks his ear.

"You're marrying mine," he reminds her, then turns back to Essie.

"Sorry, Flip, but you're at the bottom of my list." She flashes him a coy smile.

"Come on, Ess. I've changed. You could be the one for me."

Essie laughs and rolls her eyes. "We all know you prefer blondes." She pulls a binder and a tablet out of her purse and sets them on the table beside her. She props up the tablet and opens a spreadsheet.

"What is that?" I'm equally thankful that Flip has stopped flirting with her for five fucking seconds and annoyed that I give a shit.

Flip and I have become good friends since I moved into his place last fall, but he's no better with relationships than I am. I don't want him making moves on Essie and finding out how good her lips taste.

"It's how I keep track of everything," Essie explains. "You have access. Everyone does. I email whenever I update it with pertinent details."

"Oh." I pull my phone out and open my personal email, which admittedly, I don't check as often as I should. I have thirty new emails, four of which are from Essie with spreadsheet updates. I click on one, and the sheet pops up on my phone. It's color coded, and there are different tabs, sections, and even dropdown menus.

"Should we discuss the bridal shower first? Since that's next weekend and it's co-ed?" Essie asks brightly.

"Sounds good," Rix agrees.

Tristan kisses her temple.

I have no idea what a co-ed bridal shower is, so I keep my mouth shut.

"The whole team has RSVP'd, and almost everyone is bringing a plus-one," Essie reports. "Kodiak and Lavender send their regrets, but I'm pleased to report that Lavender can make our girls-only party, *and* they can make the wedding."

"That's good news," Tristan says.

"Lavender is so fun!" Rix is all smiles.

Kodiak Bowman, my brother, and Flip all went to the Hockey Academy together before they turned pro. Kodiak plays for New York now, and they've remained friends all these years.

"Oh, and I have confirmation from both of your families, including aunts and uncles, that they can attend the shower as well." Essie flips to the guest list tab.

I'm suddenly on alert. Maybe the phone calls that seemed to come from nowhere aren't so out of left field. But Tristan would have said something before now. "What do you mean both of our families?"

Tristan holds up a hand. "Mom is excluded, don't worry." It's probably the hundredth time he's had to reassure me. "I don't want that drama. Especially with Dad finally dating."

It's only been a few months since my dad started seeing someone. Her name is Sophia, and she's a lot younger than he is. I've met her once, briefly. She seems nice enough, even if she is closer to Tristan's age than my dad's. They met at the Toronto Terror fundraiser gala in the spring.

"Right. Okay." Heat works its way up my neck and wraps around my ears. "Sorry."

"Nothing to be sorry about." Rix's tone softens with empathy.

I'd love to be over my mother abandoning our family, but unfortunately I'm not. One day she was there, and the next she was gone. For a couple of years she called on birthdays, but eventually she just…ghosted us. Then last year when our younger brother Brody graduated high school, suddenly she wanted to be involved again. Dad and Tristan shut that down. Thank fucking God. I couldn't handle her coming back into our lives on top of the breakup with Lisa.

I tune back in to the conversation, which Essie is once again dominating. I wish I didn't find it attractive that she's so adept at creating spreadsheets and organizing events. But I do love order and organization.

"As requested, it's a no-gifts shower, but attendees are welcome to donate to the Food for Kids program or Supplies for Success. I'm happy to report that more than fifty filled backpacks have been donated, and you've already raised over four thousand dollars for Food for Kids." Essie turns her tablet to Rix and Tristan, where the total is highlighted at the bottom.

"That's incredible. Thank you so much for setting that up!" Rix smiles at Tristan. "Isn't that great?"

"It's fantastic." He kisses her temple. Again.

Essie waves the comment away. "It was just a couple of phone calls and emails with links. It was no big deal."

I frown at her easy dismissal, and the fact that I've had no part in any of this. I scroll down the list and discover there are actual formulas in the spreadsheet.

"Don't downplay it, Ess. You really went above and beyond," Flip adds.

I refrain from commenting. I've been over here planning the bachelor party and slacking on everything else, it seems. And here's Little Miss Sunshine and Rainbows making pretty spreadsheets. I can make a fucking spreadsheet. With formulas. I do it all the time. She's not the only organizational wizard at the table.

The server arrives with appetizers. He must ask Essie three times if he can get her anything else, to which she always replies with a *no thank you* and a smile.

We hit pause on the planning and pass the plates around.

Essie taps her lip, surveying her plate and the ones scattered around the table.

"What are you missing? I can give you whatever you need, Ess," Flip offers.

"I'm good." She bites back a smile. "Nate, can you pass the cauliflower?"

"Oh come on, Ess." Flip waves a hand in my direction. "This

guy doesn't even believe in love! Why would you look to him to fulfill your needs when I'm right here?"

"Keep me out of your flirting. I'm not looking to be part of your throuple," I grumble and stab some potato-poof thing.

"Am I not good to you, honey bear?" Flip winks at me.

I scratch my temple with my middle finger.

"Okay. Back to business." Essie looks expectantly at me.

"What?"

"Please pass the cauliflower."

"Right." I hand them to her.

Her fingers graze mine, and the hairs on my arm rise. She takes three pieces and passes them to Flip, who takes one while eyeing it with skepticism. The guy would live on KD—Kraft Dinner—if Rix didn't drop off meals for him twice a week. On top of being an accountant, she's also a full-time student and develops meal plans for my brother, her brother, and some of their Terror teammates.

Essie continues to lead this dinner meeting by reviewing all the food, games, and decorations for the bridal shower.

"Do you have a rough estimate for the cost per person?" Rix asks.

"Whatever it is, I'll cut a check," Tristan assures her.

"I can figure it out for you right now." Essie glances at the totals while setting up a new formula. "Roughly eighty-seven dollars a person based on food and drink," she says before she's even had a chance to complete the formula. She highlights the row, the total appearing.

I had no idea Essie was math smart. I also had no idea I'd be attending a bridal shower.

Since I haven't looked at Essie's emails, I can't make any valuable contributions, and asking questions will only highlight my complete lack of involvement. So I just sit here and continue to be annoyingly impressed with her attention to detail, exceptional organizational skills, and ability to run numbers in her head. I feel like I've underestimated her—not just now, but in the past—and that bothers me for a lot of reasons.

In high school, she was the girl everyone wanted to date. She was voted hottest girl in the school all four years, and she was fun, a literal ray of sunshine. She didn't hide the fact that she loved all things princess, and she always had a new boyfriend. For some reason I assumed she floated through every part of her life the same way, but now I have to wonder what else I've been wrong about.

Eventually we move on to the stag and doe, which is also a co-ed event. Again, the point is to raise money. This time for a local women's shelter.

"I have a list of prizes and the corresponding games they would be best suited for." Essie consults another beautiful spreadsheet with projected earning potential for each game already outlined, based on prizes. "I'm still on the hunt for a Plinko board, though."

"You mean from *The Price is Right*?" I ask.

"Exactly!"

"I'll make it. I can make a Plinko board. What else do you need made? Or done? I'm good at organizing things, too." I can't allow this to continue. Not when I'm literally the king of organization.

"My shoes have never been lined up so perfectly," Flip agrees.

I give him a look.

"And my towels have never been folded so uniformly. If you want to make my bed for me too, I'm down, honey bear." Flip winks again.

I like neat and orderly. I function better when everything is in the right place.

I ignore Flip. "Seriously, though. I've got the Plinko board." I have an engineering degree. It should be straightforward.

"Okay, great!" Essie makes a note. "Oh! I almost forgot. I have something for you."

I expect her to hand it to Rix, or literally anyone but me. It's book shaped. "What is this for?"

"I saw it and thought of you." She blinks up at me, all innocent-like.

"That was so nice of you," Rix says.

"Thanks?" I peel the tape, careful not to rip the paper. My neck itches like it's wrapped in a wool scarf because everyone is watching me. I frown as I read the title. *A Guide to Happiness: 100 strategies for a happier, healthier you*!

Flip barks out a laugh. Tristan snickers. Essie smiles, and Rix hides hers behind her drink. I bite the inside of my cheek as it heats. "Ha-ha, thanks." I have nowhere to hide it, so I flip the book over and set it on the table between us.

Essie steers the conversation back to the stag and doe, and then it's on to wedding-wear updates. "I've already stopped by the tuxedo shop to confirm that the handkerchiefs and ties match the bridesmaid dresses. And Nate has been for his fitting, so we are good to go there."

"Isn't that my job?"

"Mm-hmm." Essie's voice pitches up. "I emailed you about it, but I didn't get a response, so I took care of it. You should have all the details if you want to follow up."

"Right, yeah. You should probably just text instead of email."

Essie's smile turns wooden. "Okay. I can do that."

By the end of dinner, my competitive side has been fully activated. Essie's here with a fucking binder of information, taking over everything, and I look like a complete slacker—and a shitty brother and best man. It's fucking on. Whatever games she has for this stag and doe, I'll have better ones. And prizes. I work for one of the top sports-equipment companies in Canada. I should be able to score some awesome stuff.

Flip holds the door open for Essie as we leave the restaurant. I want to charley horse him when he leans in and whispers something that makes her laugh. The fuck is wrong with me?

"You okay, man? You seem...more tense than usual," Tristan

says quietly. "Work still super busy? You know Flip will help out with whatever you need."

"Work is fine. Good, actually. And I can handle things. I just didn't realize Essie was communicating everything through the email I don't check very often," I explain. "Once we switch to text, we'll be good."

"Okay. Cool. And thanks again for picking up Ess. It took the pressure off Bea." He pats my back.

Essie waves and hops into the back of Rix's SUV while Flip joins me in my car.

He reclines in the passenger seat and stares at me as I fasten my seat belt, check all my mirrors, and adjust the air. "What?"

"There's a vibe between you and Essie."

Of course he's noticed. He's irritatingly perceptive. "There's no vibe between me and Essie."

"The way you're gripping the steering wheel tells me that's a load of bullshit." He nods toward my hands. "But if you're not ready to talk about it, that's fine."

"There's nothing to talk about."

My phone buzzes in the holder, and the screen lights up with a new message.

"Who's Cotton Candy?" Flip asks.

"No one." I manage to grab it a split second before Flip. Thank fuck. He tries to steal it out of my hand, but I slide it into my pants pocket.

"No one, eh? Is that why your face is beet red and you look like you're halfway between a heart attack and jizzing in your pants?"

"Leave it alone, Flip."

He holds up his hands. "All right. Backing off."

He talks about how much fun the stag and doe will be since his teammate, Dallas Bright, has offered to host it at his parents' place on Lake Vernon in Huntsville. I've been there once, for Dallas and Hemi's engagement party. I let him talk while I sweat. I swear my phone is burning in my pocket.

As soon as we get home, I lock myself in my bedroom and pull my phone out.

I quickly change Cotton Candy to Essie in my contacts and open her message.

My stomach flips and sinks.

There's only one new one.

ESSIE

Here are the links to all the spreadsheets. I hope you enjoy the book.

I swallow down guilt as I read the ones above it, dating back six years ago.

NATE

I'll call you tomorrow.

ESSIE

Can't wait 🩶

But I didn't call. Or message. I ghosted her and moved to Kingston for university a few weeks later. It wouldn't have worked out. She stayed in Toronto with Rix. Kingston was a three-hour drive away. But I was still an asshole. Still am an asshole now.

NATE

Got it. Thx.

ESSIE

So you can text back. Good to know.

What else can I say when it's far too late for *sorry*?

CHAPTER 3

ESSIE

NATE

I don't have edit access to the spreadsheets, and I found an error.

ESSIE

No you didn't.

NATE

I did.

ESSIE

Screenshot it.

I'm not sure if you're aware, but there's a bridal shower happening today, and I'm a little busy.

NATE

So am I. Give me edit access and I'll fix it.

ESSIE

Say please.

NATE

Please.

ESSIE

In a voice memo. Three times.

NATE

shifty eyes GIF Why?

ESSIE

bats lashes GIF

I pocket my phone. As fun as this is, I don't have time to pander to Nate. My tablet is in hand, checklist ready for ticking—I love a good checklist—as I survey the hall. The decorations are on point, everything looks perfect, and guests should start arriving soon.

"What can I help with?" Tally, the Toronto Terror's head coach's daughter and good friend to me and my younger sister Cammie, appears at my side with her friend Fee. She's the younger sister of Terror assistant coach Lexi Forrester. Well, Lexi was a Forrester until she married the team's recently retired goalie, Roman Hammerstein. Now they are both Forrest-Hammers.

"Put us both to work," Fee insists.

"Can you two help Rix's mom with the centerpieces, please? There should be one for every table. They come in two parts, and there is some assembly required."

"Absolutely." They turn toward the table behind me. "Oh! Oh my gosh! Did Rix's mom make these?"

I nod. "Hand painted every single one." Wooden figurines of Rix and Tristan sit on a flat wooden circle, cut from a birch tree, surrounded by mini flower wreaths.

"They are adorable," Tally gushes.

Rix's mom, who everyone calls Muffy, appears. She's wearing a pretty summer dress, with hair and makeup done by yours truly, looking nervous and excited. My own mother is right behind her. She's dressed in pants and a pale blouse, also fitting for the summer weather.

"Everything looks wonderful!" Mom pulls me in for a quick hug. "You've done an amazing job, honey."

"Thanks, Mom." I grew up in a home full of love and

support. "I have two volunteers to help you and Momma Muffy with the centerpieces."

"This is so fantastic, Essie." Muffy is on the verge of tears, and has been for the past hour. "You really went above and beyond."

"Rix deserves the best and more." I kiss her cheek and turn toward our friends. "Tally and Fee, this is Muffy, Rix's mom and Athena, my mom."

The girls wave hello.

"Tally and Fee." She glances between them. "Are you part of Rix's Babe Brigade?" She looks to me for confirmation. "Isn't that what your group of girlfriends is called?"

I grin. "That's right."

"It's so lovely to finally meet you." She hugs both girls, her smile wide and soft, eyes a little watery. "Rixie is surrounded by so many wonderful people."

"She's an amazing friend." I give Muffy another little squeeze.

"And an incredible daughter." Pride lights up Muffy's face. "Always so responsible. Dinner would have been a sad affair in our house without her."

"She could make a gourmet meal out of onions, bread, and cheese," I agree.

And she often did when she was young. She was the only nine-year-old I knew who could make French onion soup like a pro. Rix also had a paper route to make extra money, and Flip was forever mowing lawns in the summer, raking leaves in the fall, and shoveling snow in the winter as a side hustle. Both of their parents worked two jobs to make ends meet and help cover the cost of hockey for Flip. Sometimes in grade school my mom would pack an extra lunch, and I would slip it in Rix's backpack before we went inside so we didn't get in trouble for sharing.

Tally and Fee follow the mom's back into the party room to set up the centerpieces.

"More food coming through! Where should I put this stuff?"

Flip appears in the doorway, followed by Nate and the rest of the guys.

I refuse to acknowledge the flutter in my belly, or the way traitorous parts of my body tighten at the sight of Nate wearing black slacks, a black button-down, and a floral-printed tie—a sliver of the side of him I never get to see. "Straight through to the kitchen," I call, heading for the doors at the other end of the room so I can hold one open.

Rix trails behind them, wringing her hands. "I need to check all the food platters and make sure we have everything we need."

Last night she was worried we ordered too much. Now she's worried we don't have enough.

"We got everything on the list, Bea. It'll be fine." Tristan tries to reassure her.

"I just need to double-check."

"Okay, if that's what you want, babe." He looks to me like he's unsure this is the right response.

I nod. "I've got this. You manage whatever you need to manage."

He gives me two thumbs-up and heads back out, probably to bring in more food. I follow Rix into the kitchen. It's mostly empty except for Nate, who is carefully unloading a box of artful charcuterie cones.

"Are you sure we ordered enough food?" Rix's hands try to strangle each other. "What about the vegan and gluten-free boards? Are they here yet? I don't see them. We need the vegan and gluten-free boards. Tristan's aunt Freida is gluten intolerant, and she doesn't eat anything that comes from an animal."

"Nate, can you grab me the bottle of prosecco from the fridge and a glass, *please*?" I call over my shoulder, stressing the *please*, to make a point.

He freezes for a moment, gaze bouncing between me and Rix. "Sure." He sets the cones gently in their holder and crosses to the fridge.

"Some of the boards are already on the food table, so we can check to make sure," I tell her. "But I have photographic evidence of all the boards, and the vegan and gluten free were clearly labeled and among them."

Nate passes me the glass of prosecco. "Thank you." I hand it to Rix and encourage her to take a sip before I turn back to Nate, who is still close enough that I can smell his cologne. "Can you do me a favor and check the food table in the party room to make sure the boards in question are already placed?"

He nods once. "Yup. On it."

I'm surprised and grateful he's being so helpful. He's detail oriented, so I trust he'll come back with data to match the order. Also, his rear view is nice, so I don't mind watching him walk away. I wait until he disappears through the door before I turn back to Rix.

"Have another sip." I tap the edge of the glass.

She does. "I'm so jittery."

"Take a deep breath. The bridal shower will kick ass." I note the hint of shadow under her eyes. I wanted to do her makeup, but there wasn't time. "Did you sleep at all last night?"

She bites her lips together for a moment before she answers. "Did you?"

"Yup." Like four hours, but I plan to make up for it when I get home. "Were you stressed about the shower and stayed up running numbers?"

She glances over her shoulder before she whispers, "One of my clients was audited, and there's a whole bunch of paperwork that needs to be handled."

"Did you stay up all night working on it?" I ask.

"I couldn't sleep. I stayed up until like three. Then woke up at six because I was worried about the food. I should have just made it all."

I arch a brow.

"Okay. That would not have been a good idea, but I could

have at least made the charcuterie boards and the mini crème brûlée."

"You could have, but you'd be even more stressed than you are now." I encourage her to take another sip. "This comes from a place of love, okay? Maybe you should consider time off from the accounting firm and focus on just the guys from the team who already use you. Namely your brother, Tristan, and Dallas."

"This is just a blip. It's normally not this intense," she argues.

"You're getting married in a handful of weeks. Again, I say this with love, but we all want you to enjoy the process and not be stressed about work on top of everything else."

"I really hate not having my own income," she whispers. "I don't want to be kept."

This is such a deep-seated issue for Rix, and it pains me to see her so overwhelmed and on edge. But we're not solving this problem today, so I'll do what I can to help alleviate her tension with humor and a little encouragement.

I settle my hands on her shoulders. "Oh my sweet, sweet best friend. Tristan already asked if there's a cucumber salad. If anyone is being kept, it's that man."

She barks out a laugh. "He did not."

"He totally did. Last word on this for now, but that man *wants* to take care of you. We both know you don't need taking care of, but you don't have to keep proving it." I push her hair over her shoulders. "Now, we are going to have the best time this afternoon, and we're going to play stupid games and make our aunties and moms and grandparents happy, and those boys are going to wait on us hand and foot, and it will be glorious."

"It will be glorious," Rix repeats.

Nate reappears. "There are two vegan and two gluten-free charcuterie boards, and they are very clearly marked as such. I made sure with the help of Tally and Fee and some neon chalk things. I reviewed the entire spreadsheet, and everything is accounted for. And there's also some kind of vegan meringue that is really freaking tasty, which is wild, because I thought those were made with egg whites."

"You can use chickpea liquid," Rix explains.

"Huh. Well, I have a new, deep appreciation for the liquid chickpeas swim in."

Muffy pokes her head into the kitchen. "Trixie Rixie! There you are. The cake arrived, and I thought you might want to decide where it should go."

"Yes. Absolutely." Rix passes me her glass of prosecco and kisses me on the cheek. "Thank you. I love you."

"I love you, too."

She links arms with her mom, and Muffy guides her out of the room.

I deflate a little and gulp her prosecco.

For a second I forget Nate is still in here. He's staring at me, a furrow etched in his brow. He opens his mouth to speak, but I raise a hand. "Do not ask me about the spreadsheet."

"But there—"

"—is no error."

"The formula—"

"—is not wrong."

"Why are you being so difficult?"

"I don't know, Nathan, why am I being so difficult?"

I changed the formula so Rix wouldn't stress about the cost after I sent the specs to Tristan, but I won't type that in a message or say it out loud right now. I pull my compact and my lip gloss out of my purse so I have something to focus on that isn't the delicious furrow in his brow.

"Why do you hide behind that?"

"Hide behind what?" Like I want to go out there with smudged eyeliner.

He stares at me.

I stare back, feeling increasingly unsettled by the intense way he's looking at me.

He kissed me.

He ghosted me.

He never apologized.

He can't stand me.

But instead of either of us walking away, we're bickering like teenagers.

"Take your broody asshole down a notch, Nathan. Your black cloud is dimming my shine."

I brush past him. I can't let him get to me. Today is about Rix and celebrating her forever. I have plenty of time to fixate on why I never seem to get any closer to my own.

CHAPTER 4
NATE

"Excellent presentation, Nate. Great work." My boss pats me on the shoulder as we leave the boardroom on Monday.

"Thanks, Andrew. I appreciate your support." Under my suit jacket I'm sweating, but the stress has been worth it. I've only been with the company for a handful of months, and I'm already proving my worth. Even more exciting, I've been given a half-million-dollar budget to develop the prototype for my new skate and blade design. It's a huge deal, considering how new I am. But I have career goals and a plan to attain them. If this project goes well, it could give us an edge against the competition, get us big contracts with the Terror hockey team, and make a name for me in the industry. It's the start of something awesome.

"We should go for lunch to celebrate," Greg, one of my colleagues, suggests.

He's always up for a party as he's on the rebound after his girlfriend of six years broke it off with him recently. She said she'd fallen out of love. He just reinforces my belief that love doesn't last, and his single status makes him an easy work friend.

"Sure. Let me just drop my things in my office." *And change my shirt so I don't have to wear my suit jacket in the sweltering July heat.*

I stop short when I spot Essie sitting in the waiting room outside our offices. She looks like she stepped out of a summer advertisement. Her long, dark hair falls in waves over her shoulders, contrasting with her pale, floral-print dress and strappy sandals. Her bag matches her dress, and she has a binder in her lap, as well as a tablet and her phone.

Panic makes my heart race, and my already sweaty palms dampen further. "What are you doing here?"

Her head lifts and a wide, beautiful smile curves her annoyingly luscious lips. "Waiting for you."

"But...why? Are Rix and Tristan okay? Did something happen?" I remind myself she wouldn't be sitting here smiling if things had gone sideways.

"Rix and Tristan are fine." She pushes to her feet. "I need to discuss a few things with you, and they're pressing."

Greg is still standing beside me, and Jennie, the head receptionist, is watching this go down with more interest than I would like. She keeps telling me about her niece who just graduated from university. Like I would ever date someone related to a person I work with.

"Come into my office." I take the binder and tablet from her and lead her down the hall, closing the door once we're inside. "You couldn't have messaged?"

"I tried. Several times. You didn't respond." Her smile stays firmly in place.

I dig my phone out of my pocket. I have unread messages from last night and more from this morning. "I had a big presentation. I would have responded this afternoon."

"I need an answer before this afternoon, so here I am. How did the presentation go?" That smile stays firmly on her pretty, glossy lips.

"Huh?"

"The presentation? How did it go?" Her attention catches on the wall across the room, and she heads toward it.

"It was fine." I can't imagine Essie giving a shit about my career goals.

While my office lacks a lot of personal touches, that particular wall feels a lot like diary entries for work. All my sketches are tacked to the corkboard. Organized neatly, of course, but still, that wall is the only space in this office that isn't clutter free. The whiteboard is full of notes and formulas, all of which pertain to the presentation I just gave. I came in early to review before the meeting to be sure I had it all locked down.

She tilts her head. "What's all this?"

"Just stuff I'm working on." I could literally talk for hours about what I do for a living, but most people gap out after about thirty seconds.

She reaches out and brushes her long, delicate fingers along the edge of one of my earliest designs. It's basic, and unfinished, but also a reminder of how far I've come in the past several months.

She glances over her shoulder. I don't know how to read her expression, but her eyes move over me on a sweep that makes my body feel like a live wire. Her voice is soft and reverent when she speaks. "This is like…scientific art."

I brush off the compliment. "It's rudimentary."

"What are these formulas for?" she asks.

Like she's genuinely curious. Like she actually wants to know what I do, beyond the title of engineer.

But I like to keep my workspace devoid of distractions. Which means I need her out of here as soon as possible. I don't want the memory of Essie looking intrigued, and sexy, and determined, smelling like cotton fucking candy haunting me while I'm trying to design. I already think about her in the shower every damn morning these days.

"You wouldn't understand." I've tried to explain it to people outside of work, and their eyes just glaze over.

Essie shoots me a look.

I redirect the conversation before it turns into another one I get to feel bad about. "You had something you want to discuss. What is it?"

She rolls her shoulders back, eyes no longer lit up with interest. "The Plinko board, have you made it?"

"It's handled." I haven't started it, but I still have time.

"So you have it?" she presses. "Do you need help finishing it?"

"No. I definitely don't need help." It's bad enough that I'll have the memory of her standing in my office. I don't need her in my apartment trying to help me build something. "I'll have it ready for the weekend." Which is when we need it.

She crosses her arms. This draws attention to her chest and reminds me that I've seen her nipples. My dick tingles. I think about the day my mom left. It works, but also darkens my mood.

"If you can't follow through, Nathan, I need to know. We are five days away from the stag and doe. I'd like it to go as smoothly as possible for Tristan and Rix. Do you have a way to get it to Huntsville? Because if you don't, we need to make a plan."

"I'll figure it out."

She huffs, and her right cheek tics with irritation. It's hot, which is frustrating. Why does she have to be so brain-meltingly attractive and sassy and competent?

"Look, Nate, I get that maybe this stuff isn't your top priority, and you obviously have other things going on." She motions to my whiteboard. "But Rix deserves to have the best stag and doe in the history of the universe, and that's what I'm trying to plan. If you're going to flake out, or be a hindrance, step the fuck out of the way and let me run things."

Work me takes that as a challenge. But as I gaze down at this tiny, polished, annoyed woman, I realize she truly loves Rix. Why else would she come all the way across town just to make sure I'll follow through? She has no reason to believe I will since

33

I've let her down in the past, and I've been letting her down by not being engaged in all this planning shit. More than that, I'm letting my brother down by not showing up the way I should. Tristan deserves the same special experience Essie wants to give her best friend.

"The presentation took up all my bandwidth," I confess. "But it's done now. I promise I will send photographic evidence of the Plinko board as soon as I can, and I will have a means to transport it to Huntsville for the weekend." *There.* I'm stepping up and assuaging her concerns. "Is there anything else you're concerned about that needs my attention?" *Like your nipples.*

I really need her out of my office. She smells fantastic, and she's far too good a friend to Rix, and I'm so fucking antsy and full of self-loathing over my inability to stop thinking about her pretty mouth, and other body parts I'd like to explore. Not to mention my inability to be anything but a constant dick when she's around.

"I'll hold you to it with the photographic evidence. Also, I sent you a calendar invitation days ago, and you haven't accepted." Essie scrolls through her calendar and taps a button.

"For what?"

She holds up her tablet. "Dance lessons."

"Dance lessons?"

"Rix would like to be prepared with more than our dance routine from junior high. Tristan is game because he loves her and wants what she wants. I told her we'd join them for solidarity, and so we don't look like bumbling idiots during the wedding reception."

"I can dance just fine," I argue. I also don't know if I can handle touching Essie for an extended period without drowning in my own disdain.

She blinks up at me, wearing a placid smile. "Are you saying you won't support Tristan and Rix? Because if that's the case, I can ask Flip. I'm sure he'd be happy to take dance lessons with me."

"No. Don't ask Flip."

"Are you afraid Flip will show you up?"

"No, that's not—"

"That he'll have better moves than you?"

"No, I—"

"Then what's stopping you, Nathan?"

"I'm accepting the invitation right now." I'll never hear the end of it if Flip takes my place at the dance lessons. And I won't let Tristan down. I scroll through my calendar notifications and reply yes. The lessons populate in my phone. I show it to Essie. "There. Happy?"

"Immensely." Her tone drips sarcasm. She glances at her phone. "I have to stop at The Party Place to pick up decorations."

"I can pick up decorations," I offer.

She pats me on the chest. "Just get that Plinko board ready." She spins, and her long, dark hair fans out impressively.

Why the hell do I suddenly have the desire to shove my hands and face into it and inhale?

"I'll walk you out." I saw the heads turn when we were coming to my office.

"That's not necessary."

"I have to meet a colleague." There. Now she can't read into my motives.

Greg perks up as we pass his office. Every single head turns in our direction as I walk her to the elevator. Guys I don't even know say hello. Essie smiles and murmurs a greeting in response while I just nod, my irritation growing with every lingering look.

I work in an office full of engineers. We're all science nerds. Women like Essie—who look like they stepped out of a magazine—are infrequent around here. I place a protective hand at the base of her spine and rush her to the elevators, pushing the button with the side of my wrist.

"I'll have the Plinko board done. And I'll check your spreadsheet and see what else I can tackle." I also plan to add a couple of games, but I won't put them on the list.

"Most of it is already handled."

The doors slide open.

"I'll see you on Friday in Huntsville." I shove my hands in my pockets because I don't know what else to do with them.

She steps into the elevator, hits the button, flips her hair over her shoulder, and smiles the smile that brings back good and bad memories. "Yes, you will."

The doors slide closed, and I can finally take a full breath again.

"Who's the hottie?" Greg asks.

"Shut the fuck up, Greg. Let's go for lunch."

CHAPTER 5

ESSIE

ESSIE

We're twelve hours away from leaving for Huntsville, and I'm still waiting on photographic evidence of the Plinko board.

NATE

thumbs up emoji

ESSIE

You are not instilling confidence, Nathan.

Please tell me you're finished and just being your jerk self.

NATE

Send that in a voice memo.

ESSIE

middle finger emoji

F ive minutes pass.

ESSIE

I'm serious, Nate. I need photographic evidence now.

NATE

Sounds like a threat. What's your plan? To annoy me to death with incessant messages?

ESSIE

I will come to your apartment.

NATE

I'm almost done.

ESSIE

So you have been procrastinating! I knew it!

NATE

I've been working on it all week. I don't half-ass shit.

ESSIE

I'm grabbing my keys.

I'm calling an Uber.

An image appears of a mostly finished Plinko board.

NATE

Satisfied?

ESSIE

I'd be more satisfied if it was finished.

NATE

Stop messaging me and it will be.

"The weather is ideal." I prop my fists on my hips and survey the Brights' backyard.

"It really couldn't be more perfect. Thank you for organizing this." Rix hugs me.

"I had some help." It was pulling teeth with Nate until I

showed up at his work. After that he was all over task management, almost to an annoyingly adept degree. "Besides, it was fun, and if there's ever a relationship to celebrate, it's yours and Tristan's. You two are an inspiration."

Rix's smile grows soft. "He's really come a long way, hasn't he?"

"You both have." I nudge her shoulder with mine. "I love the way you love each other."

The guy went from completely relationship adverse to completely dedicated. They attend couples therapy together so they can deal with their personal issues. They're awe-inspiring, and I'm rooting for them so hard. If anyone deserves to be loved with such ferocity, it's my bestie.

"Me too." She links her arm with mine. "You'll find your person one day."

I shrug. "I'm turning over a new leaf. No more looking for the one." Especially not in the wrong guy. I have the worst habit of falling for guys who will never give as much as they take. Moving back to Ontario got me out of another bad relationship, but I fell into the same trap a month later. He was attracted to the shell. He wanted arm candy, not someone to contribute to discussions. I'm tired of men who can't see past the surface. So I went on a self-imposed dating hiatus so I could focus on my best friend and her wedding. Between my job and organizing events for Rix and Tristan, I haven't had time for dating, which means my plan is working.

My gaze catches on Nate and Flip, who are wheeling something into the yard. Nate cut it close—the photo of the finished product came in at two a.m.—but it does look like the real deal.

I squint. "What is that?"

"I think it's one of those carnival things where you hit the target and try to ring the bell," Rix says.

I frown and consult my games spreadsheet. "That wasn't on the list."

"Bea, baby?" Tristan strides across the lawn. "Hey, Ess, sorry to interrupt, but do you want to check out the appetizer plates before we bring them to the food tent? And yes, we have cooling plates so no one has to worry about food poisoning."

"And it's all set up in the shady tent?" Rix clarifies.

"Yup." Tristan nods.

"I love you so much." She wraps her arms around his waist and tips her chin up.

He gently curves his hand around her throat, drops his head, and brushes his nose against hers. "I love you, too. I'll show you later how much."

"I'm going to check out what's happening over there." I leave them to their foreplay, my smile fading as I spot yet another game that wasn't added to the spreadsheet.

I surreptitiously check to make sure my makeup is on point and my hair isn't doing anything wonky before I head for Nate. My pink, jewel-encrusted flip-flops kick sand up the back of my legs as I hit the beach. Nate is wearing a pair of board shorts, a Terror T-shirt, and sandals. My eyeballs appreciate him more than I would like.

Which, of course, makes me snippy. "Where did this come from?" I motion to the paddleboards and modified paddles. "*What* is this?"

"It's paddleboard jousting," Nate explains.

"But, but…it wasn't on the list." I hold up my tablet. "All the donated prizes have been allocated." I was meticulous in my planning, and I won't have Nate, of all people, messing it up for me with last-minute additions.

"I scored a few donations of my own, so I added extra games. We didn't even have a pie-throwing contest, Essie." He says this like it's the most heinous crime.

"Who the hell wants to get pie in their face?" I spent half an hour perfecting my makeup this morning and setting it so it doesn't melt off my face in the summer sun.

"It's all in fun, and so is the paddleboard jousting. The guys will love it." His smile widens, and he leans in closer. "You didn't honestly think I would let you take over the entire event, did you, Ess?"

I narrow my eyes as heat travels down my spine. "Are you trying to one-up me?"

His voice is whisper quiet. "I know you're used to being the center of attention, Ess, and I'm sure it burns your ass to share the limelight. But I'm happy to knock you off a paddleboard later to cool you down."

I've been planning this for months, and he's pulling stuff out of his ass in the eleventh hour. "I see your competitive edge has finally kicked in." I pat his chest, shoving my irritation aside while trying not to appreciate how solid he is. "It's on, Nathan. May the best woman win." I wink and spin around, walking away before he can get the last word.

CHAPTER 6
ESSIE

Half an hour later, the food is set out and Rix and Tristan's friends and family start to arrive. My younger sister, Cammie, rolls in with Tally, Fee, and her boyfriend, Chase. He plays hockey for their university team, the Tilton Blaze. It's hilariously ironic, because until they started dating, Cammie had never even watched a game.

"Oh my gosh! This is so cool!" Cammie hugs me. "Well done, sis. When I get married, you're planning all the things."

"You mean when *we* get married," Chase says.

"Yes, that's exactly what I meant." Cammie pushes up on her toes and kisses him.

"We're going to have the best time tonight!" Tally steps in to hug me, too.

"I wish I was nineteen," Fee mutters.

"I promise it'll still be fun," I assure her. "Your group are right next to Brody in yurts eighteen and nineteen, and I swear that was just a coincidence."

"Sure it was." Tally bumps my shoulder.

"Thank god our parents are staying at the lodge and not here," Cammie says.

"How far behind you are they?" I ask.

"They left about an hour after us, but we had to stop at Weber's for burgers, so they should be here soon."

Flip appears out of nowhere. "Talls, Fee, when did you get here?"

"We just arrived."

He gives Chase an appraising once-over and extends his hand. "Flip Madden, brother of the bride."

"I know who you are." His eyes are wide with awe. "I'm Chase, boyfriend of Cammie, the maid of honor's sister. This is like—wow. Mind blown. It's so cool to meet you."

"Ah, Cammie's boyfriend." Flip nods slowly. "You play hockey?"

"I do, yeah."

"Cool. It's good to have you here."

"It's great to be here." Chase looks like he might pass out.

Flip turns to Tally. "Where's your boyfriend?"

"Home in Winnipeg for the summer." Tally rolls her eyes. "Besides, there's no way my dad would let me stay in the yurts if he'd come, so it's better he didn't."

"Right, good thinking, yeah." Flip nods on repeat.

"We'll just drop our stuff off and come help, if you need it." Cammie leads Chase toward the yurts.

"I think Chase is a little starstruck." Tally pats Flip's arm, then withdraws like his skin is on fire. "I'm going to settle in."

"Me too!" Fee waves as she joins Tally and heads across the yard.

Flip runs a rough hand through his hair. "I can't believe they're old enough to party with us."

"Tally's parents are coming, and so are Fee's sister and Roman, so lots of eyes watching out for them."

"Right. Cool." He rubs his bottom lip and watches them disappear into one of the yurts. "I'm going to see what else needs doing."

"Sounds good. I'll check on the bride-to-be."

"If you get tired of sleeping alone tonight, you know which yurt to find me in."

I wiggle my fingers. "My girls are good company."

He wiggles his back and winks. "My boys are better."

I bite my tongue and avoid saying something that might hurt his feelings, like how I'm sure many women can confirm that is true. Flip has made some big changes in the past couple of years. He used to be an over-the-top playboy, but he's settled down. I have a feeling his prolific love life had less to do with wanting to fuck his way through half the population of Toronto and more to do with personal issues. I get it. Despite growing up with incredible parents whose relationship is a fairy tale come true, I keep falling for the wrong guys. But not anymore. I won't give my heart to another man who doesn't deserve it.

"What's going on? Do you need something?" Nate comes busting between us.

I frown at his furrowed brow and slightly manic expression. "Yeah, for you and your black cloud of doom to go rain on someone else's parade. I need to find Rix."

I have a stag and doe to run, and my games must outshine his.

It's not long before more guests roll in, including my parents. They look adorable in their coordinated outfits.

"Honey, this is incredible!" Mom hugs me.

"I had a lot of help, I promise."

"Always so modest." Dad gives me a squeeze.

"Why don't you bring our stuff to the lodge, and I'll see if Muffy needs any help setting up?" Mom says to Dad.

"Dallas's mom is probably in the main house. I can take you over and introduce you," I offer.

Mom waves me off. "I met most of these people at the shower, and you have lots to do, I'll check in with you later." She kisses me on the cheek. "You're a wonderful best friend."

"Thanks, Mom."

My dad winks and settles a hand on her lower back, guiding her toward the house. I love their love.

The team arrives in waves, interspersed with family and other friends, and things get underway. As far as stag and does go, this one is taking the cake. I'd like to say it's all my doing, but the freaking Plinko board has a never-ending line, and so does the stupid paddleboard jousting, which I refrain from experiencing because I didn't spend all this time on my hair and makeup to have it ruined.

Also, Nate is hella competitive. He's beaten almost everyone at the paddleboard jousting. And he looks stupidly delicious in nothing but a pair of board shorts. Although, so does every other one of these hockey boys. I manage to avoid being tossed in the water by commandeering the megaphone. Every time someone tries to get me close to the lake, I call for Flip, which seems to irritate Nate.

I don't get it. I'm forever nagging him with messages, which are met with his constant disdain. He's made it clear that he can't stand me or my zeal for everything romance. So why does he feel compelled to intervene every time Flip gets within five feet of me? Despite my confusion, it is fun to annoy him, and he's hot when he gets all growly.

When Flip makes a move to be my partner in the mini-cucumber-pass game, Nate steps in and makes Tally do it with me. Which I guess is better than Tally passing a cucumber with Nate or Flip.

"Why the hell are we using mini cucumbers? Don't they usually do this with a balloon or a potato or something?" The furrow is back in Nate's brow.

"You seriously don't know?" Pretty much our entire girl-friend group has the inside scoop on this.

"Obviously you do." His gaze shifts from me to Tally, whose face is now beet red. "And you." He looks at Flip, who seems less confused and more disturbed.

"I would like to remain in the dark about this." Flip's eyes are anywhere but at me or Tally.

"Ask your brother," I tell Nate with a wink, then turn to Tally. "Ready to pass the cucumber?"

"So ready. Let's hand them their asses."

"Oh, it's on." Nate tries to clamp the cucumber between his knees, but this is the one instance where height and breadth are a disadvantage.

We kick their butts. It's the stupidest, most hilarious game.

When we move on to pin the veil on the bride, Nate pushes his way in, so we're once again competing. I'm pretty sure he cheats, which is the only reason he freaking wins. We vie for the top spot in the toonie toss, which I win, but then Nate beats me in the beanbag toss.

And then it's time for the limbo stick. By now I'm several glasses of prosecco into this night. I'm feeling no pain, and I'm also pretty limber, thanks to years of cheerleading. If ever there was a time to limbo, it's now. Of course, because Nate is in full-on competition mode with me, he also lines up in the queue. He and Chase are the only guys. The height differential isn't quite fair. All the girls are under five eight, and they're well over six feet.

It doesn't take long to whittle it down to just me and Nate. I'm surprised he's so bendy.

He strips off his shirt and tosses it aside, then rolls his head on his shoulders and does a couple of arm pinwheels, followed by deep knee bends. For a guy who works in an office, he's fit as fuck.

"Watch how it's done, sweetheart." He struts to the limbo stick, all seven hundred abs rippling as he leans back and expertly passes underneath. The crowd cheers and whistles. He chest-bumps Flip.

It's freaking ridiculous. Why is he good at something so random?

But I have more than twenty years of gymnastics on my side.

And two can play at the no-shirt game. As he approaches, probably to gloat, I pull my shirt over my head. I'm wearing a bikini top, but it isn't padded.

His eyes immediately drop to my chest and spring back to my face.

"Hold this for me please, Nathan." I purposely brush against him while also skimming his nipple as I hand him my shirt. "Two can play this game, pretty boy."

I take my place in front of the limbo stick, winking at him as I bend backwards, fingers dragging up my calves as I pass under the bar.

Nate's eyes are on fire and his breath is a little ragged as he thrusts my shirt at me.

"Thanks and good luck." I glance down. "Looks like you're a little...overstimulated."

Flip, who is quickly becoming my new favorite person, calls out, "Come on, honey bear, you're up!"

"I could use a minute," Nate grumbles, eyeing me with a familiar discontent.

"We've got a line of people waiting for their chance to play round two. Bring it, honey bear." Flip is all feigned oblivious smiles as he motions him forward.

Nate exhales harshly through his nose. "I'll get you back for this."

"I look forward to the challenge." I smile serenely.

Nate gives me a dark look that makes my entire body break out in goose bumps. He's always so...in control. But right now, he looks like he wants to shred my swimsuit and toss me in the lake. He attempts a surreptitious adjustment in his swim trunks, but the material is unforgiving. The sun has mostly set, and the tiki torches light the area, creating wonderful, telling shadows all over his body.

His air of cocky confidence has dissipated, and for a moment I almost feel bad. *Almost.* But then I consider the way he's tried to upstage me tonight with his surprise fun games and his cool prizes. He's also underestimated me multiple times, and made me feel like an annoyance every time I ask for assistance. So when he gives me an imploring look, I just cock a brow and nod to the limbo stick. It's time for comeuppance.

Resigned, he moves into position, bends backwards at the waist, and edges forward. His knees make it under, and so do his thighs, but the problem in his shorts isn't deflating despite the growing crowd of onlookers and high potential for embarrassment. He attempts to drop his hips so his problem clears the bar, but that sets him off-balance. His special parts skim the stick. Someone snaps a picture.

He lands on his back in the sand and jabs an angry finger in my direction. "You cheated!"

I bat my lashes and offer him a hand. "How could I possibly have cheated?"

He rolls to his feet, fires the double bird at me, and stalks toward the dock, where he dives gracefully into the water.

I pass under the stick with no problem, but the high of my win is slightly dampened since my challenger is cooling off in the lake.

"Seriously, Ess, the right side of my bed is yours tonight, if you want it," Flip offers.

Rix tweaks his nipple. "Stop hitting on my best friend! She does not want to hook up with you!"

"Ow! Where the hell did you come from?" Flip rubs his chest. "And I'm just playing."

She crosses her arms over her chest. "Are you, though?"

He holds up both his hands. "Ninety-percent playing and ten-percent hopeful." He winks at me.

Rix rolls her eyes and grabs my hand. "Come on. I need your help with the music!"

"Are you having fun?" I ask as we weave through the crowd.

"So much fun! I've had a lot of prosecco, though, so there's a good chance tomorrow will be rough. Also, can I just say I'm glad Tristan booked us our own little cabin because I'm liable to let him do filthy things to me when I'm in this state."

I laugh. "You're always willing to let him do filthy things to you."

She bites her lip. "This is true."

We pull up the playlist and connect the laptop to the sound system, adjusting the volume so the neighbors don't totally hate us. But they're also all invited, so we're not too worried.

I don't bother to put my shirt back on. It's a hot summer night, and the energy in the air turns frenetic and sensual as more people join us.

Tristan and Rix start grinding, and people begin to pair off, as often happens when music and too much booze are combined. I spot Nate at the edge of the action. He's changed his clothes, now wearing a black T-shirt and shorts. His gaze shifts to me and darkens as I move through the crowd.

He tucks a hand in his pocket when I reach him.

"No hard feelings about limbo." I adjust my bikini top.

He follows the movement with his eyes. "You do that on purpose."

"Do what on purpose?"

"Draw attention to yourself. Become a distraction. Make me…" His nostrils flare.

"Make you what?" I tip my head. I've heard this before. I'm always a distraction. I've been one my entire life. As a child I was the cutest kid in the room. My university degree was funded by all the flyer advertisements I posed for. As a teenager I was envied and hated by most of my peers, except Rix. Now at least I have the Babe Brigade—thanks once again to Rix—who love me as I am. But my role has been set for me by society without my permission. I'm used to the attention, but it doesn't mean I always want or like it. I asked for it tonight, though.

"Nothing. Never mind."

I roll my eyes and step into the shoes I always wear. "Lighten up, Nathan. This is a party. You're supposed to be having fun. Let loose. Come on." I grab his wrist and tug.

He doesn't budge.

"I'm not trying to get you to date me, Nate." He's brilliant and broody and beautiful. My personal kryptonite. "Put your black cloud away and relax for a minute. Tristan has looked over here fifteen times in as many minutes because he's worried. At least pretend you're having a good time."

He sighs and lets me drag him to the bar, where I order shots.

He eyes them skeptically. "Are you sure these are a good idea?"

"Positive." I'm pretty sure they're the opposite, but I'm committed to this bad decision. "Give me your hand."

He does. Albeit reluctantly.

I run the lemon wedge along the webbing between his thumb and forefinger, then sprinkle it with salt and do the same with my own. I hook my arm through his and lift a brow in challenge.

He can't resist a dare. Not when it comes to me, apparently. He's proven that tonight.

We shoot our shots, but before he can lick the webbing on his own hand, I grab his wrist, lock eyes, and suck his skin.

His eyes widen, then narrow as his fingers encircle my wrist, firmly but gently. Warmth shoots up my spine. Nate lowers his head, chocolate eyes fixed on mine as he bares his teeth and they press into my skin—just enough to be a warning. His tongue swipes, and he sucks, hard. Heat floods my center.

My heart thunders in my chest, and all the air leaves my lungs on a whoosh.

Nate's full lips pull up into a devilish grin, and his teeth press in a little harder before they finally release. He picks up the lemon, sucks that too, tosses it to the ground, and walks away.

Maybe he was right about this being a bad idea after all.

Not that I'll ever admit it.

CHAPTER 7

NATE

I walk away from Essie before I do or say something else I'll regret. Putting my mouth on her was the worst idea. Because now I won't be able to stop fantasizing about doing it again—all over her incredible body.

She keeps pushing my buttons, and I keep letting her. In fact, I fucking enjoy it. I can't stop being a competitive jerk, or feeling guilty about the past, or wanting to peel back all the layers of her so I can see what's underneath the gorgeous veneer.

Beyond my internal turmoil, though, I can fully admit that Essie has gone all out on this party. It's impossible not to appreciate how much she cares about Rix and my brother.

This means I need to do better when it comes to Tristan's bachelor weekend. It's planned, but I want his to be just as good as Essie's party for Rix, if not better. It needs to be a showstopper. And once again, I feel like a dick for wanting to outshine her, but she's a freaking organizational, event-planning genius, and I can't help myself.

Flip appears and hands me a drink.

"What is this?"

"Spiced rum and soda water with a dash of cranberry. It's

pretty good." He scans the dance floor. "Have you seen the girls?"

"Which girls?" I sucked on Essie's skin ten minutes ago, and my body is still overstimulated from that not-quite-innocent experience.

"Tally, Fee, and Cammie." He shakes the ice around in his glass. "Tally can drink, and it's an open bar. I don't want those girls getting wasted and making bad choices."

"Fee's sister is here, and so are Tally's parents," I remind him.

"The 'rents went back to the lodge already. Someone has to monitor them."

I tip my head.

"What?"

"Nothing." I could call him out, but that would open the door for him to do the same with me. I've seen the way Tally looks at him. Not with stars in her eyes, but some kind of aware-ness. And Flip is always hyper-alert when she's around, always looking out for her. Always worried. Always protective. If he gets a clue, that could change. It could also really fuck him up, and the guy has enough emotional baggage, so I keep my mouth shut.

I spot Tally sitting with her friends in the corner of the food tent. She's lost that teenage softness over the last year. I point toward them. "They're over there, with Brody and Chase."

"Okay, good." His shoulders come down from his ears, and he sips his drink. "So Essie—"

"Nope."

"She's—"

"I'm going to use the bathroom."

His laughter follows me as I go.

Halfway across the lawn, I spot Essie heading away from the party and into the dark. Alone. We're in the north. There are wild animals out here. Raccoons. Bears, even. Where in the world is her self-preservation? Did she tell anyone where she was heading? What if I'm the only one who knows she's out there on her own? I change course and follow her.

She lifts the old-school wooden latch on the shed door and disappears inside. I should turn around, or stay where I am and wait until she rejoins the party. But I don't. I slip inside the shed with her. I don't know what's wrong with me. Why do I feel compelled to follow Essie around, even though I behave like a massive asshole with every interaction?

I glance around the space. It's a typical shed, with a shelving unit that holds a bunch of random items and a few paper products, and next to that is a riding lawn mower—a nice one with a zero-turn radius. I used to fix those a lot when I took small engines in high school.

Essie strains to reach the paper towels on the top shelf as my shadow passes over her. She shrieks and spins around. "What the hell are you doing? You scared the shit out of me." She shoves my shoulder, and I stumble back a step, bumping into the door.

"Why are you wandering around in the dark on your own?" I fire back.

"I'm getting paper towels." She throws a roll at me.

It hits me in the chest and falls to the floor.

She props a fist on her hip. "Why are you following me?"

"There are bears out here." It sounds ridiculous even to my ears.

She gives me a disbelieving look.

"There are signs posted at the dump!" I've latched on to this faulty logic like a burr on a wool sweater.

She rolls her big, beautiful eyes at me. "Because it's the *dump*, and bears love a free meal."

I have no defense, and anything else I say will probably make me look even more pathetic or dickish.

She turns back to the shelf and jumps up, nabbing another roll of paper towels. She skirts around me and frowns at the lack of handle. I push on the wooden door, but nothing happens.

"Ha-ha. Open the freaking door, Nate."

I push again, but it doesn't budge. I can see very clearly through the quarter-inch gap that the wooden bar, which holds the door closed from the outside, has fallen back in place. That means we're trapped in here. Together. Just me and Essie and six years of not dealing with the shit I pulled before I left for university. "Okay, I need you to not freak out." And I need to not say something offensive or hurtful.

She crosses her arms. "You can't say that and not expect that exact thing to happen."

I give her a look and mentally plead with my eyeballs to stay above her neck. It's tough since she's still wearing only a bikini top, through which I could see her nipple shields earlier.

She returns the look and ups the ante when her pretty, pink tongue drags across her equally pretty, pink bottom lip. "Please tell me we're not locked in here, Nathan."

"I can tell you that, but I would be lying." Good work. Not offensive and truthful.

"Oh my God! *Oh my God.*" Her voice rises, and her eyes flare with the panic I was hoping to avoid. She throws the roll of paper towels at me, but we're standing close to each other, so it bumps between us and drops to the ground with the other one. She pokes me in the chest with a manicured nail. "This is your fault."

"You pushed me," I remind her.

"You followed me in here!"

"Because you were wandering around in the dark on your own!" *Why do I even care?*

"There's a party fifty feet away!" She motions to the other side of the door.

"The bears are real!"

"Why are you obsessed with the fucking bears, Nate?"

"I don't fucking know!"

"What is this really about? Are you still angry about limbo

dick?" Her eyes drop for a second, and she wrinkles her nose. "Stick."

"That was a dirty move."

She grins. "So dirty."

"Pretty proud of yourself for that one, aren't you?"

She tips her chin up. "Absolutely."

"I'm already plotting my revenge tour," I warn.

"And this is where it starts? By locking us in a shed together?" Her voice pitches up, real panic setting in as she pushes me out of the way and starts banging on the wood. "Hey! Someone let us out!" *Bang, bang.* "Anyone! We're stuck thanks to fucking Nate."

I grab her hands before she can slam them against the door again. "Stop! You'll hurt yourself." And that would also be my fault, which I can't have. I already carry around enough guilt when it comes to Essie.

Her eyes are wide, and her voice trembles. "What if we're stuck in here all night? What if we can't get out? What if no one realizes we're missing, and we die in here from inhaling riding lawn mower fumes?"

"We won't die in here. Where's your phone?"

"In my yurt, because all the people I text are outside this shed. Where's yours?" She looks hopeful and less panicked for a second.

"Also in my yurt." I let go of her wrists.

"Fuck." She throws her hands in the air. "We are going to die in here."

"That's highly improbable." But there is a chance we could be in here for a while. No one can hear us over the music. It's only ten thirty, and the party is still going strong.

"What if we do? What if we pass out from the gas fumes? What if I irritate you to the point that you put me in a sleeper hold and end up accidentally killing me?" She sucks in an unsteady breath.

I curve my palms around her shoulders. Her skin is so soft, and smooth, and warm. "Take a breath, Essie."

"You can't be the last person I see!" she laments. "You hate me!"

"I don't hate you." But I do hate the way I feel when I'm around her—guilty, on edge, overstimulated, needy. I also dislike my inability to keep my distance or my feelings in check when she's close to me. Like now.

"Liar! Every time I walk into the room, your black cloud of doom expands exponentially!"

"You're giving yourself an awful lot of credit for my bad moods."

I tighten my grip on her shoulders when she tries to move toward the door again.

"We need to figure out how to get out of here!"

"If you try to break down the door with your fists again, I will kiss you," I threaten.

Well, it's sort of a threat, because the longer I stand here, the more I really want to do just that. Feel her soft lips again. Find out whether the memory has been exaggerated in my head. And if I kiss her, I can't say anything assholey, and we'll stop bickering.

Her eyes flare. "You wouldn't."

"Are you sure about that?" We stare each other down.

Her chest is heaving.

My dick is raging.

And just as I hoped, she reaches for the door.

"Don't do it." I ease my grip on her shoulders.

"Don't boss me around."

"Keep testing me, Essie."

"Keep making idle threats, Nathan."

"I'll do it. You know I will."

"You don't always keep your promises."

My cold, dead heart lurches. "This time I will."

"We'll see about that, won't we?" She reaches behind her and touches the door.

I move my hands to her face, thumbs settling under her chin to tip it up. "God, you get under my skin."

"Good. That's been my goal from the start."

"Mission accomplished."

Essie exhales a shuddering breath, and her warm, cotton-candy-scented breath fans across my lips. I'm really going to do this. I'm going to open the lid on Pandora's box and dive right the fuck in.

Her tongue darts out. It's the permission I need.

I drop my head, and the moment our lips meet, I'm flooded with a host of emotions. I'm angry, I'm relieved, and I'm suddenly desperate for this kiss to never fucking end, because it's not just as good as I remembered, it's *better*.

Essie's lips part for me, and our tongues brush. All that aggression and frustration melts away as she loops her arms around my neck and presses against me. Soft. Sweet. Warm.

I snake one arm around her waist, holding her close, though I worry she'll come to her senses and slap me across the face or bite me. Based on the way my dick kicks at the possibility, I'm not opposed to the latter.

I run my hand down her back, curving it around her ass as I walk her back toward the riding lawn mower. When she bumps into it, I help her up onto the steel hood and groan as she wraps her legs around my waist.

She does this swirl thing with her tongue that makes my knees turn liquid. The hard steel of her nipple piercings rubs against my chest. What I wouldn't give to feel those under my fingers. To suck on the soft skin and warm metal, to get her naked and just...do all the things I thought about, dreamed about, fantasized about all those years ago. Then robbed myself of the possibility when I ghosted her.

Her hands are in my hair, nails running down the back of my neck as we make out like ravenous, hormonal teenagers.

"You taste so fucking good…" I groan against her lips.

"I know." She rolls her hips.

I almost laugh. Of course she knows. Essie was the most sought-after girl in high school. Nothing has changed, and yet everything has. "This is a bad idea."

"The worst," she agrees.

I kiss my way down her neck. "Why do you have to feel this good?"

"Because I like tormenting you," she replies.

"Well, you're doing a really fucking awesome job. I can't stop thinking about your nipples."

"I'm glad they left a lasting impression." She sucks my bottom lip.

And then we're back to making out. Hands roaming, tongues exploring. Her fingers skim along my belt line. I trail my fingers up her side. Bad idea or not, I'm suddenly desperate to know what those nipple piercings feel like under my fingertips.

The door to the shed swings open, and Essie tears her mouth from mine. I spin to face the intruder, ready to give them shit for interrupting, except it's Mrs. Bright—the owner of this shed and the lawn tractor we're making out on, and the mother of Dallas Bright.

"We got locked in," Essie rushes to explain as she smooths out her skirt.

The corner of Mrs. Bright's mouth twitches. "You don't have to defile the lawn mower. We have plenty of more comfortable spots available, which you can use like civilized folk."

"I panicked. Nate was distracting me."

"Seems like it worked," Mrs. Bright observes.

"I should deliver the paper towels." Essie grabs them from the ground and rushes out, disappearing around the corner.

I take a step toward the door. "I'm going to…just…go. Sorry, Mrs. Bright." I head toward the lake instead of following Essie back to the party.

What the hell did I just do? Worse, why do I want to do it again as soon as humanly possible?

CHAPTER 8

NATE

"That prototype is gorgeous," Greg says as we step into the local pub to grab an after-work drink.

"Super impressive," Bill agrees.

"Imagine how cool it would be to have your skate promoted by your brother's team," Patrick adds, voice filled with awe and envy.

"It would be great for my career," I agree.

Greg elbows me. "Is that the hottie who stopped by our office last week?"

I follow his gaze as we head for our usual table. Standing less than fifteen feet away is Essie. "Uh, yeah, it is."

She's dressed in a pink crop top with poofy sleeves, high-waisted jeans, and a pair of pink heels. Her hair hangs over her shoulders in artful waves, her makeup runway ready. She looks gorgeous—as usual—and also uncomfortable. A smile is plastered on her face. Her head is tipped slightly to the side, and she's twirling a lock of hair around her finger. It seems more like a nervous habit than flirtatious. It's so different from the feisty, competitive, sharp-tongued Essie I deal with.

My gaze shifts to follow hers. She's talking to a behemoth of a guy. He looks like he was carved out of marble and brought to life. Their level of attractiveness matches. I immediately dislike him.

Essie's eyes flare slightly when they find me. Mere feet separate me from her and the Adonis. Her entire demeanor shifts. She stops twirling her hair and a wide, heart-stopping smile lights up her face. "Nathan, baby, there you are!" She grabs my hand and pulls me over, ducking under my arm and snuggling into my side. I'm hit with her cotton candy and lightly floral scent. She fits perfectly against my side.

"Hey, Ess," I say slowly, going along with whatever this is, mostly out of curiosity and also because I like touching her and don't want to stop.

"Jason, this is my boyfriend, Nathan."

I swallow my shock. I'm not a small guy, far from it, but Jason looks like he eats guys like me for lunch. He could snap me like a twig. Still, I don't drop my arm, or call her out. "Hey."

"Hey." Jason looks disappointed as fuck, and like he's assessing this pairing.

Essie presses her hand against my chest and looks up at me with adoring eyes. "Nate is an engineer. He designs sports equipment. Right now he's working on a design for a new ice skate, and it's just beautiful."

"Cool. That's cool." Jason nods like things are starting to make sense.

"Nate, Jason is a fitness influencer. He has a younger sister who follows my socials," Essie explains.

"She loves Essie's makeup tutorials and skin care stuff. Essie inspired her to apply for makeup artist programs in the city." Jason's face is turning red.

I bet Jason's sister isn't the only one who watches Essie's makeup tutorials. I don't spend much time on social media, but I might have to start.

"Essie's an inspiration." I pull her tighter against my side, like a proud boyfriend would. "The way she transforms people is a real art."

"Totally, yeah, man," Jason agrees, eyes bouncing between me and Essie.

Essie smiles up at me. "I just make people look good. You're the real artist."

"Don't downplay your skill set, sweetness. You make people look and feel like the best versions of themselves."

Except me, obviously, but that's not her fault, it's mine.

"That's really sweet," she says.

"*You're* really sweet," I counter.

"I'm gonna go." Jason thumbs over his shoulder. "Thanks for the photo. My sister will be so excited."

"You're welcome," Essie says with genuine sincerity.

"Nice to meet you, man." Jason nods to me.

"You too," I lie.

Jason heads for the door. He barely clears it as he leaves the bar.

Essie elbows me in the side. "He's gone. Why are you still touching me?"

The whiplash is strong. "You put *my* arm around *you*."

She fluffs her hair and smooths her hands over her hips. That smile I know so well is plastered on her face again. "And you couldn't text me back six years ago. Thanks for your help. I accept your apology." She pats me on the chest. "You're absolved of your crimes against me."

I'm dumbstruck for a moment, but I tuck that away with all the other things I've learned about Essie lately.

It seems she didn't forget that kiss either.

It also seems like I hurt her more than she's ever let on.

That makes me feel worse, but better. Because if given the chance back then, I probably would have mishandled her soft heart. Probably even crushed it. And then maybe it wouldn't be only me who doesn't believe in love.

CHAPTER 9

ESSIE

I snap a selfie in my bathroom mirror and hit send, then apply another coat of lip gloss. My phone buzzes with new messages. Except they're not from Rix.

NATE

I feel good about it. The tiara is a nice touch.
Very on-brand princess vibes.

But it would look better on my bedroom floor.

"Shit." Heat works its way up my chest and into my cheeks. Also, I wonder, *yet again*, what Nate is like in the bedroom. Would he pay attention to detail? Is he as good with his hands as he is his mouth?

ESSIE

That wasn't for you. Disregard.

NATE

Then why did it end up in my messages?

> And who else would you be dressing up for?

> ESSIE
> The instructor, obviously.

Another message pops up.

> RIX
> Be there in ten.

Nate goes silent. I grab my purse, slip my feet into heels, leave my tiara on the vanity—it's probably a little much—and rush down to the lobby to meet my bestie.

Rix lets out a low whistle as I climb into the passenger side of her SUV. "Wow, looking hot for dance lessons."

"Is it too much?" I run my hands down my mostly bare thighs. I picked a spaghetti strap summer dress with a skirt that flares and ends about eight inches above my knee. Underneath are a pair of matching bike shorts. Nate has already seen my underwear and more of me than he probably meant to, and we don't need a repeat of that. Or for Tristan and our instructors to also get an eyeful of my butt.

"Not even a little too much." She pulls away from the front door and signals into traffic.

"I thought Tristan would be with us?" And possibly Nate, but I can't even say his name without it coming out all breathless and needy. That stupid kiss in the shed has been taking an excessive amount of bandwidth lately. It was hot, and Nate's tongue, while usually barbed when it comes to me, was toe-curlingly perfect. Despite the smell of cut grass, dirt, and gasoline, and the distinct lack of ambiance, it's now my second-favorite kiss. Irritatingly, Nate owns spot number one as well. And then there was the run-in at the bar the other day. He was so...*nice*. But I'm attributing that to his being caught off guard. Needless to say, I'm a little on edge tonight.

"He and Nate had to pick some stuff up for their boys' weekend, so they're meeting us there," Rix explains as she heads toward the highway.

"Any idea what they have planned?" I rummage around in my bag for my travel makeup kit. I need to highlight every asset I have.

"Nope. Any hints on our plan?"

"I'm maintaining the surprise. Your job is to pack a bag for a weekend of fun." I'm impressed that I've been able to keep the girls' weekend completely under wraps. The Babes know they need their passports and clothes for going out and sightseeing, plus a bathing suit, but that's it. I'm confident it will blow the guys' weekend out of the water, whatever they're doing.

"You won't even give me a hint?" She turns her pouty, sad-puppy face on me.

I stay focused on dusting bronzer on my cheeks since I'm not immune to that look. "You know I wouldn't plan something you didn't love."

"This is true."

And I don't trust that Tristan wouldn't find a way to coerce the information out of her post-orgasm. That man is fully dedicated to meeting every single filthy need she has. I switch the subject to avoid spilling the beans. "How are you feeling about everything? Are there things you need to offload onto me?"

"I'm mostly excited, and you're already handling so much."

"That's what I'm here for." I'm a helper by nature, so organizing things and taking stuff off her plate is my love language. "What are the other feelings aside from excited, and what's the ratio of those compared to the excitement?" Rix has a degree in accounting, and I love data, so percentages are a safe way to gauge how she's feeling.

She taps the wheel. "I'm eighty-five-percent excited, five-percent overwhelmed, and ten-percent nervous."

"What's overwhelming you?" I have access to her wedding plan document and spreadsheet. If I see things that are highlighted or need to be tackled, I'll just do them and mark them as done to ease her nerves and lower her stress.

"I just want it all to go smoothly, and I'm worried there will be glitches," she admits.

"Glitches are normal. And you're good at rolling with things. You have the support system in place, and everyone attending the wedding will step in to help, if it's needed."

"I know. I have to remember that." She squeezes the steering wheel. "Tristan wants it to be perfect too, but he has his own worries."

"Is that what's making you nervous?" That would make sense. Tristan is head over heels for Rix, and all he wants is to make her happy—and not fuck things up with her ever again. It's not entirely reasonable, because people make mistakes, but it's understandable considering how hard things were at the beginning of their relationship.

She nods. "His mother has called a few times, but Tristan didn't feel ready to talk to her, so he let it go to voicemail, which I completely understand. She's been absent from his life for more than a decade and a half, apart from the Christmas cards sent to their dad's house." Her grip on the steering wheel tightens. "But then she called Nate."

My stomach sinks. "Oh no."

Tristan's mom bailed when he was twelve. Nate was eight, and Brody was four. Their dad raised them on his own, and Tristan hasn't seen her since the day she left. But since last year, when Brody graduated high school, she's been making half-assed attempts to reinsert herself into their lives. None of them are particularly interested after the damage she's done, though.

"She's a real piece of work." Rix's cheek tics with irritation.

"How did Nate handle that?" I slide my mini makeup case back into my purse and focus on Rix.

"Not particularly well. He was pretty upset about it, and so was Tristan. I guess his dad stepped in and told her to back off. I'm worried she'll show up out of the blue and ruin things. And

Tristan's dad is finally dating again. It's his first girlfriend in years, and he's happy. Tristan's mom coming back into the picture is just...opening a lot of old wounds."

"I can imagine. I'm so sorry, Rix."

That woman must be a special kind of selfish to pop back into their lives all these years later, seemingly without considering how difficult it would be for them.

"Don't mention anything to Tristan, though—or Nate. It's a sensitive topic, and we're dealing with it in therapy, but Nate is struggling, and talking about it is hard for him." She turns into the dance studio parking lot and takes the empty spot beside Nate's car.

Nate is guarded on a good day, so this must be a heavy weight for him to carry. I nod. "I'll keep it between us, and if you need to vent or talk things out, you know I'm here."

We lean across the center console to share a hug. "I know, and thank you," she says. "I'm so grateful for you and everything you're doing to make this wedding a success. I know it's been a lot."

"I love this kind of thing," I assure her. "Weddings and party planning are my happy place. Anything you need, I'm here for you." Even if I never find my own Prince Charming, at least I get to help Rix tie the knot with hers.

"I'm so lucky to have you."

"Same."

We get out of the car and head inside. Tristan and Nate are waiting for us, along with another couple, who have their backs to us. As soon as Tristan spots Rix, he crosses over to us. "Hey, Ess. Hi, Bea." He pulls a modified version of his signature move, his hand at the side of her neck, thumb sweeping the edge of her jaw as he dips down to rub his nose against hers.

It's so freaking sweet. I look away, my smile faltering as my gaze lands on Nate. He's dressed in his black pants and black shirt uniform. Except instead of a button-down, he's wearing a

T-shirt, which is somehow even hotter. He does not look excited to be here. Although, he never looks excited to be anywhere.

His furrowed brow deepens as his eyes move from my feet all the way to my face. He runs a hand through his hair. "Ess," he grinds out.

"Nathan."

I'm awarded with another glower.

This should be fun—in a stepping-on-a-Lego-barefoot kind of way.

"Essie?" A deep, familiar voice drags my attention away from Nate.

My heart plummets into my feet as I take in the other couple. *What are the freaking chances?* "Barton?"

"Hey! Wow. It's been a long time." Barton's eyes move over me. He puts his arm around the woman next to him. "This is my fiancée, Alison."

"It's so nice to meet you." I extend a hand and she takes it, looking questioningly at Barton.

"You too," she says. "How do you and Barton know each other?"

"Oh, uh, we're old friends." Barton chuckles uncomfortably.

My stomach lurches, and I fight to keep the smile on my face. We dated for several months before I took the job in Vancouver. He told me he loved me, I thought maybe he was the one—although I think they're all the one—and then he got a slick job offer in Sri Lanka and didn't tell me he was moving. He broke up with me in a text message. That was three years ago.

"How's your job? Are you still a photographer?"

Alison threads his arm through hers. "He's been featured in *National Geographic*. We met a few years ago when he was stationed in Sri Lanka. We just came from Granada."

"Oh, that must have been wonderful," I choke out.

Just then our instructors enter to introduce themselves. *Thank God.* I move to stand beside Nate. He gives me a questioning look. I ignore him and focus on Fernando and Martina.

Fernando is a tall, lean, dark-haired man dressed in black pants, matching shoes, and a mostly unbuttoned flower-print shirt. He has an impressive swath of chest hair. Martina is a petite, dark-haired woman with a dancer's figure, wearing a siren red dress and matching stilettos.

"Such beautiful couples!" Fernando praises.

Nate mutters something I don't catch. I stay silent and plaster a smile on my face, even though I'm reeling.

Fernando and Martina give us a rundown of the routines we'll learn today. I try to follow along, but I'm already in a weird spiral. After Barton told me he loved me, I'd moved us in together and started planning our wedding—something exotic, of course. And here he is, three years later, engaged. And here I am, single with no prospect of my own happily ever after on the horizon.

"We'll start with the two-step, then move on to ballroom, and finish with the salsa." Martina punctuates the sentence with a swish of her hips.

"The purpose of this class is to give you the basics, and don't forget to have fun!" Fernando adds, directing a loving smile at his partner.

I side-eye Nate, wishing I hadn't pretended he was my boyfriend to escape Jason, who probably doesn't have a younger sister. Nate was so nice that night. It's confusing.

And I've dreamed about that shed kiss escalating past first base every night this week. Last night we made out in front of Jason and made him cry. *What's wrong with me?* My body is already pinging with pent-up sexual frustration, mostly because I've refused to handle my situation on principle. Getting myself off to the fantasy of a guy who can't stand me is a low I don't want to stoop to.

I turn to face Nate as instructed and slip one palm into his, settling the other hand on his shoulder, while his hand curves around my waist. He tries to pull me closer, but I resist.

His deliciously furrowed brow deepens. "There's a foot of space between us. This isn't a grade-eight dance, Ess."

"This is fine. We don't need to be closer." I keep my eyes firmly fixed on his chin.

He sighs and tries to close the gap, while I try to maintain it.

"Let your partner lead." Martina adjusts our hands, then places a palm on both of our backs to move us closer together.

Nate arches an I-told-you-so brow.

"Nice and loose. Relax. And dancing is sensual. You want your eyes on his." She taps her chin.

I drag my eyes to Nate's and hate how pretty they are. He smirks. I step on his toe and get told to watch my feet by the instructor.

It takes an eternity to get everyone into position. Or at least that's how it feels with Nate making uncomfortable eye contact and my vagina having all kinds of feelings about his hands on my body while my ex and his fiancée giggle and smile.

"Who is that guy, and why do you feel like a piece of plywood?" Nate grouses.

"He's an ex."

Nate's narrowed gaze shifts his way. "From how long ago?"

"A few years. Pretty sure he broke up with me for that woman. Over text."

Nate's expression darkens further. I wish he was less sexy. I wish I didn't give my heart away so easily, and that it didn't get beaten up so badly when I do.

"You two need to give each other a little space," Martina calls to Rix and Tristan.

I feel horribly awkward and stiff as we learn the two-step. I try not to look over at Barton and Alison. But focusing on the heat of Nate's palm burning through my thin dress isn't any better.

Nate dips down until his mouth is at my ear, lips brushing my cheek as he speaks. "Get out of your head, Essie."

A shiver runs along my spine. "I'm not." *Such a lie.*

"Stay focused on me. That guy's a fucking idiot, and you're better off without him."

"His photographs have been featured in *National Geographic*."

"Impressive, but he's still an idiot." His eyebrows lift. "We can outdance him."

He's probably being nice out of guilt or pity, but I'm all for using his competitive edge for face-saving purposes.

"Relax! Have fun!" Martina instructs, breaking the tension between us.

Tristan and Rix are laughing and having a great time. Barton and Alison seem to have already mastered the two-step and are dancing around the room with ease.

I will not be outdanced by my ex.

I relax into Nate's arms.

He smirks and takes the lead.

Surprisingly, he's a good dancer. I don't want to find it sexy, but the way he takes control and guides me around the room is irritatingly hot. And it's wildly satisfying that we're infinitely better than Barton and his fiancée.

We move on to ballroom dancing. Nate proves to be a versatile partner, and he's just as good at this as he was at the two-step. We dance circles around my ex while Tristan and Rix are called out several times because his hand placement is inappropriate. They will for sure bone like bunnies when they get home. And I will have to take a cold shower so I don't give in and get myself off to thoughts of Nate.

Salsa is the most complicated of the routines, but our competitive sides have been fully engaged, especially since Barton and Alison already seem to be salsa pros. But determination, Nate's attention to detail, and my bendiness give us an advantage. He lifts and spins and twirls and dips me. My leg ends up on his shoulder in some complicated spin-dip move. And then our bodies press tight against each other. His hot gaze is locked on mine, and I can't look away. Nate's knee finds its way between my thighs, and he hooks my knee over his hip as we attempt another advanced-level combo.

I'm sweaty and breathless by the time the song comes to an end. I can't break free from Nate's dark, satisfied gaze. This feels like the most incredible foreplay, and every part of me is hot with desire.

Clapping startles us. Nate and I release each other and step back. He shoves his hands in his pockets, and I smooth mine over my hips. I'd completely forgotten about Barton and Alison.

Our instructors are beaming. My ex is staring at us, his fiancée looks annoyed, and Rix and Tristan are sitting on one of the benches, both of them regarding us with more interest than I'd like.

Rix hugs Tristan's biceps. "You two have been so weird tonight."

I smile and flick the end of my ponytail over my shoulder, feigning nonchalance and avoiding direct eye contact. "Nate's really competitive," I explain. "Seems to run in the family."

CHAPTER 10

NATE

"What's in the box?" I check my pockets to make sure I have everything I need before I head over to see my brother.

"Dunno. It has my sister's name on it. She probably sent it here by accident." Flip stands in front of the stove, stirring cheese powder into the pot. The guy loves neon noodles. There is a salad on the counter, as well as seasoned, cooked chicken breast—both provided by Rix—so at least all his food groups are covered and there's some balance.

"I can drop it off at their place."

"Are you sure you don't mind?" Flip dumps most of the pot onto his plate alongside the chicken.

"Not at all. I'm on my way there now." The guys' weekend is around the corner. I've kept the location under wraps, so it'll be a sweet surprise, but there are a few details to iron out.

"Okay, cool. Rix will appreciate it." He turns to face me. "Heard you're quite the dancer."

"Fuck off." I shoot him the bird, shove my feet into my shoes, grab the box—it's surprisingly light—and head for the door. Of course Tristan or Rix said something to him. Essie was a cheerleader and a gymnast. So maybe I watched a couple of tutorial videos prior to our lessons. I wasn't going to be upstaged by Little Miss Sunshine and Rainbows.

Her ex being there shifted things, though. If that had been Lisa with the guy she dumped me for, I don't know that I would have been able to keep my shit together. I probably would have turned into a giant asshole instead of a sheet of plywood. The more time I spend with Essie, the more intrigued I become. Sure she bounces back after heartbreak, but it still hurts her. I could see it on her face, feel it in her stiff posture. How many scars does her heart have? How deep are they?

Flip's laughter follows me into the hall.

I take the elevator to the lobby and walk the two blocks to my brother's building. We're experiencing a typical July heatwave, so even this late in the day, the blast of air conditioning when I step into the foyer is a welcome reprieve from the humidity.

My brother buzzes me in. The door is propped open with the safety latch when I arrive. I still knock and poke my head in, to be safe. "Tris? You here and decent?"

He rounds the corner wearing a pair of gray shorts and a black T-shirt with the word BAE in pink block letters. "Hey, bro. How's it going?"

"It's going."

He pulls me in for a one-armed back pat, then steps back, glancing at the box tucked under my arm. "What you got there? Something for the guys' weekend?"

"This was dropped off at Flip's, but it's for Rix." I set the box on the counter.

"Oh. I bet that's the thing she's been checking for compulsively this week. Thanks for bringing that over." He heads for the fridge. "Can I get you something to drink? Or eat? Bea made blueberry muffins, and raisin bran, and banana walnut."

"She on a nervous baking kick?" Rix loves to make food, but when she's stressed, she makes *a lot* of food. As of late there have been more deliveries than usual for Flip, and he and I have been invited for impromptu dinners because they have no room in their fridge.

"You know it."

"All of Rix's muffins are magical, so I'll take whatever. Where is she, anyway?" I've come to really enjoy Rix. She's soft and kind and like the sister I never had.

Tristan sets the container of blueberry muffins on the counter. "She's at Essie's."

"Everything okay?" I haven't said a word to anyone about that kiss/make-out session at the stag and doe, but I don't know if Essie kept it to herself. I doubt Tristan would be all that enthused if he knew.

"Yeah, it's all good. I think they're planning their girls' weekend." He loads a plate and puts it in the microwave for thirty seconds.

"You find out where they're going yet?"

He shakes his head. "I can't really push Essie to tell me when you're keeping the boys' weekend all hush-hush."

"I can't believe Ess hasn't even told you," I muse. It's been hard enough keeping the boys' weekend to myself, and Tristan hasn't been needling me for information.

"She knows it wouldn't take much for me to spill the secret to Bea under the right circumstances." He snaps a quick pic of the box and sends it to Rix.

The microwave dings, and I retrieve the butter dish from the cupboard and a knife from the drawer. Flip and I come over for dinner at least once a week, so I'm familiar with where everything is. Rix always sends us home with leftovers. It's the closest thing to a family dinner I've had apart from holidays since I went away to university. Growing up we were always eating on the run. Tristan had hockey and so did Brody, and I had robotics competitions. It was a lot for a single dad to juggle.

Tristan and I take seats at the kitchen island. I pop the top off two muffins, add a pat of butter to each, and pass the knife to my brother.

"What's in the box, anyway?" I ask.

"Don't know. There've been a lot of deliveries lately, and unless they're addressed to me, I leave them alone. Last week I accidentally opened a box from a lingerie store and got in trouble because it was supposed to be for the wedding night, and I ruined the surprise."

"Shit."

"Yeah. She had to order something new, and I almost made her cry, so now I just steer clear," he explains.

"She cried over lingerie?" Rix is pretty levelheaded most of the time.

"She spent hours searching for the perfect set, and it was expensive. I wish she wouldn't stress over money so much, but hopefully with time that'll ease up." He slathers butter over his muffin tops.

"She and Flip had it rough when they were young." I see hints of his thriftiness all the time. He always grabs extra vegetable bags from the grocery store, and he never throws out leftovers, even if they would barely qualify as a snack. I bite into the muffin and groan. "Man, these are good."

"I know," he mumbles around a mouthful.

"Mom never made us treats like this." The words are out before I can call them back. It feels like a bad omen to talk about her.

He pauses, his muffin an inch from his mouth. "She call you again?"

"Not in the past week or so." My stomach twists. I wish I hadn't opened this can of worms, and that I could lie to him about it.

His eyes narrow. "When did she call last?"

"Before the stag and doe. I didn't answer." But I stupidly listened to the voicemail again.

Tristan nods. "I left her a message a week ago. It wasn't particularly kind or friendly, so I'm hopeful she got the message

76

to fuck off. I just want to keep her away from Brody." He sighs and runs a hand through his hair. "I don't want her to fuck with his head the way she keeps trying to fuck with ours."

"It was easier when she just stayed gone," I agree. Easier to bury the memories, easier to pretend she wasn't still out there, that she hadn't left us.

Tristan leans back in his chair. "You know, if you want to talk to someone about it, I can hook you up with my therapist."

"There's nothing to talk about." I take another big bite, but it tastes like cardboard now.

Tristan sighs and laces his hands behind his head. "I felt the same way for a long time. But I know I'm fucked up because of the way Mom left. We all are. Talking about it sucks. It hurts."

"So why do it then?" I can't think about it without having feelings, and hashing those out with some stranger is a hard nope.

"Because I was hurting Bea, and I hated myself for it," he says somberly.

My head snaps in his direction.

He raises a hand, reading the shock on my face. "Not physically."

Relief dissolves the weight in my stomach. "Then how?"

"Emotionally, which is just as bad, if not worse in a lot of ways." He swallows and fidgets with his napkin.

It's clear this makes him feel...something. Sadness? Guilt? Discomfort? I get the last two. I feel those every time I think about Essie. Along with lust.

Tristan and Rix didn't have the easiest start, but they're here, trying to make it work. Even after all the shit we've been through, Tristan managed to find love and keep it. For now. "Worse how?"

"I didn't know how to deal with my feelings, and I have a lot of them when it comes to Bea. In the beginning, sometimes they came out in unhealthy ways, and I couldn't give her the parts of me she deserved because I was too fucking afraid. But therapy has helped. It's not easy, and some days I feel like a giant bag of shit."

"But why do it if it makes you feel like trash?" Every call I avoided from our mother put me in a mood for days. I can't even fathom what talking about it would do.

"Because Bea doesn't deserve to feel bad because I can't handle my feelings. I used to shut down when things got hard, but that's not fair to her. I can't walk away from the person I want to spend the rest of my life with. I love her so fucking much. I want to deserve her, deserve the love she gives, deserve her patience and kindness and goodness, but that won't happen if I don't deal with the shit that made me so closed off and angry. So I talk to someone every other week, and Bea and I go together once a month. We talk it through now, and she calls me on my shit when I'm being a dick. It's a leap of faith, and she's worth it."

"I thought Lisa was worth it." For a year and a half I thought I had stability, someone to lean on, someone to love. And then she found someone else, someone better, took it all away, and left me with more holes in my stupid heart.

"I know. I'm sorry that didn't work out."

"It was for the best." She's still dating the guy she cheated on me with, so they're obviously better suited for each other.

His phone buzzes with a message. "Looks like that package was supposed to go to Essie's."

"I'll drop it off." I finish the rest of my second muffin.

"You want to go through the guys' weekend stuff first?"

"Nah. I can stop by tomorrow." I stand and round the counter, putting my plate in the dishwasher and washing my hands.

His brow furrows. "You sure you don't mind?"

"It's really no problem." I don't know why I'm in such a hurry to leave, other than this conversation makes me uncomfortable and for whatever reason, I want to see Essie. Maybe so I can get the details on their girls' weekend.

That's probably it. I'm competitive. I need the guys' weekend to rock. What other reason would there be?

CHAPTER 11
ESSIE

I am not dressed for a visit from Nate, and yet he's here. I check my reflection in the hall mirror on the way to the door and wish I was still wearing my cute jean shorts and top and not my ratty jogger shorts and an oversized, baggy crop top. The latter is totally bestie-appropriate wear. The former is better for greeting the hot, smart guy I made out with on a lawn tractor, who posed as my boyfriend for no reason I can understand, and who danced like it was his job to show up my ex.

Most of the time he's an insufferable jerk, but recently he's done some things to balance it out. And I can't stop thinking about that kiss. Or how good his arms feel around me. It's such a problem.

I take a steadying breath, adopt a smile, and open my apartment door. "Hey, Nate."

"Essie." His gaze meets mine, then drops for a couple of beats before it lifts again. "This was delivered to the wrong location." He taps the box under his arm.

"Thanks for bringing it over."

"I was in the neighborhood." He doesn't make a move to hand it to me.

Maybe it's heavy. "Do you want to come in for a minute?"

Looks like we're being formal and appropriate, not antagonistic and competitive. At least for now.

His eyes dart briefly to my mouth. "Sure."

Rix appears, purse slung over her shoulder. "Hey, Nate."

His expression softens. "Hey, Rix."

She comes in for a hug, which he returns. "Thanks for bringing that all the way over here."

"It's not a problem," he assures her.

She kisses me on the cheek. "I'll message when I get home, and I'll probably see you tomorrow, unless work gets in the way."

"Sounds good."

She slips on her flip-flops, waves, and walks out the door. I secure the safety out of habit, then turn to Nate, who's now standing inside my apartment looking uncomfortable and unreasonably sexy in a pair of black shorts and a black shirt. The bulk of his wardrobe is funeral appropriate.

I remind myself that I've sworn off men. Then in the next beat, I internally debate the merits of a fuck buddy. I need to learn not to get attached. Nate has made his stance on love and relationships clear. He's not interested. Our life goals do not align. Which could make him a good option for no-strings fun, if I could learn how to do that…

After a moment I realize that while I've been up in my head, he's been standing in my kitchen, still holding the box. My manners kick in. "Can I offer you something to drink? I have a few beers and some white wine."

"I could have a beer." He sets the box on the counter.

I head for the fridge, glad to have somewhere else to look.

The telling buzz of a phone has me looking for mine—my mom is supposed to call after her pottery class tonight—but Nate pulls his out of his pocket, frowns, jabs a button, and shoves it back in. His mood seems to shift, eyes darkening. I swear it's like a rain cloud has just rolled into my apartment.

I grab a beer and the bottle of wine Rix and I opened earlier. I uncap the beer and pass it to Nate. "Everything okay?" I pour myself a little wine.

"There's a lot of color in here." Nate's gaze moves around my apartment. It makes me self-conscious, especially knowing what I do about him, and how people perceive me. There are pink bows adorning my bookshelves, and a *Once Upon a Time* poster is hanging in the living room. I'm in love with love. I always have been. Fairy tales bring me joy.

"I like bright things." And apparently dark things with the way my body is responding to his presence in my apartment.

"You've really leaned into the whole princess fantasy, eh?"

"You're really leaning into the total asshole fantasy, eh?" I fire back.

His expression shifts, and he runs a hand down his face. "Sorry. It was my mom that just called. I've been avoiding her for a while."

"Oh." My defensiveness tones down a notch. "Do you want to talk about it?"

"We're not the kind of people who talk about things, are we?" His gaze moves over me in an assessing, not unappreciative sweep.

"I guess not." I pull my hair over my shoulder, exposing my neck.

I'm used to being looked at. Admired. As a teenager, I was flattered. As an adult, it's become a curse I can't escape. Yet also a reflex.

Nate could have just dropped off the box and left, especially after dodging a call from his mother. But he didn't. He's still here, of his own free will. "Do you want the grand tour?" There isn't much to my apartment, but it's better than standing here staring at each other.

"Sure." He takes a long swig of his beer.

"This is the kitchen." I motion to our surroundings, then beckon him to follow me to the living room. A series of framed art prints featuring princesses and their princes line the wall. The bookshelves are filled with books based on fairy tales.

"You and pink are a thing, eh?" he observes, pausing to examine the photo collage comprised of pictures of me and Rix over the years.

"It's a happy color." And related to love and sexuality. I straighten a heart-shaped throw pillow and fold a blanket, draping it over the arm of the couch, which is a dusty rose color.

Nate stops at the bookshelf, scanning the titles. One shelf consists solely of special-edition fairy tales, but the one below still holds a handful of my textbooks from university—the ones I sometimes refer back to when I need to look up the chemical structure of a specific makeup or skin care product.

"Quite the eclectic array of reading material." He plucks a textbook on the science of skin care from the shelf and leafs through it before sliding it back in place. "I didn't realize how much chemistry is involved."

"Combining the wrong products can cause unpleasant interactions," I explain.

Nate tips his head. "It's science and art. You went to university just like I did. Don't downplay the challenge or the accomplishment."

"It's a vastly different skill set, and mine won't change lives." I point toward the next door and change the subject. "The bathroom is through there."

Nate leaves it alone and pokes his head inside the bathroom. His eyebrows lift, but he doesn't comment. The pink theme is strong, but no other guy who's been in my apartment has focused on the color, the décor, or my bookshelves.

Nate heads for the last door, which is my bedroom. The one room I hadn't planned to show him.

I set my wineglass on the coffee table and gazelle leap past him to barricade the doorway. My bedroom is an homage to every princess fairy tale I've ever read. He will one-hundred percent make fun of me if he sees it.

His body collides with mine, and I slap a hand over his eyes. "You can't see my bedroom."

"Why not? What's the worst that could happen?" His fingers curve around my mine as he pries them away from his eyes.

I could try to seduce him, and he could reject me, and the next few weeks would be unbearably awkward. I reach behind me and pull my bedroom door closed. "It's a mess because Rix and I were narrowing down my wardrobe choices for our girls' weekend. All my bathing suits and pretty lingerie are lying on my bed."

Nate's fingers stay wrapped around mine, and his nostrils flare. "Why do you need lingerie for a girls' weekend?"

I smile up at him, enjoying the dark look on his face. "I like to be prepared for every possible adventure."

He scowls and clears his throat.

I wish everything about him wasn't such a turn-on.

"Are you saying that to push my buttons?"

"Do you want me to push your buttons, Nathan?"

"Maybe." His voice softens. "I bet your lingerie is all pink and lacy."

"Wouldn't you like to know?"

"Yeah, actually, I would." His brow creases. "And it's driving me up the fucking wall."

His admission shocks and emboldens me. He doesn't believe in love, doesn't want the same things I do, so hooking up with him will never lead to anything else. He won't fall for me, and I won't fall for someone who thinks love isn't even real. He's safe because he can't hurt me. So I needle him. "Can't stop thinking about that kiss, huh?"

"No. I can't. I also can't stop thinking about dance lessons and that idiot ex of yours." He's sincere *and* annoyed.

Our eyes lock, and then drop to each other's mouths.

I want him to break.

And he does. "Fuck it."

One second, we're standing in the middle of the hallway, and the next, I'm pressed against the wall, Nate's knee between my thighs and his lips dragging along the column of my throat.

"Why do you have to be so fucking tempting?" He groans and bites the edge of my jaw.

"Because the dark is always trying to consume the light."

He pauses for a moment, eyes on me. "Not inaccurate." Then he slants his mouth over mine.

I part for him, and we both make needy, relieved noises as our tongues brush. Those dance lessons earlier in the week felt like the best kind of foreplay, but my self-administered orgasm later that night was lackluster at best. I'd been angry for caving in, but I needed the release.

Nate is the most competitive man I know. And that's saying something because I've been surrounded by hockey players and actors for years. I bet he's just as driven in the bedroom. It suits his personality.

We could relieve some of the tension between us. Maybe then I'll stop fixating on that damn kiss.

I move his hand under my shirt. His fingers skate up my ribs, and he makes a deep sound of approval as his thumb finds my nipple. It sends an electric jolt through my body that settles between my thighs and comes out of my mouth as a moan.

"Shit, that's hot." He rolls my nipple between his thumb and forefinger.

I slip a single digit into the waistband of his shorts. When I'm not met with a reprimand, I pop the button. He's already hard. Surely we can get each other off without me mentally marrying his brilliant, grumpy, unpleasant, hot ass.

I can touch his dick and not envision walking down the aisle with him. Hell, we made out over a week ago and at no point have I moved him into my apartment. Not even in a dream. I can get mine and not become emotionally attached.

I slide my hand into the front of his boxers and grip his exceptionally generous erection. I shut down any thoughts about it probably being a pretty boyfriend dick. Nate is the opposite of boyfriend material, but he's excellent fuck-buddy fodder. He groans and squeezes my breast.

But then he wrenches his mouth from mine and pulls back.

For a second I think he's about to tell me it's a bad idea. Which honestly, it really is, even if neither of us is willing to voice that, *again*.

Instead, he pushes his shorts and boxers down, revealing his big, beautiful cock in my fist. I stroke the length, rubbing my thumb over the weeping tip. I'm so glad I took Rix out for a mani a few days ago.

"Fuck yes, that's..." He drops his head and turns his face toward my neck, lips parting against the skin. His tongue sweeps out, followed by his teeth. "So fucking good, Ess."

"How long do you think you'll last before you come all over my hand?" I taunt.

He lifts his head again, desire-heavy eyes meeting mine as his other hand skims my ribs and travels along the waistband of my shorts. "I bet I can get you off first."

Of course he'd turn it into a competition. "I'd love to see you try."

His long, thick fingers slip beneath the waistband of my shorts and into my panties. They glide over smooth skin and dip between my thighs. His brow furrows as he skims my clit.

Anxiety skitters across my skin like biting ants. I wait for the judgment.

"Are you...? Is that..." He brushes over it again. "Do you have a hood piercing?"

"Yeah."

He skims it again, sending another jolt of desire echoing through me.

"Didn't it hurt?"

He circles my clit, and my eyes roll up. "Less than you'd think, to be honest."

"Did you get it to make sex feel better?" His curiosity is distracting, but also...endearing.

"I dated a tattoo artist for a couple of months. He did them all for free. We broke up before they healed fully." Turns out mine wasn't the only clit he was playing with.

"But you kept them." He keeps circling my clit, light touches that make my entire body sing with need.

"They heighten the experience," I explain.

"It's sexy. I like it."

His approval eases the tension slightly.

He moves past my clit and slides one finger inside me.

A sigh leaves my lips, and my head falls back. It's been months since anyone has touched me. Months since I've had anything but self-administered orgasms. And I don't understand the logic, or lack of it, but how satisfying is it that the man who ghosted me all those years ago can't keep his hands off me now?

We find a rhythm, my hand moving over his length and his fingers pumping inside me, palm rubbing my clit, bringing me closer and closer to the edge. I try to hold back, to increase my pace and tighten my grip on his stunningly hard erection. But his expression is one of sheer determination, and when he finds *the spot* that makes me gasp and moan, he doubles down.

"That's it, Ess." He kisses my neck. "I know you're close."

My legs shake, and everything below the waist tightens. I whimper and try to hold on to my control, but it's slipping away.

"It's okay. You can let go." He cups my cheek in his palm as he strokes inside me again. "You're so soft." His lips brush over mine. "So fucking sweet and pretty." He pushes deeper, stretching me, filling me, making my body come alive under his touch. "I want to feel you come all over my fingers, Essie. Show me I affect you, too."

I grip his shoulder and grind down into his palm. The world is a wash of stars and white as the orgasm rushes through me. It's incredible, mind-blowingly fantastic. My body hums with pleasure. My eyes flutter open and meet Nate's feral, satisfied gaze.

He won. Of course he won.

This round. But the game is far from over.

His admission gives me courage. This man, who is always stoic and in control, loses it with me.

I resume stroking him. "Imagine how good it would feel if you were fucking my mouth and not my hand, Nathan." I suck his bottom lip. "My lips stretched around you." I let the plush flesh slide through my teeth. "How much of your cock do you think I could take?"

Dark desire makes his lip curl. "You'd take all of it, because you wouldn't want to lose again."

A coy smile tips the corner of my mouth as I nibble across his jaw. "Did I really lose, Nate? Now you have the memory of me coming just for you, and it'll be right there every time you think of me."

"Just like you'll think about me," he counters.

"Imagine me on my knees for you, Nate."

His gaze drops as I lace the fingers of my free hand with the one already stroking him.

"Shit. Fuck—" He groans.

"My mouth full of your thick cock." I slide both thumbs up his shaft and circle the crown. "Your hands in my hair." Slow stroke. "Guiding me." Tight squeeze. "Your cum sliding down my throat, because I'd swallow for you, Nathan, like a good girl does."

"For fuck's sake, Ess." His eyes roll up, and he slaps a palm against the wall as he pulses in my hands. It's a powerful feeling, knowing I broke him, that his careful control snapped because of me. That he wants me, even though he shouldn't.

"Your mouth is filthy." He drops his head to my shoulder, following with a soft kiss.

"You didn't seem to mind."

"No. I really didn't, did I?"

"Don't you feel better?" I ask brightly.

He snorts a laugh and straightens. A rare, pretty smile curves one corner of his mouth. "Yeah. I feel better."

"You made a big old mess, by the way." There's cum on my shirt, my hands, and the floor.

His cheeks flush an adorable shade of pink. "Let me get something to clean that up with."

"I'll get it." I slip out from between him and the wall, needing to get away before any potential awkwardness has a chance to settle in.

I wash my hands, blot the residue on my shirt with a damp face cloth, and grab a few tissues to manage the mess on the floor.

But when I return, Nate has already handled it with paper towels from the kitchen.

He stands there, one hand tucked in his pocket. The other he runs through his hair.

And there's the awkwardness I wanted to escape.

"So thanks for stopping by." I head for the box on the counter. "And for dropping this off." I pull a pair of scissors from the drawer and run them across the edge.

"What's in there that was so important, anyway?"

I show him the contents.

"Are you fucking kidding me? This is what I wasted my entire night for?"

I pat him on the chest. "Did you not get an outstanding handy out of the deal?"

He side-eyes me but offers a grudging smile. "It was an excellent handy. And I did get to play with your clit ring, so I guess it was worth the trouble."

CHAPTER 12
NATE

"I cannot believe this shit," I mutter as we board the plane.

"What are the chances, right?" Flip is all smiles.

"We're not changing seats. The girls sit with the girls, and the guys sit with the guys, and that's that," I snap. "This is not a couples' weekend." I thought I was being all sly, keeping the destination of Tristan's boys' weekend under wraps. But here we are.

"I'm not part of a couple," Flip reminds me.

"Neither am I." Essie's sunshine-and-rainbows voice comes from behind us.

"Or me!" adds Dred Reformer, Flip's neighbor and firmly platonic friend.

"The rest of you better not pair off," I grumble.

"Do you hear that, sweetheart? You sit with Tristan, and I sit with Aurora." Lavender pats Kodiak on the chest. She's his wife, and a tiny thing. She's wearing a dress the color of her name with lime green infinity symbols edging the hem and winding around her waist and over her shoulders. It's more like art than clothing. "I'm right across from you."

Kodiak frowns. He and my brother played hockey together for a summer when they were teens at the Hockey Academy.

"What's the holdup?" Essie asks from behind me.

"Kodiak doesn't want to be separated from Lavender," Flip explains.

"Everyone needs to sit in their assigned seat so we don't hold up boarding!" I call.

Lavender unwraps the scarf from her neck and winds it around his hand. "You'll be fine. Until an hour ago, you thought you were spending three days away from me. You can handle sitting across the aisle for five hours."

He sighs and flops into his seat. Aurora, also often referred to as Hammer because the hockey boys like to use last names, takes the spot beside Lavender, and they share a giggle. Aurora works for the Terror; she's also Roman's daughter and Hollis's girlfriend. Roman and Hollis retired from the league at the end of last season, they're best friends, so the levels of complication are high.

There are sixteen seats in first class, and we take up all of them. My group includes me, Kodiak, and my brother's current and recently retired teammates.

The girls in Rix's friend group have dubbed themselves the Badass Babe Brigade. Today they're wearing shirts proclaiming them as *Bea's Babes*. Two of them are pregnant, so we get them seated quickly. Rix and Essie end up across from me and Flip.

Everyone takes their seat, and because karma is clearly having a laugh at my expense, Essie makes eye contact while applying her lip gloss. I immediately want to take her to the bathroom so I can kiss it right off her perfect lips.

"What are the fucking chances, eh?" Flip says jovially.

I drag my gaze away from Essie. "Seriously."

If everyone pairs off, I'll be super pissed. But at the same time…I sure wouldn't mind getting my hands on Essie again. Or having her hands on me. I'm also hella impressed that she single-handedly managed to wrangle all these women onto a plane without anyone finding out where they were going. I finally had to cave a couple of days ago and tell Flip so I could get his help on a few things.

More passengers board the plane. It doesn't take long for people to realize first class is full of professional hockey players. The poor flight attendants keep redirecting people to their seats, and boarding takes way longer than it should. Women and children shriek, and men turn into starstruck fools. It's quite the experience.

Eventually everyone is where they're supposed to be, and the flight attendants pass out glasses of champagne to our group, except for Shilpa and Lexi, who accept orange juice and crackers. People keep trying to use the bathroom at the front of the plane so they can get things signed.

Once we're in the air, it turns into a freaking party. The girls clean them out of sparkling wine. I'm half-hoping they get plane drunk and all need a two-hour nap once we land in Vegas.

Rix gets up to use the bathroom.

I connect to the Wi-Fi so I can get free messaging and warn my brother to keep his mouth shut, but I have new messages from Essie, so I check those first.

> **ESSIE**
>
> This is super suss.
>
> Did you find my travel plans while I was cleaning your jizz off my hands?

I shoot her a look.

She bats her lashes and refocuses on her phone.

> **ESSIE**
>
> Where are you boys staying?

> **NATE**
>
> Why?

> **ESSIE**
>
> 👀

NATE

You want me to play with your clit ring again?

I want to play with her clit ring again. And I want to get my mouth on her nipples.

ESSIE

My clit could be persuaded.

But also because Kodiak can't be separated from Lavender.

NATE

I'm not telling you.

ESSIE

Hard for you to find out how pretty I look with my mouth full of your cock if you don't. 🔒

She pockets her phone when Rix returns to her seat.

"What hotel are you guys staying at?" Rix asks.

I shake my head. "I'm not telling you."

"The Drake," Flip says at the same time.

I shoot him a look.

"They were going to find out eventually."

He's not wrong, but still. And Essie is right about not being able to play with her if I don't know where she's staying.

"Seriously?" Essie narrows her eyes. "How is this even possible? Did you go snooping around when you stopped by the other night?"

"You stopped by Essie's?" Flip leans forward. "I keep telling you, I could be the one."

"The one I don't need," she quips, batting her long lashes.

This trip is turning into a shitstorm. "Can you two stop talking around me?" The last thing I need is Flip flirting with Essie all weekend. "I had to drop something off because apparently it couldn't wait twenty-four hours. I wasted a whole night running around," I grouse.

But mostly I'm frustrated that I can't get the sound, smell, and feel of Essie coming for me out of my damn head. And I really, really want to do it again. Soon.

"I really appreciated your dedication to seeing it through, though," Essie says sweetly.

I give her a look.

She winks.

My dick wants to get involved.

This is going to be a long-ass flight.

CHAPTER 13
NATE

The text conversation keeps rolling over in my head. It doesn't matter how many vodka sodas I consume, they don't dull my awareness of Essie's proximity and all the things we could do this weekend when no one is looking. The memory of her hands on me and the taste of her mouth is all I can think about.

How good would it feel to have those pretty, soft lips of hers wrapped around my cock? How much would I love to suck on her clit piercing while I bury my fingers inside her? How much do I want to be the one to make her come?

"Are you a nervous flier?" Flip asks.

"Huh?" I drag my brain out of the gutter and look his way.

He glances at the armrest, which I'm gripping so tightly my knuckles have turned white. "Oh. Yeah. Sort of."

I stop drinking and try to ignore Essie. I'm zero percent successful.

She spends the entire flight fully focused on making sure everyone is comfortable, being sweet to the flight attendants, and reviewing her unbelievable spreadsheets. The more I see Essie in action, the harder it is to ignore what's right in front of me. Yes, she's otherworldly gorgeous, but she's also thoughtful, amazingly organized, and intelligent.

I'm relieved when we finally land and are forced to take separate limos to the same hotel. "You and Essie for sure didn't plan this?" Tristan asks for the tenth time.

"No, man. This is supposed to be your bachelor party, not a couples' retreat." I thought I'd have a three-day reprieve from Essie—not because I don't want to see her, but because I do.

I had this idea of who she was and what mattered to her, and the more I learn, the more I realize I was wrong about all of it. Except for her obsession with love and weddings. But that makes her an outstanding maid of honor and the main reason I put this much effort into Tristan's boys' weekend.

"It's just wild, right? Who would have thought we'd end up on the same flight and at the same hotel?" Dallas can't stop grinning.

"I'm not complaining." Kodiak's phone is in his hand. He's probably texting his wife. He spent ninety percent of the flight trying to get her to link pinkies with him across the aisle.

"I'm actually glad we're in the same city—you know, in case Shilpa has any issues," Ash adds. Of all the guys, I can't blame him since his wife, who is also the team lawyer, is pretty damn pregnant.

"I'm with you on that," Roman agrees, although Lexi isn't as far along.

I want to remind them this is supposed to be about the boys, but seeing as the uncoupled people are outnumbered three to one, and all their partners are here, it's pretty much a lost cause.

The girls have just finished checking in when we arrive at the hotel. Most of the guys beeline over to them, while Flip follows me to the front desk.

He glances over his shoulder and drops his voice to a whisper, "I hope you don't mind, but I got myself a separate room—you know, since it's Vegas and all."

"Sure, man, whatever works for you," I say.

He claps me on the shoulder. "And there might be someone here you want to spend time with."

I grunt. I spent the entire flight spinning fantasies in which Essie ended up back in my room. Hell, I even thought about joining the mile high club, and I try my best never to use plane bathrooms because they're disgusting.

By the time we're done checking in, the girls have disappeared up to their rooms. Ironically, we're on the same floor, though thankfully at the other end of the hall. According to Tristan, they have a spa afternoon planned, which means they can't be a distraction.

After everyone has dropped off their stuff, I corral all the guys so we can do some necessary bonding. At the racetrack.

"This is fucking awesome, Nate." Tristan slings his arm over my shoulder a little while later, grinning from ear to ear.

Pride swells in my chest. Racing cars is way cooler than a spa. "I thought you'd like this. Obviously, you get first dibs on whatever car you want to drive." I motion to the lineup of sweet rides.

"Tristan's definitely picking the one with the most balls." Flip fist-bumps my brother, and they share a chuckle.

Kodiak snaps a bunch of pictures, thumb-types for a few seconds, then tucks his phone back in his pocket.

"Everything good?" Tristan asks.

"Yeah. Everything is awesome. Just checking on Lav. Thanks for the invitation. It's nice to see you guys somewhere other than the ice when we're playing against each other."

"Right? I'm glad you and Lavender could swing it," Tristan says.

"Me too. Lavender has been super busy with work. I'm

thankful this fell between productions. She really needed a break, and this is the perfect getaway for us."

"She works off Broadway, right?" Tristan told me she's a costume designer. That tracks since the dress she was wearing on the plane was a real head turner.

"For now, yeah."

"New York will probably renew your contract when it's time, right?" Tristan says.

"They might, but our parents are out in Chicago, and with her dad opening a satellite campus for the Hockey Academy in Toronto, we've been talking about options. We want to start a family eventually, and we want to be closer to our parents when that happens."

"You're still young, though. You've got time and a lot of years of hockey left to play," Hollis assures him.

"I know, but Lavender's happiness is more important than anything else. She's my world. Has been since I could say her name." He smiles fondly. "I've loved her my entire life. I want what she wants."

"Even if that means you end your hockey career prematurely?" I can't fathom having that kind of faith in someone else's love.

He nods. "Nothing is as important as she is."

He means it.

The attendant comes over with the paperwork, and we all pair up and pick our cars. Tristan takes the wheel, and I take my place in the passenger seat since the Ferrari is a top choice for both of us.

"You sure you're cool with me driving first?" he asks.

"Yeah, absolutely. This is your weekend."

Tristan and I switch places after a few laps. It's a real rush driving a car with as much speed as this one. It's an awesome first pick for the afternoon. Then we break for a few minutes while we wait for the next car to be free. We lean against the rails, watching the cars zip by.

"Thanks for this, Nate. I know the wedding stuff isn't your favorite, and having the girls at the same hotel isn't what you expected, but I appreciate you putting this together. I know you're juggling work to make it happen."

"I don't mind. It's been fun, and I needed to get out of the grind for a bit." I've been putting in long days at the office, and if it wasn't for my brother and Flip, I'd have no social life. Which is why I was looking forward to this weekend with him and the guys.

"How is the skate prototype coming along, anyway?" he asks.

"Good. Great. The 3D printers make all the difference in getting things right. I think we'll have something testable in the next few weeks." I leave it at that. It's easy to get overly excited about this and start talking above people's heads. The guys in my office understand, but most other people glaze over when I nerd out.

"You know I'm all for helping test them."

"Yeah, I appreciate it. We should be at that stage soon." If things go well, we could have a cutting-edge hockey skate in our fall catalog, and I could end up with an awesome bonus.

We're called up for round two. This time it's a Lamborghini, and I get behind the wheel first. Car racing is a blast. We trade spots after a while, and then we switch to the final car. Afterward, we return to the hotel to shower and get ready for dinner. The guys can't stop talking about their racetrack exploits. You'd think they were pro drivers, not hockey players. They're like giant twelve-year-olds. I mean, me too, I guess. It was pretty great.

When everyone's ready, we all head out together. I check my phone and find a new message. The guys are busy either texting their partners or sharing videos they took of the cars they drove.

ESSIE

Where are you going for dinner?

NATE

Where are you going for dinner?

ESSIE

I asked first.

A picture of her holding a banana pops up. Her fingernails are a pretty pale pink, and they feature stars in yellow that shoot across her fingers.

NATE

Is this a bribe?

ESSIE

Is it working?

NATE

No.

It absolutely is. I'm already picturing my cock sliding through her hand, thumb rubbing the crown.

Two more pictures pop up. One is a neck-down shot of Essie standing in front of the bathroom mirror wearing a sparkly, black dress with little pink hearts edging the hem, and a plunging neckline that highlights her cleavage. The second shows off the back of the dress, which dips low in the back. There's no bra. There can't be. Which means her nipples are just a thin piece of fabric away.

ESSIE

eyelash batting GIF

Are you sure you don't want to give me a hint?

NATE

So you can torture me for two hours in that dress? Not a chance.

Another picture comes through. This time it's a close-up of her mouth, and her lips are wrapped around the banana.

ESSIE

Suit yourself.

"Everything good, man?" Tristan asks.

"Huh?" I click the side button and my screen goes blank.

"Everything cool?" He glances at my phone.

"Oh, yeah, just checking on dinner reservations."

I booked a table at a steakhouse. And of course, because this seems to be a weekend of six degrees of separation, we're seated next to the girls.

They're all wearing little black dresses and the sashes I spent my entire night running around to deliver. They read BEA'S BABES, and I guess they're essential to the evening. I'm suppressing an eye roll even now. Whatever. What I do know is that the picture Essie sent has nothing on how good she looks in three dimensions. Her hair falls in loose waves over her bare shoulders, her makeup is artfully applied, and her dress highlights every damn one of her physical assets. As per usual, she receives a lot of double takes and flirty smiles.

"You don't mind if we move the tables together, do you, bro?" Tristan claps me on the shoulder.

"Not at all," I lie.

The host and servers jump into action, pulling out Essie's chair, falling all over themselves to offer their assistance. She bats her lashes and smiles.

It irks me that these guys keep treating her like a pretty object to admire and she just…allows it. Or maybe I'm just pissed because she's aiming the same smile she gives me at someone else. Or it could be that back in high school, I fit into that category, and I still feel shitty about it.

I end up next to Essie once our tables are pushed together. She pulls a compact out of her purse and fluffs her hair.

"You don't need to keep checking to make sure you're still beautiful," I murmur. "Just ask me, and I'll tell you."

Her gaze lifts to my eyebrows. "How is it possible for you to look angry while giving a compliment?"

"It's not a compliment. It's a fact."

She reaches up and smooths her finger between my eyebrows.

"What are you doing?"

"We're in Vegas, Nate. Your furrowed brow belongs back in Canada."

I roll my eyes. "You hijacked my boys' weekend."

"And *you* hijacked my girls' weekend, so it looks like we're even. All this moping will give you wrinkles, so you should try having a little fun."

She winks and turns her attention to Rix, who thinks everything on the menu sounds good.

And just like the last time we were at a restaurant, I end up constantly passing things to Essie.

She leans in, fingers dragging along my forearm. "Can you pass me your balls?"

I quirk a brow. "They're not detachable."

Her nose wrinkles and she tips her head, pointing with one pretty nail to the dish on my left. "The chicken balls, Nathan."

"That's not what you said," I grumble and pass her the plate.

"I think your mind is in the gutter," she whispers.

"I wonder why." But maybe I am hearing things.

She crosses her legs under the table, and her bare foot slides up the back of my calf and rests there. "Where are you boys headed after this?" she asks the table.

The guys look to me. "Nate is keeping the itinerary under wraps," Tristan notes.

"It's staying that way, too." I side-eye Essie.

I won't be able to handle Essie in this dress, at a club, being hit on.

After dinner, the girls head up to their rooms to get ready for their night out. I need a minute to come down from the over-stimulation of sitting next to Essie and not being able to kiss the knowing smirk off her face. I convince the guys to go to the hotel bar for drinks and not follow them up to their rooms.

"We should play a drinking game." If I get good and wasted, I might not cave and send Essie late-night messages asking for all the things she's been texting me today.

"What are we doing tomorrow?" Tristan asks.

"I'm not telling you until tomorrow." I don't trust him or any of the other guys not to blab to their girlfriends and wives.

"What about a hint?" Roman asks.

"No hints."

"What time do we have to be awake?" Flip asks.

"We won't leave the hotel until eleven." I planned it so we could have fun tonight and not regret it too much tomorrow.

The bartender arrives with drinks.

"Okay. How about a round of Never Have I Ever? I'll go first." It's been ages since I've played a drinking game. "Never have I ever gone more than a year without sex." I take a swig of my beer.

"Wait, you drank. Does that mean you have or haven't gone more than a year without sex?" Flip asks.

"I *have* gone without it."

"We've all gone without sex for more than a year if you count all the years prior to losing our virginity," Dallas says.

"I mean in the last decade," I clarify.

Both Roman and Hollis drink, then side-eye each other. It must be really fucking weird to have your best friend in a relationship with your daughter.

"You've gotten action since you and Lisa broke up, haven't you?" Tristan asks.

"Of course." I scoff. I don't need to tell him it only happened recently, or that it was a handy provided by Rix's best friend. There was one night at a bar just after Lisa and I broke up, but it ended badly, and there was definitely no sex. I'm just glad I moved back to Toronto, so I'll never run into that woman again.

Flip frowns. "Really? Because you've been living with me for almost a year, and I'm pretty sure you've never gone on a date or brought anyone home."

"You're on the road half the year. You don't know what happens when you're gone."

"Yeah, but Dred would tell me if you brought someone home. She worries about you, honey bear."

"This is supposed to be a drinking game, not a psychoanalyze-Nate game," I snap. "Tristan. Your turn."

"Check out this picture of a mousse cake in the shape of a peach Bea just sent me." He shows the table his phone.

"Dude, this is supposed to be a boys' weekend." I slap the table to get their attention. "Put your freaking phones away! You can handle a few hours of separation from your girlfriends and wives." I make meaningful eye contact with everyone, then check my watch. "We should hit the club." Hopefully that will distract these guys enough to keep them off their phones and in the freaking moment.

Flip pays the tab, and we finish our drinks, then head to the club—conveniently attached to our hotel—where I've reserved table service.

The bass is pumping, forcing us to yell over the music to hear each other. The dance floor is crowded with gyrating bodies. We climb the stairs to the VIP lounge, and I'm hit with a wave of emotion.

Annoyance is the first thing to wash through me, followed by unsettling relief. Because sitting front and center are the girls. And in the middle of them is Essie.

As much as I don't want them to keep hijacking our weekend, I also don't love the idea of them partying it up without a bodyguard or two. Sure, they can handle themselves, but I feel infinitely better knowing we're here as backup.

And tonight, they look like they might need it. Essie has changed into a sparkly, pale pink number that hugs every curve of her magnificent body. Her long hair is now pinned up, so it spills down her back in waves and exposes the elegant curve of her neck. Her eyes are rimmed in dark liner and her lips are a glossy pink. I already know they taste as good as they look.

"You didn't plan this, did you?" Flip asks.

"Nope. I sure didn't."

"Seems like the universe might be trying to tell you something."

I give him a questioning look.

His grin turns wry. "I'm going to use the bathroom."

Rix is the first to notice us. She jumps up from the table and flounces over to Tristan, throwing her arms around his neck. "Did you use the tracking app to hunt me down?"

"I didn't even think to check, to be honest. I was trying to give you girl time and not piss my brother off." He nods my way.

"I'm getting a drink," I announce.

"We have a bottle already; just join our table," Rix says.

If you can't get away from them, drink with them, I guess. My frown deepens as Essie's smile widens. "You're so gleeful about this."

She passes me a glass full of liquid and ice. I take a tentative sip. It's tequila.

"And you're such a grumpy bear." She presses her finger to the edge of my lips and tugs up. "You're pretty when you smile." She winks and brushes past me, linking fingers with Rix as they move to the dance floor.

It doesn't take long for the couples to join them. Shilpa, Lexi, and Dred hang out in the VIP booth with Roman and Ash. I lean against the railing and observe from a distance, trying and failing to keep my eyes off Essie. And I'm not alone. There are plenty of guys checking her out. It's fucking infuriating.

She crooks her finger at me, an invitation to join them. I sure as hell don't want Flip dancing with her. I knock back the rest of my drink and make my way through the throng of bodies until I finally reach the group.

She settles her palm on my shoulder, and I bend until her lips brush the shell of my ear. "I can't decide if you look angry or horny."

"Definitely both, but probably more the latter than the former."

She pulls me away from the group by my belt loop. No one notices, too caught up in their partners to pay attention to us. Essie drapes one hand over my shoulder. "What are you angry about? You showed up at the same club as us, not the other way around. If anyone should be annoyed, it's me. Especially since you've been watching me like a hawk for the past half hour. You're scaring all the prey away." She waggles her brows.

I laugh. "You think *you're* the predator?"

"People like pretty things. Even if they might bite them."

"You haven't bitten me."

"Not yet, no." Her expression softens. "I meant what I said. You're beautiful when you smile."

"You're drunk," I observe. But secretly I like that she thinks this about me.

"I'm tipsy and happy and horny," she clarifies.

"Sounds like a dangerous combination." And possibly my favorite.

She runs her nails down the back of my neck, sending a shiver along my spine. "Or the perfect combination."

CHAPTER 14
ESSIE

Nate's palm settles on my hip and he pulls me closer. I feel his belt buckle and, more excitingly, his erection pressed against my stomach.

I'm kind of obsessed with the dark look on his face every time his eyes find me. Serious, intelligent, broody Nate is attracted to me, even when I'm tipsy and not on my best behavior. Maybe especially then.

"You look good in this dress." He's still wearing his dark, annoyed expression.

"You look good all the time," I reply. "Edible, really."

He smiles faintly, and his gaze drops to my mouth.

"Thinking about my text messages from earlier?" *I sure am.* How good his hands felt on my body and how I could kiss him for hours and never get tired of his mouth has been on a constant loop all day.

His eyes narrow. "Is it that obvious?"

I shift my hips. "You are poking me in the stomach."

He drops his head, lips only inches from mine. But my phone buzzes between us, and his permanent scowl deepens. "Where are you keeping your phone, anyway?"

He loosens his grip, and I remove it from the iron-on pouch

attached to the inside of my dress, just above my chest. "I made a pocket since there aren't a lot of places to keep things in this."

"Smart."

My stomach flutters at the compliment. A pocket inside my dress is more resourceful than anything, but coming from Nate, I'll take it. I open my messages.

"Dred went back to the hotel to read her Swedish thriller because the oonsing was too much," I tell him.

"What the hell is oonsing?" Nate asks.

"The bass—*oonse, oonse, oonse.*" I mimic the sound pumping through the speakers.

"Ah, got it."

SHILPA

Ash and I did the same. My feet are the size of cars.

LEXI

My ankles have no definition and my husband wanted to snuggle. Sorry we bailed.

RIX

Tristan persuaded me to go back to the hotel for some alone time. #sorrynotsorry

HAMMER

Hollis is old and it's his bedtime.

LAVENDER

We also left. See you in the morning.

HEMI

Dallas and I went for late-night ice cream and I have no regrets.

A private message comes through from my bestie.

RIX

Please tell me you're still with Nate.

ESSIE

I'm still with Nate.

RIX

Thank God. I was worried when I saw all the girls were gone.

ESSIE

Have fun!

I glance around, searching the VIP area for Flip, but the table we had has been taken over by a new group of dudes, and Flip is not with them. "We're the only ones left."

His furrow deepens again. "Everyone's gone?"

"Seems that way." I shrug.

Nate's jaw tics. I can't read his expression. "Flip has his own room."

"Okay." Flip has been on the straight and narrow for a while, but this is Vegas. At least he's being considerate of his roommate, I guess. I hope he doesn't do something he feels bad about later.

"So I have mine to myself." His fingers flex on my hip, like he's waiting for something.

Me, I realize. He's waiting for me. "Do you want to go back to your room and make out?"

"Yeah." His throat bobs. "Yes. It's all I can fucking think about."

"Me too." I take his hand. "Let's go."

He stays close, his other hand on my hip as we navigate our way through the crowd toward the exit. I'm all turned around, so we end up at the wrong bank of elevators and backtrack, but we finally make it to our floor. I'm determined to be stealthy as we walk down the hall. I don't want anyone to catch us and potentially thwart whatever is about to happen. Because hopefully it will include orgasms.

Nate swipes his keycard across the door and ushers me inside. This room is much tidier than mine and Rix's, which looks like a windstorm of clothing blew through it.

Nate closes the door, flips the safety lock, and tosses his keycard on the table. He turns to me, fists clenching and releasing at his sides. "I've been thinking about your mouth all night."

"And about how good I am at pushing all of your buttons with it?"

"Among other things." He moves closer until the tips of his shoes touch mine.

"Want to tell me about those other things?" I smooth my hand over his chest.

"I can't stop thinking about the way you taste." He drops his head and sucks my bottom lip on a low groan. "So fucking sweet." He pulls me closer.

I sink into the kiss as he explores my mouth with a soft sureness that makes my toes curl. He breaks the kiss and nibbles along the edge of my jaw.

"What else?" I run my hands through his hair.

There's something so exciting about firsts. First kiss. First touch. First orgasm. First fuck. It's the newness of experience. Of learning what makes someone else tick. Of discovering their secrets one at a time.

"I've been dreaming about those pierced nipples of yours and how much I can't wait to finally see them again." He brushes his thumb over one through the fabric of my dress.

"Anything else?" I open the first button on his shirt.

He trails his hand down my side, skimming the hem of my dress. "I want to know what kind of sounds you make when I suck on that hood piercing." He drags his fingers along the inside of my thigh. "Will you let me do that, Essie?" His knuckle brushes over my panties. "Will you let me kiss you here?" He's so politely dirty.

"Yes, please." I grab the hem of my dress and pull it over my head, tossing it on the floor.

Nate's eyes darken, and his lip curls as he takes me in. That furrow in his brow deepens as his gaze drops to my breasts.

He reaches out to skim a covered nipple. "Tape?"

"Protects them so they don't get caught on the fabric," I explain, suddenly self-conscious. Initially I had some regrets after the thing with the tattoo artist ended, especially since the nipple piercings took another two months to heal. But they really do heighten the experience, and I can decorate them with pretty jewelry. I make a move to peel the tape off, but Nate covers my hand with his.

"I would like to do that, if it's okay with you."

"Yes." I nod and lick my lips. "I would also like that."

He steps closer, pushing my hair over my shoulders. His fingers trail over my collarbones, and he exhales a heavy breath. "Do you have any idea how intriguing you are, Essie?"

My breath catches. I've been called a lot of things by men, most often referring to how attractive they find me. Pretty. Gorgeous. Stunning. Hot. Beautiful. But no one has ever called me intriguing. Especially not when all I'm wearing are a couple of pieces of tape and a pair of pink satin panties.

I shake my head and bite my lip.

"You are." His gaze moves over my face. "Endlessly intriguing." He traces the edge of the tape covering my right nipple. "A lovely puzzle I want to solve." He makes a sound in the back of his throat, and his tongue peeks out to push at his top lip as he carefully peels the tape free—exactly like he did when he opened the present I gave him. So gentle, so careful. His hand curves around my breast and he drops his head, eyes lifting to mine as he captures the peak between his lips and sucks softly.

"Oh fuck, that is..." My knees go weak as his tongue laves me. "I like that."

"What else do you like, Essie?" His teeth sink in gently for a moment.

"That. I would like more of your tongue and your teeth." I groan.

"I'm making a checklist for all the yeses." He peels the other nipple free, giving it the same attention before returning to my mouth, claiming it in a searing kiss.

He smooths his hands down my back, our lips still fused as he picks me up and carries me to the bed. Nate lays me down, hips settling in the cradle of mine. I feel him, thick and hot behind his fly.

I love the way he presses into me, but… "I want to feel your skin on mine."

He pushes up on one arm, dark eyes shining with lust. "I want those little hearts scraping against my chest while I dry fuck you."

I approve. "I also want that."

I kick off my heels as he braces his weight on one arm and quickly works through the top buttons while I tackle the ones at the bottom. His shirt joins our clothes on the floor.

He's still wearing pants, and possibly shoes, but when he stretches out over me again, all his warm, soft skin meets mine. His hungry gaze stays locked on me, and I moan at the feel of his erection between my thighs and the light tug on my nipples.

"Say something scientific," I whimper.

"What?" He stills for a moment, his frown moving toward confused.

I scramble for a specific question that will require science speak. "What's the chemical composition of stainless steel?"

"Why?"

"Because you know, and I want you to explain it to me."

"Right now?"

"Yes, please." I roll my hips against him, body zinging with anticipation.

His cheeks puff out. "It depends on the grade of steel."

"Just typical steel. Normal grade." I gaze up at him expectantly, then tack on, "With percentage breakdowns." I rub myself against him, hot all over as I wait for him to tell me what I want to know.

"Sixteen to eighteen percent chromium, ten to fourteen percent nickel, two to three percent molybdenum, and trace amounts of carbon, with a mix of other, less-prevalent things."

My pussy clenches. "That kind of information is just rolling around in your head all the time, isn't it?"

"It took a little work to recall it, to be honest. Can I kiss you now?"

"Yes, please."

He covers my mouth with his and hooks my leg over his hip. We make out, bodies gliding against each other, the sensation muted by layers of fabric on our lower halves. But I want this slow build, to take our time to touch and kiss.

"So many times I thought about what this would be like." He sucks my bottom lip. "How good you'd feel wrapped around me. The way you'd sound when I made you come."

The disappointed high school graduate who waited for him to call revels in this new power. But the other part, the one I've always struggled to keep on lock when I get into a new…thing, wants to know why he never called, why he ghosted me all those years ago, even though he lusted after me. But I can't let that part of me out. Not now. Not with Nate.

"This is just about sex," I declare. There's conviction in my words. I mean it. I know better than to give my heart to this man. He's beautiful, and delightfully grumpy, and competitive. And he's smart, and driven, but he doesn't want the same things I do.

He finds me intriguing now, but what happens when he sees behind the pretty veneer? I can't keep someone like Nate's attention for long. It doesn't matter that the girl in me who craves acceptance and love wants to be the one to fix him. Or that he's appealing in so many damning, damaging ways. The woman in me who's cried endless tears over the wrong guy knows better. I've given my heart to so many men who had no intention of keeping it safe. I won't add him to the list.

He pulls back. For a moment I'm terrified of what he's going to say. He drags a single finger from my temple to my chin, so wildly tender. "Is that what you want this to be?"

I nod, relieved, and run my fingers through his thick hair. "We can have an orgasm competition."

His grin turns salacious. "Oh, sweetness, this is one wager I'd put money on." He folds back on his knees and hooks his fingers into my pink lace and satin panties. "I love these, by the way. They are perfectly you."

That small compliment tugs at soft places inside me. "Thanks."

I lift my hips, and he drags them down my legs, tossing them over the edge of the bed. He quickly rids himself of his pants, and then his hands find the backs of my knees. He spreads me wide, his dark gaze locked on the glittering jewel piercing my clit. He runs his hands up the inside of my thighs, utterly transfixed as he brushes his thumb over the piercing.

I groan and swivel my hips.

"That's a sound I want on repeat." He leans in and bites the sensitive flesh on the inside of my knee, sucking softly. And then he kisses a path along my inner thigh. Warm lips. Soft tongue. Sharp nip of teeth. When he reaches the juncture, he frames my pussy with his palms, looks me in the eye, and flicks my hood piercing with his tongue.

I jolt. "Ah, fuck."

"Too much?"

"Unexpected," I clarify.

This time he laps gently at me, and I sigh.

"Better?"

"Yeah, better." I nod.

He does it again, but the third time he covers the piercing with his mouth and sucks, tenderly, sweetly, like he's testing me, learning what I like. "You taste so fucking good."

He licks me again, and then sucks the piercing until I moan his name.

"You like that?"

I stroke his cheek. "I like that."

He smiles and does it again, gauging my reaction, adjusting with every sigh and whimper and moan. It's exactly what I'd expect from Nate. Of course he's a determined, conscientious lover. Of course he wants to know what I like, because he's on a quest to make me come, and if there is one thing Nate doesn't do, it's fail.

Except at love. So he doesn't even try.

I drag myself back into the moment. He swirls his tongue, and my moan smooths the line between his eyes. I can't look away. He's too beautiful, too intense, too perfect. And when he shifts to ease a single finger inside and stroke me with the same rhythm as his tongue, I'm done for. I come in waves, body humming with a torrent of sensation. I'm drenched in desire, swirling in bliss. He doesn't stop, but he slows, gentles. I float like a feather back to earth before he takes me to the edge again and pushes me over. Three times I come, each one more intense than the last.

I'm boneless and mindless by the time he pushes his boxers over his hips and kisses his way back up my body. He presses his lips softly to my cheek, body hovering above mine, eyes hot with need. "Can I kiss you?"

I nod, and he cups my face in his palms and claims my mouth. I grip his hair tightly, but he pulls back, dark eyes alight with curiosity as his bottom lip slides through his teeth. "Do you like the way you taste on my tongue?"

"I don't *not* like it," I hedge.

"I love the way you taste. I'd eat you for hours if I wasn't worried about licking you raw," he declares.

I laugh, and he smiles, and suddenly his erection slides across my slick skin and we both make needy, desperate sounds.

He strokes my cheek. "I want to be inside you. Can I be inside you? It's okay if it's not...if you're not ready for...that. For me."

There's such vulnerability lurking under that dark-cloud

façade. I feel like I'm seeing a very different version of this man, one I want more of. I'm so used to staying, even when I shouldn't, but I can give him connection without letting him take my heart.

I sweep my finger along the edge of his jaw. "I would like you to fuck me, please, Nathan."

He blinks down at me, and his cock kicks. "I'll get a condom."

"Okay."

He finds his pants and retrieves a foil square. I take it from him and tear it open. He braces himself on one arm, watching as I roll it down his length. And then he settles between my thighs again and slides low.

His face contorts as I tilt my hips up and he fills me, one glorious inch at a time.

"Oh fuck." He drops his head, and his lips find my neck. "Shit, Ess." His entire body quakes, and he fists the sheets beside my head.

I stroke his cheek and encourage him to look at me. "Hey. Hi."

"Essie, baby..." He groans.

"Feels good, huh?"

He laughs and drops his forehead to mine. "So much better than good." His eyes are a little wild. "Are you okay? Is it okay?"

"It's awesome. You've got a fantastically large cock, and I'm super full of it, so whenever you're ready, you can fuck me right through this mattress to the floor." I grin and tap his ass with my foot.

"I don't know if you want to give me permission to do that."

"Oh, I know I want that." I bite his chin. "Come on, Nathan, teach my pussy a lesson."

He shakes his head and frames my face with his hands. "You're fucking perfect, you know that?"

I don't have time to come up with a saucy retort. Because he pulls his hips back and snaps them forward. At my loud, encouraging moan, he picks up the pace. And does what I asked—hips slapping, bodies colliding, hands caressing. He changes the angle so he hits just the right spot, and I come again. I'm spinning in pleasure, drowning in the intensity of his eyes. And when he comes, it's fucking magnificent. And definitely, without a shadow of a doubt, the best sex of my entire life.

Especially when he lies on top of me for minutes afterward, stroking my hair and kissing my neck. "That was fucking phenomenal." He rolls to the side, manages the spent condom, and shifts to face me. "Want to order room service and then do that again?"

I grin. "Yes, absolutely."

"Cool." Nate grabs his phone from the nightstand and arranges the pillows so we're half-sitting up. He stretches his arm across the pillows and pats them. "Come check out the menu."

I bite my lip. "Are you trying to cuddle with me?"

His expression shifts to uncertainty, and my silly heart clenches. I think about the way he softens every time Rix hugs him. He was abandoned by his mother and raised in a house of competitive athletes. Inside this grumpy man is a boy who was probably starved for affection.

I roll into the space he's made for me and drape myself over him like a human blanket. "I vote nothing with garlic, and we should definitely get dessert." I scroll up the page. "Everything looks good."

"Burger and fries?" he suggests.

"No onions, though."

"Agreed. How about a fruit platter for some balance?"

"Good idea, and we can round it out with the brownie sundae?" I add.

"Sounds perfect." He places the order and tosses the phone aside. "We have half an hour." He rolls over on top of me and fits himself between my thighs. "I vote you let me play with your clit piercing again until the food arrives."

"I mean, if that's what you want to do."

His smile makes my thighs and chest clench. "Oh, I want to."

He kisses his way back down my body and makes himself comfortable. I've just come for the second time when there's a knock at the door. I clap a hand over my mouth as Nate rolls off the bed. He's naked and very, very erect. He swipes across his chin with the back of his hand.

"You can't answer the door like that." I point to his hard-on.

"If you answer the door naked, I'll have to murder whoever is on the other side," he states flatly, then calls out, "Just a second!"

I shrug into his shirt, fasten several buttons, and push him back so no one else gets an eyeful of dick.

I throw the door open, but immediately attempt to close it because it's not room service on the other side. It's Flip.

His mouth opens and closes.

"Did they bring extra chocolate sauce?" Nate asks.

"Honey bear, I would have brought you extra chocolate sauce if I'd known that was what you wanted."

"Fuck. Flip?" Nate steps out from his hiding spot. His boxers don't conceal his hard-on. "You said you got your own room."

"I changed my mind. Too much temptation." He turns to me. "Ess, come on, I can show you the time of your life."

"I have known you since before you hit puberty, Flip. I was there for the voice cracks. I like you a lot better now, but still no."

"You'll fall for me one day."

"I'll think about it."

The food shows up.

Flip surveys the tray eagerly. "I'm taking the fruit platter back to my other room. Ess, you know where to find me if he underperforms. 'Night, honey bear!" Flip grabs a handful of fries and the fruit platter and disappears down the hall.

Nate tips the delivery guy, and we sit on the couch to eat.

Nate cuts the burger in half and offers me the bigger piece. I take the smaller one because I plan to do a lot of damage to the sundae.

"You don't think Flip will say anything to Tristan, do you?" I pop a fry into my mouth.

"It's not really his style." Nate rearranges the pickle so it's not hanging out of the bun. "Why? Are you worried about Rix finding out?"

"No, are you?" I abandon the fries and get to work on the sundae.

"About Rix? No."

"But Tristan, yes?" I keep my voice light.

"I don't know."

My phone buzzes. I grab it from the floor in case it's Rix. It's not.

FLIP

I'm getting drunk on tiny bottles of liquor.

See how good we are together?

Several pictures pop up, all of them with a sleeping Flip in the background and my smiling face superimposed on random women.

ESSIE

This is not the way.

"What the fuck? Why are you in bed with Flip?" Nate looks like he's about to throw down.

"It's photoshop." The *you idiot* is implied in my tone. Flip has always been like family to me, and that will never change. I'm pretty sure he's only flirting with me because it irritates Nate.

"Right. Yeah. I knew that."

"I do not shit where I eat. Which is why what's happening here is just sex and nothing else." Literally everyone else is getting laid, and no-commitment Nate is the perfect dick to ride into the Vegas dawn. "I have a really great idea." I hold up the extra chocolate sauce.

Nate arches a brow.

I sink to my knees in front of him. "Wanna find out how much chocolate-dipped cock I can swallow?"

CHAPTER 15
NATE

"Thanks for coming over." I usher Essie into my apartment. We've been back in Toronto for three days. In another three we get on a plane to Aruba for Rix and Tristan's wedding. Do we really need to meet to go over the plan? Nope. Did I just want a reason to see Essie so she can push my buttons? Maybe.

"It's a whole lot neater than it was when Rix lived here," Essie remarks.

"I like things tidy," I admit.

"Most of the time, anyway." She winks. "We're both messy eaters."

I hook my finger into her belt loop and pull her to me. "I could use a snack."

She laughs and covers my mouth with her palm. "Work first, play later."

"Play first, work later sounds like more fun," I say from behind her hand.

She widens her eyes and takes my face in her palms, turning my head this way and that. "Who are you, and what have you done with Nathan Stiles?"

"Ha-ha." I slip a hand under her shirt. "Just let me play with your nipple piercings for a minute."

She grins coyly and catches my hand with hers. "First we discuss the itinerary, then my nipples are yours to play with." She spins out of my reach and hops up onto a stool at the kitchen island.

"Where's fun Essie when I need her?" I grumble.

She pats the stool beside her. "Come on. The sooner we get this done, the sooner you'll have access to fun Essie."

I sigh but do as she asks while she opens her tablet and pulls up her itinerary. I bring the spreadsheet up on my laptop so we can compare notes. "I didn't want to fill the pre-wedding days with too much stuff, so we only have one or two projected activities each day, with a potential cost breakdown. I tried to keep the budget reasonable for Rix's peace of mind, but Tristan gave me a float to work with that I can run everything through on my end, especially for people like me and Dred who aren't making the big bucks."

"You must do okay, though." She works on a popular TV show, and her apartment, while small, is nice.

"Oh yeah, but the resort is high end, and you know how Rix worries. It'll take time before she can really settle into this life, and Tristan gets that. We just want this to be as stress-free as possible for her." She taps the column with the totals. "I'm trying to keep it balanced, so each person is allocated a daily spend."

The version of her I thought I knew was completely inaccurate. Yes, she's a pink princess-loving woman who is always polished, and she's still the life of the party. But that's only a little slice of her. She's not two-dimensional. Essie is smart, determined, creative and considerate. "You have a great mind for numbers. You could easily run your own business if you wanted."

Her eyes flare, maybe with surprise. "Maybe one day, but right now I'm honing my craft and building my skills and my industry knowledge. I'd have to pick a niche and I'm not ready to narrow it down quite yet." She props her chin on her fist. "How's the skate prototype coming?"

"Good. Great. We're trying to get the blade exactly right for the best friction and speed."

"How do you figure that out?"

"There are a bunch of formulas we use; some of it can be boring and repetitive. Lots of testing and trial and error. It's probably the same for you too," I say.

"It can be when I'm putting the same makeup on the same person day after day, but then we'll have a cool episode with a guest appearance, or I get to work on something in fantasy and it changes things up, makes it exciting again."

Her passion for what she does is written on her face. I hate that I put her in a box and gave her a label she didn't deserve. She's the one who reached out to me when the wedding planning started. She tolerated my assholery, met it with a smile, even. "You're incredible," I blurt.

She laughs and looks away, brushing away the compliment. "In bed."

"Don't." I skim the edge of her jaw, urging her to look at me. "Don't do that."

Her face softens. "I'm used to people telling me I'm pretty, not that I'm smart."

"Well, you're both, so you should own them equally."

"So are you." Her fingers skim the back of my hand.

We lean in, tipping our heads. Our lips brush, once, twice, a third time.

But before I have a chance to kiss her, the door swings open.

We separate in a rush.

"Honey bear! Essie! Have you finally come to your senses? Realized I'm the one?"

"It's still a no from me, Flip, but I applaud your tenacity." Essie tucks her tablet back into her purse. "I should probably head out. I have an early morning."

I scramble for a reason for her to stay. "Don't we have a few more things to go over?"

"I'll message if I have any questions." She winks and pats my chest as she heads for the door.

I follow, seeing her out.

When she's gone, I turn to Flip. "Seriously, dude, your timing is the worst."

"You have a bedroom with a door. You could have taken her in there. Or didn't you want her to see your serial-killer-level tidiness?"

"I don't think you've ever hit the laundry basket. And that isn't even the point. You could have warned me you were coming home early."

"And you could have gone to Essie's apartment, where she lives, on her own. But you didn't, and that's on you, isn't it, honey bear?" He pats me on the shoulder. "I'm going to leave you and your sexual frustration to fester."

His bedroom door closes with a quiet snick, cutting off his low chuckle.

Lesson learned, I guess.

CHAPTER 16

ESSIE

"How excited are you for an actual vacation?" Indigo, one of my colleagues, sips her lemon drop martini.

"With an entire hockey team," Cosmo adds.

"Literally, you're living the dream," Tanvi sighs.

"It'll be so fun," I agree.

The hockey players are hot, but it's the broody engineer I'm looking forward to spending time with naked. The hairs on the back of my neck stand on end as I glance over to find the very man who has been living rent free in my head since Vegas, walking through the door of the bar.

Cosmo's gaze follows mine. "The hot nerd vibe is so strong."

"Isn't that the guy you were talking to last week? The one who chased off your creepy influencer stalker?"

"It is." My heart rate spikes, and I turn back to my work friends. "Do I have anything in my teeth?"

"You are runway ready, girl," Tanvi assures me.

I fluff out my hair, roll my shoulders back, and adopt a warm smile as he approaches. Other parts of me warm as his gaze finds mine. His friends head to the pool tables, but he crosses to me.

"Hey, Ess." A smile curves his full mouth and his gaze roves over me on a slow sweep.

"Hi, Nate. Here for a little after work unwind?" I ask.

"Yeah. It's our regular spot."

"It's becoming ours, too." Cosmo extends their hand. "We've heard all about you. Good things, though." They wink. "I'm Cosmo."

"And this is Indigo and Tanvi. They work on set with me."

"It's great to meet you." Nate waves at them, then turns back to me. "We're about to rack up. If you want to join, we could play doubles. If pool is your jam."

"Essie loves playing with balls," Indigo offers.

Cosmo snorts and Tanvi elbows them in the side.

Nate smirks.

My cheeks and everything else heat.

"She would love to," Indigo says for me.

"Ess?" He extends his hand.

"Sure, why not." I slip my fingers into his and let him help me down.

"You should have stuck around the other night. Flip went over to Dred's and got his ass kicked at chess," Nate says quietly.

"You miss my nipples that much, eh?"

"We both know I'm a sucker for pretty things that sparkle." He settles his palm on my lower back. "And I happen to love the way you moan my name when my mouth is on you."

"Are you getting me back for all the texts in Vegas?"

"Is it working?" We reach the pool tables, and his thumb sweeps along the exposed skin of my back, sending a shiver down my spine.

"Maybe." There was no way I could disappear into Nate's bedroom with him while my best friend's brother was wandering around the apartment. Nate is far too pleasure focused, and I don't have the ability to stay quiet when he's working his magic tongue.

Two guys, both of whom are vaguely familiar, look up at our approach.

"Essie, these are my colleagues, Greg and Malcom."

"We met briefly before when you stopped by the office, but we weren't formally introduced." Greg shakes my hand enthusiastically.

Malcom is shy and subdued, blushing as he says hello, and ducks his head.

"You guys okay to play doubles?" Nate asks.

"Yeah, of course," Greg says, and Malcom nods his agreement.

Greg breaks and Nate offers to let me go first, but I decline, happy to stand behind him and check out his ass while he lines up his shot. "Twelve, corner pocket." He motions to his intended target and takes the shot, easily sinking the ball. He sinks one more before it's Malcom's turn.

"Do you guys come here a lot?" I tap my cue from side to side as Malcom lines up his shot.

"More often as of late." He glances at me. "How about you?"

"Same."

Malcom sinks one ball, but misses the second, making it my turn. I survey the table, looking for the path of least resistance. "Nine, right corner," I call out, then line up the shot. It bounces off the left side and rolls right, landing neatly in the corner pocket.

"Nice shot." Nate high-fives me.

I sink two more balls before it's Greg's turn.

A couple of guys in suits come over to say hello while Nate grabs another round of drinks. I feel a little out of place in my high-waisted black pants, heels, and pink cropped tank. Their names are Neil and Gordon and apparently they work in the finance department at the same company as Nate.

Neil tips his head. "Do you work with these guys?"

I laugh. "No. I'm a friend of Nate's."

"Right, yeah. I'm pretty sure we would have noticed you in the break room." Gordon gives Nate a quirked brow.

"What do you do? Are you a model or something?" Neil asks. I'm sure he's just trying to make polite conversation.

"I'm a makeup artist."

"Like at the mall?"

I fight not to roll my eyes. This is so awkward. I don't want to feel self-conscious, or less than, but Nate is brilliant, and surrounded by book-smart people. "You're probably thinking of a cosmetics store. I work with TV actors on set," I explain.

Neil's eyes glaze over. "Right. Got it."

"It's an art, really." Nate sweeps my hair over my shoulder and wraps his arm possessively around me. "Essie sees beauty in everything and knows exactly how to enhance it." He gazes down at me, expression intense. "But you're not an alchemist; you're a chemist and a creative."

"I wouldn't say I'm a chemist," I hedge.

"Really? You know the chemical composition of the products you use, just like I know the chemical composition of steel."

I grin, remembering how sexy it was to have him reciting that random fact while naked between my thighs. "You should never combine alpha or beta hydroxy or vitamin C with niacinamide or you'll look like you were running in the August heat."

"I wish you'd been my chemistry partner in high school," Nate murmurs.

"I'm not sure we would have gotten much work done, but after-school study sessions would have been way more exciting."

"I wouldn't mind a time travel machine right about now," Nate says.

I smile sweetly up at him. "That's what role play is for."

Greg clears his throat.

I'd completely forgotten we had an audience.

All of the guys are staring at us. Malcom's face is red.

"Nate's up," Greg says helpfully.

"Right. Yeah." Nate releases me and steps up to the table.

None of the remaining shots are easy.

Nate rubs his chin.

I want to rub my thighs together.

He moves around the table, eyeing the shot, and gets into position. But I can see from this angle that he'll be off, not by much, but enough.

"Hold on." I come around behind him.

He looks over his shoulder as I press my body against his.

He raises a brow. "We're on the same team, sweetheart. You're not supposed to be distracting me."

I lean over him. "You want me to distract everyone else?"

"Not like this, no."

"You're going to miss the shot; I'm helping." I adjust his left hand, fingers dragging across his broad back as I circle him, and adjust the right one, then kiss him on the cheek. "You're all set."

He takes the shot and sinks the ball.

I wink; he smiles.

He calls the eight ball and sinks it, too, giving us the win.

I grab my purse as the guys rack up.

Nate frowns. "What are you doing?"

"I have a dinner date with Trixie Rixie."

"You're leaving?"

"I'll see you in forty-eight hours."

He links our pinkies and drops his head. "When will you be done with dinner?"

"I don't know." I kiss his cheek. "Stay hungry for me."

CHAPTER 17
NATE

E ssie is in front of me, applying her lip gloss.

Do not think about the blow job you got in Vegas last weekend.

It's too late, though. She's already drawn attention to those gorgeous, luscious, talented lips, and the head in my pants is waking up. I make a noise in the back of my throat. She smiles coyly.

She clearly does this on purpose. Which also begs the question, how long has she known about the effect that lip gloss and her mouth have on me? That's a conversation for later.

Essie lifts her carry-on into a bin, then follows with her oversized purse before passing through the sensors. They ding, and the security guy on the other side waves his wand over her. It lights up when it passes her chest and again when it dips below her waist. She seems completely unfazed.

I, on the other hand, am remembering all the little moans and sighs and gasps that tumbled from her lips when I sucked on her pretty little pierced nipples and clit.

"Does Essie have body jewelry?" Flip asks from behind me.

"Shut the fuck up," I mutter as I toss my phone and jacket in a bin.

The security guy across from me frowns. "Excuse me?"

Flip jumps in. "Hopefully the pretty one doesn't hold us all up." He tips his head toward Essie.

Security guy nods, his expression slightly wistful. "Looks like a full pat-down."

I want to punch him in the face. But I want a criminal record less, and I want to go to Aruba more, so I force a smile.

Essie has been pulled off to the side. Based on her expression, this isn't the first time this has happened. She's lost her cropped sweatshirt and is wearing a pale pink tank. And no bra, which means I, and every single other person passing by, can clearly see the outline of her pierced nipples. Our eyes lock briefly as the female security guard makes a pass under her breasts.

I look away before my body reacts in a way that will be embarrassing in the middle of airport security.

"Pierced nipples, huh?" Flip says.

"She dated a tattoo artist," I grumble.

"I guess that tracks."

"What's going on with Essie?" Tristan asks.

"She sets off the sensors every time," Rix explains.

He frowns. "She have a surgery or something?"

"Or something." Rix pats him on the chest.

Several security guards are now gathered around Essie, smiling and laughing. She finally gets the all clear and heads for our group, but her bag isn't waiting for her on the belt. Apparently, it's not Essie's day, because that's been pulled for additional screening.

"Seriously? I get felt up *and* they get to see all my lingerie?" She rolls her eyes and heads for the guy going through her bag. "You don't have to wait," she calls over her shoulder. "I can just meet you in the lounge."

"We're not going anywhere without you," Rix replies.

We move to the side. Despite all the guys wearing nondescript baseball caps, people have started to recognize them. I keep my eye on Essie. The security guy's face grows progressively redder as he sifts through pink lace. Which I hope I get to peel off her body this week.

The security dude holds up a ratty, saggy stuffed...something. It's hard to tell since it's been so well loved. "What's inside this? Are there drugs in here? Are you concealing a weapon?"

"Oh my God, no. It's a fake heart!"

He calls someone else over, and that guy reaches for a pair of scissors.

"Jeez! You don't need to hack Catalina apart!" Essie's voice goes high and reedy. "There's a Velcro opening, on her back below her head."

"Is that a stuffed animal?" Flip asks as he passes a hat back to one of the growing number of fans who recognize the Terror players.

"It's Catalina. I got it for her after her cat died when we were in grade five," Rix explains.

"I remember that. You bought it with your newspaper money, right?" Flip replies.

"Yeah. She loved that cat. She was devastated. Essie always brings Catalina on trips. Don't be dicks about it."

"I wasn't planning on it," Flip says defensively. "It's sweet."

I shoot him a look. He widens his eyes.

I return my gaze to Essie, who's now hugging her ratty stuffed cat to her chest with one arm and trying to repack her bag with the other. Rix goes over to help her.

We finally clear out of the security area, and they rush us through customs because we're causing a ruckus as the guys collect another crowd.

Once again, we board and take up the majority of first class, except this time we all have pods, so there's no need to play musical chairs. Five hours later, we land and take a private bus to our resort.

Essie and I join Rix and Tristan at the concierge desk so we can help get everyone checked in.

"We have a room block under Stiles," Tristan informs the young woman behind the desk.

Rix wraps her arms around Tristan's waist. "It's for our wedding."

"Congratulations. How exciting." The woman smiles politely and returns her attention to the screen in front of her. But that smile stiffens. "Can you just excuse me for a moment?" Her heels clip on the tile floor as she pulls a man aside and they have a hushed conversation.

"Do you think something's wrong? What if something is wrong?" Rix asks nervously.

"Everything's fine, little Bea." Tristan rubs his nose against hers.

"Tristan! Hey, man, I just got your text!" Connor Grace, another Terror player, crosses the lobby. "I'm glad you made it."

He's wearing golf shorts and a collared golf shirt, tattoos I've never seen before on display. Usually he's in a suit or hockey uniform, and they're all covered up.

"Hey! I didn't realize you were going to be here this early." Tristan fist bumps him.

"I brought my Meems here for a little holiday," he explains.

Rix tips her head. "Meems?"

"My grandma," Connor explains.

"That's so sweet," Rix replies.

From the other side of the lobby, I spot Flip with Hollis and Roman, wearing a frown.

Connor and Flip do not get along, thanks to old beef from their Hockey Academy days. But they've been at each other's throats less since they had a come-to-Jesus talk at the end of last season. I wouldn't call them friends, but they tolerate each other.

The gentleman and the woman return, both wearing awkward smiles. "Mr. Stiles, we have a small issue."

"What kind of issue?" Connor asks.

The gentleman startles. "Mr. Grace, I'm so sorry. How can I be of service?"

"It's Connor, and I don't need anything right now. I'm just welcoming my friends."

"Your friends." The man smiles and swallows compulsively. "There seems to be an issue with the booking. We have some important guests with us." The guy looks like he wants to sink into the ground as his gaze darts to Connor for a moment. "And we won't have rooms for you until—" He clicks on his screen. "—Friday."

"That's three days from now!" Rix looks like she's two seconds from crying.

"It'll be okay, Rix. We'll get it sorted out." Essie rubs her arm.

"What if it isn't, though? What if we have to find another place to stay?"

"There are plenty of hotels around here, Bea. Palace on the Beach is right next door."

"But it's so expensive," she whispers.

Essie sidles up next to me. "What are we going to do?"

"Give me a minute." Connor touches my shoulder, then nods at the slightly manic guy behind the counter.

"Doesn't Connor's family own a bunch of hotels?" I ask.

Essie nods. "Maybe he's pulling some strings?"

"Here's hoping." I glance around the lush, opulent space. Tristan has mentioned that Connor comes from money, but I don't think I realized exactly how wealthy they were until this moment.

Connor whispers something to the woman. She smiles and nods. He then ushers the very nervous man into a room.

The woman turns her attention back to us. "Just give us a few minutes. We'll bring you some complimentary champagne while you wait."

She rushes off, and I fully expect her to never come back, but she returns a minute later with a server in tow, a tray of glasses, and two bottles of expensive bubbly. I know it's expensive because I bought a bottle for my one-and-a-half-year anniversary with Lisa. She broke up with me a few weeks later.

"See, Rixie? Everything will be fine. Look how beautiful it is here. We can sleep on the beach, if we need to." Essie passes Rix a glass of champagne.

"Everything will be fine," Rix repeats then takes a hefty gulp.

They've just finished passing out the champagne when Connor and the gentleman come out of the office.

Connor approaches Tristan. "My Meems is waiting on me, so I gotta run, but Harold here will take care of you. I'll touch base later, okay?"

"Yeah, sure." Tristan frowns as Connor rushes off, then turns back to Harold.

"We're so very sorry for the misunderstanding. We've upgraded your stay, and you'll be at our sister hotel next door. You'll have all the amenities included in your original package with the addition of butler service, access to a private pool for you and your guests, and daily in-room massages or other spa services, if you prefer."

Rix's eyes look like they're about to pop out of her head. "You don't mean the Palace on the Beach, do you?"

"That's correct, ma'am. Unless there's another location you would prefer?"

"But it's twice as expensive," she whispers.

"The upgrade is on us. We're so sorry for the inconvenience, but we hope this makes up for any undue stress." He looks like he might need a drink after this.

"Yeah. Yes. This absolutely makes up for it." Rix's shoulders come down from her ears. "Oh my gosh. We're staying at my dream hotel!"

Essie bumps her shoulder. "I told you it would all work out."

"You did. You told me that."

"We'll have your bags brought to your rooms," Harold continues. "In the meantime, we'll escort you over so you can have a look around. How does that sound?"

"Great! It sounds great." Rix is practically vibrating.

"There's just one thing." Harold makes a face.

"What one thing?" Tristan asks.

"All of the rooms have been updated except for one. It's private, though. Nice and quiet," he explains.

"I'll take the private room," I offer before Essie can beat me to it. Hopefully we'll need the seclusion this week.

Harold smiles. "Wonderful."

We're provided with beaded wristbands to open our doors before we're herded out to the front of the building. We load into golf carts and make the short trip down the boardwalk to the sister resort. Which is stunning. The hotel Tristan and Rix picked for their wedding was already one of the nicest, but this is a step above.

Rix and Tristan are dropped off at the honeymoon suite first. Rix can't stop smiling as she waves at us and calls, "Text when you're settled in your room, Ess!"

"I'll give you a couple of hours!" Essie shouts back.

Tristan gives her the thumbs-up and pulls Rix toward the room as we continue down the path, dropping off couples and singles along the way. Every room is luxurious, with a walkout pool and huge private sunbeds. Essie and I are last to be dropped off. Like everyone else, Essie's room has a walkout pool and a sunbed.

"You're just around the corner." The guy points to a narrow walkway that disappears around the side of the building, then buzzes off in his golf cart.

Essie's bags are already waiting in front of her door. She gives me an appraising look. "I'm going to freshen up."

"Yeah, me too."

She drags a finger down my chest and pushes up on her toes, whispering, "If you want to fuck, you know where to find me." She winks and spins around, disappearing into her room.

Would I like a quick shower followed by a long, slow fuck? Absolutely. But I can't give in to temptation. Not yet. I need to play it cool—and take the edge off because I've been fighting an erection since security back in Canada.

I follow the path to the private room. It's a little run-down, the paint peeling around the door and the foliage close by in need of pruning. But I'm sure it'll be great inside. I let myself in and realize I'm wrong about that. Harold wasn't kidding. This room is about twenty years out of date, even with the fresh linens. Whatever. I'll mostly just sleep in here. *Unless I sleep in Essie's room with her.* In Vegas she went back to her own room after round two.

I roll my luggage into the room.

Here, we could spend the night together. It's been so long since I've slept next to another person and woken up with someone draped across me. Temporary or not, I think I'd like that. Even if it's just for a few days. *What if it could be more, though?*

I push that thought away. I'm no good at relationships, and Essie doesn't want that with me. But we can fuck. And have fun. It's a vacation. A break from reality. A week of Essie. Fun, thoughtful, creative, clever Essie.

I take a quick shower—but only because the hot water runs out after two minutes—finish myself off in the bathroom sink and change into my swim trunks. I consider texting Essie, but again, I want to play it cool. I grab my sunscreen and head for the private pool.

The girls are already there. And I almost die when I spot Essie, her long, dark hair piled on top of her head in a messy knot, sunglasses covering her dark brown eyes. She's wearing a pale pink bikini that contrasts with her summer-kissed skin. A *thong* bikini. Her entire, perfect ass is on display.

She holds up a bottle of spray suntan lotion. "Can I get help with my back?" she calls out.

"I got you!" Flip heads in her direction, but I cut him off by shoving him into the pool.

"I can help," Rix offers.

Flip launches himself out of the pool like a fucking dolphin and pulls me in. I go under with him, spluttering as I break the surface.

"Cool off, honey bear. I won't step on your toes." He pats my shoulder and flops back into the water, splashing Dred, Lexi, and Shilpa, who are gathered together on one huge, shaded sunbed.

Dred lowers her book and points at her eyes and then at me.

Tristan wades across to me. "How's your room?"

"Great. How's yours?" It's a lie, but he doesn't need to worry about me. And it will be fine, especially if I don't have to sleep there.

"It's literally Bea's dream. I'll have to thank Connor. He must have pulled some serious strings."

"He's an all-right guy, isn't he?"

Flip doesn't have much to say about him, and when he does, it's usually with disdain. But he can't be all bad if he managed to fix the hotel situation for us.

"Yeah, he really is. He can be a hard nut to crack, though." Tristan tips his head toward Rix and Essie. "You and Ess seem to be getting along okay these days."

"She's super organized, and smart, and a good friend to Rix." I shut up and stop digging my own hole.

"She is." He nods his agreement and claps me on the shoulder. "We couldn't have pulled any of this off without the two of you."

"Essie handled most of it. I basically just followed her lead," I reply.

We look across the deck to where Essie and Rix pose for selfies, laughing and smiling.

For a moment I wonder what it would be like to be in my brother's shoes.

His relationship with Rix hasn't always been easy. But he believes in what they have. He'll do anything for her. Am I capable of loving someone the way he loves Rix? Is someone capable of loving me? Or am I too broken to fix?

CHAPTER 18
ESSIE

"This place is so freaking perfect! Our room is gorgeous, Ess. It's straight out of a fairy tale!"

"You deserve the fairy tale." I clink my Badass Babe Brigade travel mug against hers. Hemi had them made for all of us.

"I'm so glad all my friends are here with me!" Rix is channeling her inner exclamation mark. "I can't believe we have a private pool!" She bumps off the edge and grabs for the tail on my beaver floatie so we don't drift to opposite ends.

"The water is perfect, and it's so nice to be weightless," Shilpa says.

"This." Lexi clinks her lemonade against Shilpa's, water lapping at their baby bellies.

"I have never been to a resort this nice," Dred muses. "Thank you for inviting me."

Rix smiles fondly. "I'm just glad you could get the time off work."

"This is exactly what we all needed before the season starts," Hemi says.

"Right? We'll be refreshed when we get back to reality," Hammer agrees. Her gaze follows Hollis, who's heading over to the rest of the guys.

Nate looks fantastic in a pair of black board shorts, broad back flexing every time he brings his drink to his delightfully full lips. Despite his mirrored sunglasses, I still detect a slight furrow in his brow. I wonder what he's worrying about now.

"You girls want to take some jet skis out?" Flip calls.

"I will pass on that." Shilpa pats her belly.

"Same," Lexi agrees.

"I only venture into freshwater bodies and pools," Lavender notes without apology.

Dred holds up her book. "I'm ninety percent of the way through and sort of desperate to finish."

The rest of us pull ourselves out of the pool, tuck our feet into slides, and follow the guys to the rental station. There are three couples and five singles, but only seven personal watercrafts available.

"I'll hang back with the girls," I offer.

Flip raises his hand, but Nate smacks it down. "You can ride with me."

Rix, Hemi, and Hammer are too busy letting their significant others adjust their life jackets to notice the way Flip snickers and Nate glares at him. And Roman is too focused on his best friend adjusting his daughter's bathing suit bottom to catch it.

I shrug. "Uh, sure, that works."

I put on my life jacket and follow Nate to our watercraft.

He flips the key around his finger. "Do you want to drive?"

"Uh, you can take the wheel for now." The water is choppy, and it's been a few years since I've been on one of these.

He grabs the handlebar to steady the machine and holds out a hand. Heat travels through my fingers and tightens my nipples as I slip my palm into his. It was tough not to invite him over a couple of nights ago, but waiting until we were in Aruba seemed like the smarter plan.

I straddle the seat and shimmy back, making room for him. He's still wearing his sunglasses, so I can't see his eyes, but his lip twitches and that space between his brow creases as he moves to sit in front of me. I slide forward until my legs bracket his. He pushes away from the dock and turns the engine over.

"Hold on!" he calls over the rev of the motor.

I grip the sides of his life jacket as he hits the gas, and we bump across the clear blue water. At first, it's super fun. How could it not be? The sun is shining, the wind is in my hair, I'm surrounded by the ocean, and I'm wrapped around the hot guy who will eventually end up in my bed later tonight, when everyone else has gone to sleep.

But Nate is Nate. And when the guys start doing donuts and jumping each other's wakes, I'm forced to hold on for dear life because Nate joins in. He launches us over a wake, making us airborne for several seconds before we hit the water again, and I nearly lose my hold.

"What the hell, Nate!" I shriek, clinging to him as he spins us around and heads for another wake.

"Hold on tight," he calls over his shoulder.

I adjust my grip, but I can't secure myself in time. He launches us over another wave, and I'm tossed into the air. A second later I hit the water, and a huge wave smacks me in the face. I splutter and cough as ocean water goes up my nose and into my mouth. Panic follows swiftly on its heels. Like most of the people in our group, I grew up swimming in fresh lake water, where there are no sharks who might think my feet are a tasty snack. It's fine near the shore, but out here...who knows what's lurking under the surface?

"Nate! Get me out of the water!" I'm annoyed at how shrill my voice is and how quickly the irrational thoughts take hold.

Nate circles me, just as I imagine a shark would.

"Now! Get me out now!" I shout.

He gets in close and cuts the engine. "Calm down, Ess. What are you afraid of?"

"Calm down?! Don't tell me to calm down! What if a shark bites my foot off? How will I walk down the aisle for my best friend if I don't have a foot?"

"You're more likely to get stung by a jellyfish than bitten by a shark."

"Not fucking helpful, Nathan!" I'm thrashing like a freaking walrus.

"Stop flailing so I can help." Nate holds out his hand, and I curl my fingers around his. He pulls me closer, and I wrap my free hand around his ankle. He moves it to his shoulder. "Now link your hands behind my neck so I can pull you up."

I do as he says, and the watercraft rocks toward me.

"It's going to tip! Don't let it tip or we'll both be in the water!" I'm back to freaking out.

"It won't tip if you don't thrash."

I stop flailing, and he winds his arms around my waist, pulling me out of the water and into his lap. I stay wrapped around him, mostly because I'm afraid if I move I'll end up in the water again with the sharks and jellyfish.

He runs his hand down my arm. "You're all right, Ess."

"Am I, though?" I lean back. "I'm soaked because of you." And all the time I spent on my makeup, that was supposed to make me look sun-kissed, was pointless.

His lip twitches. "Tonight I'll make sure you're soaked for the right reasons."

"You think I'm inviting you back to my room after you tossed me in the water?" I shove his shoulder and the watercraft rocks perilously, so I throw my arms around him again.

His lips curve against my neck. "I told you to hold on. If you let me, I'll make it up to you later and suck on that pretty little clit ring."

"And my nipples. You'll suck on those, too," I demand.

"As if I would leave them out of the fun." He repositions me so I'm nestled between his thighs, sitting in front this time.

His erection pokes me in the butt as he shifts forward. I'm about to comment, but Tristan and Rix ride up next to us.

"You okay, Ess?" Rix is wearing a worried expression, as is typical these days.

"Oh yeah, just fell off!" I say brightly.

"Be careful with Ess," Tristan warns, then speeds off. Rix's peal of laughter is drowned out by the sound of our engine turning over.

"You're poking me in the ass," I note.

"You are wearing a thong bikini, Essie. I've had to watch you parade around in it every time you got out of the pool to refresh your drink. And now your entire *bare* ass is pressed up against me. So yeah, I'm poking you with my hard-on."

"Does this mean you've spent the whole afternoon thinking about bending me over the closest surface and fucking me from behind?"

"Among other, slightly less civilized things, yes."

"Tell me about the uncivilized things."

"No." He takes my hands and puts them on the handlebars, settling his over them. I thought being wrapped around Nate was an experience, but this is so much better. His body creates a protective cage around me. His hard-on pokes me insistently in the tailbone, and it's all I can think about. I wonder what uncivilized Nate is like in the bedroom. I wonder what it takes to bring out that side of him.

Eventually his hard-on calms down in time to return the jet ski. It takes ten minutes for the guys to decide they're bored and want to play water volleyball after we return to the pool. Somehow, I get sucked into playing, along with Hemi, Rix, and Hammer.

To the shock of no one, competitive Nate is out in full force.

I'm on the same team as Flip, and the opposite team as Nate. Every chance Flip gets, he high-fives me, or chest-bumps me, and Nate keeps trying to hit him in the head with the ball. Or at least that's how it seems.

Aurora and I tap out and join Lavender and Dred on the lounge chairs when they start game two. Shilpa and Lexi have both gone to their rooms for an afternoon nap.

"Watching these guys makes me tired," Dred muses.

"Yes," Lavender agrees, slurping her drink. "Also horny. All those muscles and sluicing water."

"How much longer do you think they'll be at this? I'd really like to take Hollis back to the room and have my needs fulfilled before dinner." Hammer sighs.

"I wouldn't mind fulfilling my own needs before dinner." Dred squints and adjusts her glasses. "Holy shit, look at that hottie over by the tiki hut."

"There are a lot of hotties around here, Dred. You'll need to be more specific." I shade my eyes and follow her gaze.

"The dark-haired, tattooed Adonis. At least he has an Adonis body. We'll see about the rest if he turns around." Dred sips her drink. It's probably water or juice. She doesn't drink often.

I spot the object of her attention. His entire back is covered in a stunning design that wraps around his shoulders and trails down his biceps to his forearms. He's a human canvas, and the art is magnificent. He turns, and we get a glimpse at his profile.

"Oh my gosh, is that *Connor*?" I ask.

"Oh yeah, that's Connor," Lavender confirms.

"Why did I not know he was covered in tattoos?" Dred makes it sound like this was an intentionally kept secret.

"I had no idea, either," I reply.

"He's always so put together off the ice. He wears tailored suits; his hair is perfect and neatly cut. Even when he comes to Callie's games he looks like he's ready for a posh night out. He's been sitting beside me for months. And here he is, covered in ink, looking like a delicious bad boy." She sounds mortally offended.

"Why did we not know you have a thing for guys with tattoos?" Hammer asks.

Dred shrugs. "I don't know. Sometimes I date guys without tattoos. Although it's been ages since I've been on one. I'm just a sucker for guys that have them. Especially guys with bodies that look like they were chiseled from stone, who also attend little girl's hockey games to make them happy. Gah." She fans her face. "He's hitting all the bad boy who's really a marshmallow buttons so hard right now. Do not tell Flip I was checking out Connor. He will lose his mind."

"He did fuck Flip's sandwich," Hammer muses.

"And Flip fucked his shirt, so I'd say they're pretty even," Lavender adds.

"Are they, though? Because apparently, it was Connor's last clean shirt," Hammer notes.

"I don't get why Flip just didn't fuck his own shirt," I mutter.

Dred jumps to Flip's defense. "Based on what I know about Connor's family, his shirts were probably softer and more plentiful than whatever Flip had."

"That's probably accurate." Flip was forever doing laundry when we were teenagers, cycling through his limited wardrobe at an unprecedented rate.

"Boys are ridiculous." Lavender checks the time. "I'm getting hungry, and honestly, there is zero chance that Kodiak won't want a pre-dinner vagina snack, so I'm going to help end this game, if that's okay with the rest of you."

"I'd like to eat an actual meal before it's my bedtime," Dred agrees.

"Same," I chime in.

"Me also." Hammer nods.

Lavender adjusts her white thong bikini and stands.

Kodiak's head whips in her direction.

"I'm going to jump in the shower before dinner," she calls to him.

"I'm coming." He pulls his massive body out of the pool and eats the distance between him and his wife in two strides. He takes her bag, then dips down and tosses her over his shoulder.

"See you at dinner! Say forty-five minutes?" Lavender calls.

"Make it an hour!" Kodiak shouts over his shoulder.

"That man is gone for her," I observe.

"Totally. Absolute couple goals," Dred agrees.

Everyone else abandons the game, partnering off to have

some pre-dinner sex. I gather my things and purposely bend in the direction of the pool while doing it. When I straighten, Nate is already gone.

Guess I get to take care of my own pre-dinner needs.

I spend extra time on my hair and makeup and pick out a sexy little dress, but I end up at the opposite end of the table as Nate for once. I throw out the idea of going to the resort night club, but everyone is sun tired and wants to go back to their rooms. What they really mean is that they want more sex. Or in Lexi and Shilpa's cases, they actually want to sleep.

It starts raining on the way back to our rooms, forcing us to rush off, so I don't have a chance to toss out another invitation to Nate. Texting him is out of the question. I've already extended the offer. I won't do it again.

I've just changed into my nightshirt when there's a knock at my door. I put my eye to the peephole. It's Nate. I do a breath check before I throw the door open. It's pouring. And he's soaked.

"There's a leak in my room," he announces.

"You're just here for the pussy." It's as much a reminder to myself as it is for him.

His expression remains flat. "Your bed is dry."

I grab the front of his shirt and yank him inside. "For now."

CHAPTER 19
NATE

I fumble with the lock and make sure the latch is flipped as Essie curves her palm around the back of my neck. Her cotton-candy lip gloss and the warmth of her mouth has turned into a level-ten addiction. I suck her bottom lip and cup her face, angling her head so I can get inside. I move to pull her closer, but she puts her hand on my chest.

"Shit." I raise both hands. "Sorry. We should slow down."

She gives me a look. "I'd like to limit my soaked body parts to my vagina."

I glance down. My shirt is stuck to my body. "Right. Yeah. Let me fix that." I pull the sopping shirt over my head and toss it on the floor, where it lands with a wet thwack.

Essie tugs my shorts and boxers down, and my erection springs free. I kick them aside as she pulls her nightshirt over her head. She's gloriously naked underneath.

"Fuck me…" I groan as I take in all her smooth, tanned skin. The pretty little jeweled barbells piercing her nipples wink at me, begging to be sucked.

Another item added to the ever-growing list of things about her I'm obsessed with.

Essie tilts her head toward the bed, smile impish. "Let's test out the mattress."

"Excellent idea." I pick her up by the waist, carry her across the room, and toss her on the bed.

She lands gracefully, rolls to the pillows, props her cheek on her fist, and pats the empty space beside her. I climb up, stretching out next to her. Essie drags a single finger from my clavicle to my navel, then shifts to straddle my thighs.

Her warm palms smooth up my abs. "Finally, I have you all to myself."

I settle my hands on her thighs. "This entire week has felt like extended foreplay."

"It really has." She settles her hands on my pecs and leans in, dark hair sweeping across my skin. "You're pretty ripped for a guy who sits behind a desk designing skates."

"I work out with Flip and Tristan," I explain.

She bites my chin. "We can get all our cardio done together this week."

I laugh, and she pulls back, eyes softening. "You're so pretty when you smile." She frames my face with her hands and she presses her lips to mine. A sweet balm of relief washes over me.

I curve my palm around the nape of her neck. She parts and our tongues brush. Desire rushes through me, and I grip her hip and shift under her, seeking friction.

Her fingers curl around the bottom of my chin, lips still touching when she whispers, "Someone's in a rush to get to the good stuff."

"You're the one who got me naked seconds after I walked through the door." I arch a challenging brow. "How do you know I didn't want to just hang out and chat?"

"Your dick did not want to hang out and chat."

"He's not the boss of me."

She rolls her hips, her pussy a soft, warm counterpart to the hard steel of her piercing sliding over my shaft. I groan, fingers digging into her skin as I lift my hips.

"What was that?" She sucks my bottom lip between hers and releases it slowly.

"You're playing dirty."

She grins and bites her lip. "Fuck, I love your grumpy face."

I glare at her.

"Mmm..." She shakes her head and sighs. "You're such a smoke show when you look like you're plotting my undoing."

"I'm never plotting your demise, Ess." I keep one hand on her hip and trace the other up her side.

"Not what I said, but that furrow in your brow tells a different story."

"It's not a demise furrow." I skim her collarbones

"You really are ridiculously attractive when you're channeling your inner Grinch," she teases.

"I don't channel an inner Grinch," I grumble, basically proving her point.

She props her forearms on my chest and settles her chin on her fingers. "Say something smart."

"Something smart."

She rolls her beautiful eyes. "Smart, not *smart ass*. Pull a random fact out of your head and share it with me."

"Why?"

"Because your big brain is a turn-on, and it's even sexier when you say smart things while you're naked and wearing your serious face."

I dredge up a random, not entirely useless fact. "Your lips have over a million nerve endings and are one of the most sensitive places on the body." I suck her bottom one.

"Tell me something else," she whispers, tracing the bow of my mouth.

"There are ten thousand nerve endings in your pretty little pierced clit, which is one of the reasons it feels so good when I suck on it."

"Especially when you're wearing nothing but your determined face," she agrees with a roll of her hips.

"I can suck on it now, if you like, and I'll do my best to wear my determined face."

She smiles and bats her lashes, fingers drifting over my cheek. "Maybe later. I'd like to choke on your cock before I sit on it."

"For fuck's sake, Essie."

"I'll take that as a yes."

I can't take my eyes off her as she kisses a path down my chest. Sex with Essie is an adventure. She's fun, uninhibited, and wildly beautiful. She drops open-mouth, wet kisses, her pierced nipples dragging over my skin, as she makes her way down my body. She skirts around my erection, cheek brushing the head as she kisses across my hip.

She teases and licks and nibbles, long hair sweeping over my thighs as her palm encircles my length. Her eyes find mine and she takes me in her mouth. Soft lips, wet tongue, her satisfied hum vibrating through me.

She cups my balls, lips sliding down my shaft. Everything tightens, and I close my eyes for a moment, overwhelmed by the sight and feel of her.

She pops off, and my eyes flip open. "Too much?" She drags her lips up and down the side of my cock.

I shake my head. Then nod. Then shake it again. "You just feel so fucking good, and the way you look..." *Gorgeous, depraved, perfect. The loveliest vision.*

"Am I pretty when I'm trying to swallow your cock?" She covers the head again, cheeks hollowing out as she sucks.

"You're fucking beautiful." I push up on my elbow and slide my fingers into her hair.

Her expression turns angelic as she licks around the head, but her words nearly ruin me. "Would you like to fuck my mouth, Nathan?"

Heat travels down my spine, and I grind out a guttural, "Yes."

She curves her palm around my fingers in her hair, closing my hand into a fist. "Guide me."

I sit up and slide my other hand into her hair, taking in her expectant, needy expression. She parts her swollen lips, and I ease inside. Essie's eyes stay on mine as I move her mouth gently up and down my length.

"So good, Essie," I praise as her cheeks hollow out. "Such a lovely, sweet mouth." The head hits the back of her throat. She opens wider and takes more. "So fucking gorgeous when you're swallowing my cock."

She does this thing with her tongue that pushes me to the edge.

"I'm going to come," I warn.

She takes me deeper, and I explode in her mouth. I loosen my grip on her hair, giving her back control. She bobs a couple more times, but I'm hypersensitive, so I gently ease her off, slip my hands under her arms, and pull her up as I flop back on the mattress.

Her body is draped across mine, chin resting on the center of my chest. She grins at me with swollen lips. "Hi."

"Hi. That was outstanding."

"You seemed to enjoy yourself." She kisses my chin.

I curve my hand around the back of her neck and kiss her chastely.

"I can brush my teeth first if you want," she offers.

I frown. "Why?"

She strokes a finger between my eyes. "Because my mouth tastes like your cum, and you might not love that."

"I kissed you last time."

"There was chocolate sauce involved."

"Don't care. I want your mouth." I tip her chin down and bring her lips to mine.

She hums as our tongues meet, and I rearrange her legs so she's straddling me again.

I keep one hand on her hip while we kiss, helping her shift

against my reawakening erection while I play with her nipple piercings.

She gazes down at me, eyes hot with need.

I wind her hair around my hand, nipping the edge of her jaw. "Would you like me to fuck you now, Ess?"

She bites her lip and nods. "I'll get a condom."

She stretches across the bed, reaching to the nightstand for the pink zippered fabric pouch with a magic wand and stars on it. The heart-shaped jewel piercing her nipple catches the light. I capture the peak, sucking softly as the metal slides over my tongue.

Essie moans, clutching my hair. "I love your mouth so much when you're being nice with it." She slides a finger into the corner of it and detaches me from her nipple, then covers my mouth with her palm when I try to get back what I've lost. "You can suck on them to your heart's content once you're inside me."

"Mmmm... Fair." I kiss the swell and lie back.

She sets the pouch on my stomach, unzips it, and produces a box of condoms—the same kind I had when we were in Vegas last weekend. She pries the box open, tears one free, and rolls it down my length. And then my hands are on her hips, and she lowers herself onto me. Her eyes flutter closed, and her fingers skim her nipples as they drift down her stomach. She's an absolute vision. But she's too far away. I want her close. I want her wrapped around me, hot skin against mine.

I sit up and latch onto her breast.

Essie threads her hands through my hair, eyes soft as she watches me. I wish it could be like this between us all the time—the walls down, all my fears chased away by lust and the overwhelming need to make her feel good. I covet every sigh and moan and soft whimper. I want to bottle up this feeling and carry it around with me.

She wraps her arms around my head, body shaking as her pussy clenches. But I want more. I want to watch her face as she unravels for me. So I tip her head back, dropping my other hand between her thighs to find that little steel ball.

"Oh God, Nate." Her nails bite into my shoulders.

"That's it, Essie, keep fucking me. I want to watch you come for me."

I move her over me, finding a rhythm as she gazes down, one hand gripping my shoulder while the fingers of her other hand tremble against my cheek.

"You feel so good," she whispers.

"Let go for me. Let me see what I do to you." I brush my lips over hers. "So pretty when you're coming just for me."

She contracts around me, pussy gripping me like a fist as euphoria passes across her face. Primal satisfaction rushes through me. I make her feel this way. I give her what she needs. I'm the one who gets to see her at her most vulnerable and beautiful. My own orgasm slams through me, wiping out my thoughts, replacing them with overwhelming sensation.

I fall back against the pillows, taking Essie with me. She sprawls across my chest, and I wrap my arms around her, holding her close.

"Best sex ever." She pokes at my nipple with her tongue.

"Yeah?" I stroke her hair.

She hums and lifts her head, expression soft. "Did you have fun?"

I stroke her cheek. "So much fun."

"Me too." She kisses my chin. "I'm going to brush my teeth." Her expression shifts, uncertainty making her voice pitch up. "You're welcome to half my bed if you want to stay the night."

"Yeah. I'd like that."

She grins. "'Kay." She lifts herself off me and brushes my hands away when I reach for the condom. "I'll do it." She removes it, tying it at the top and taking it with her to the bathroom. The door closes with a soft snick.

She reappears a minute later, still naked. "There's a spare toothbrush if you want it," she offers.

"Yeah, sounds good." I trade places with her.

Neatly organized makeup lines the vanity, along with creams, hair products, and accessories. I pick up a bottle of lotion, rolling it between my fingers before I twist the top and sniff the contents. It's the scent I associate with her. Soft and feminine. Pretty and sweet. I replace the cap, put it back in its place, and use the extra toothbrush. Then I clean myself up before I leave the bathroom.

Essie is already in bed, covers pulled up, the lights off apart from the one on my side of the bed. She pats the empty space, and I stretch out next to her. I flick off the light and shift until I feel the warmth of her body. I slide an arm under her and pull her closer. She's wearing her nightshirt.

"I didn't take you for a snuggler," she murmurs.

"Usually I'm not," I admit. I rearrange her leg so it's draped over mine and cover the hand on my chest.

"Hmm…" She kisses the side of my neck. "'Night, Nate."

I kiss her forehead. "'Night, Ess."

It feels good to hold someone.

No. Not someone.

It feels good to hold *Essie*.

And that's the moment I realize this isn't just about sex. Yes, it's out-of-this-world amazing. But I like Essie. More than like Essie. This warmth in my chest, the desire to spend the night beside her, to hold her. *What if I have feelings for her?*

It's a bad idea. She doesn't want a boyfriend. Especially not one who doesn't believe love can last—that it's even real, or tenable. She wants the fairy tale.

Eventually her fondness for my bad attitude will shift and prove what I know to be true: Nothing lasts forever.

And then where will I be? Alone again.

I can keep my feelings on lock, though. I've done it for years without even trying. I can have this week with Essie. It's better than not having her at all. And it's better for both of us if I keep my feelings to myself. Because everyone leaves eventually.

CHAPTER 20

NATE

"Nate." *Poke.* "Nate." *Poke. Poke.* "Seriously, you are the soundest sleeper in the freaking universe." Essie shakes my shoulder.

I do not want to move and give away the fact that I'm awake. Essie is exactly where I want her to stay, pressed against my body, warm breath breaking against my neck. She wiggles around, waking up other parts.

Her hair tickles my face as her lips brush my earlobe. "Anal sex," she whispers.

My eyes flip open, and I slide my hand down her back to squeeze her ass cheek.

"You are such a dude." She leans back so she can see my face. "How long have you been awake, you dirty bird?"

"About five seconds before you offered anal." My voice is thick and raspy with sleep.

"That wasn't an offer; that was me trying to wake you up. And it worked." She wriggles around again, trying to worm her way out of my hold. "It's already six. You have to go back to your room."

I roll us over so I'm on top of her and bury my face in her neck. "Don't wanna."

Essie runs her fingers through my hair while I edge my knee between her thighs. "Rix gets up balls early. She's too stressed to sleep in. I don't want her to knock on my door and find you in here. Especially since I'm supposed to be on a dick hiatus, and clearly I've fallen off the wagon."

I reluctantly push up on my arms. There are sleep lines on her right cheek, and her hair is fanned across the pillow. Fresh-faced, barely awake, bedhead Essie is the most beautiful Essie in the universe. All I want to do is spend the rest of today in bed—fuck the rest of the world.

"Do you think she'd be upset?" I ask, still doing a pushup on top of her.

She smooths her thumb along the bridge of my nose. "She's worried about everything right now, and I don't want to add to that. You can come back tonight, though."

I grin.

"But anal is not on the table—"

"You put it on the table when you whispered it in my ear."

"We can do doggy or reverse cowgirl, and you can stick a finger or a plug in there, but your dick is huge."

"Fingers are a gateway."

She rolls her eyes. "And much more reasonable than your delightfully massive cock. This isn't debate class." She pats my ass. "You have to get up, Nate."

I roll off her and out of bed, hopping to my feet.

She sighs despondently, eyes on my erection. "I'm sorry I can't jump on that now, but we'll make up for it later."

"It's okay. I'm used to handling it on my own."

She slides out of bed and pads across the room, grabbing my clothes, which she apparently hung up to dry for me at some point last night. She tosses them at me. "Please put those on. I'm going to brush my teeth." She hustles into the bathroom.

I dress and am forced to tuck the head of my dick into the waistband of my shorts so it's not an embarrassment. Essie returns a minute later, hair brushed, wearing a pair of shorts and a sports bra. "Okay. Let me make sure the coast is clear."

I follow her to the door and wait while she pokes her head out. I wish I had brushed my teeth so I could kiss her before I leave, but my mouth still tastes like sleep.

She deems it safe for me to leave, but she fists my shirt and pushes up on her toes, sucking my bottom lip for a moment before she shoves me out of her room. "See you and your dick later."

She closes the door in my face. At the same time, Flip steps out of his room two doors down. He's wearing a pair of athletic shorts and running shoes. He gives me a look as he takes in my rumpled shirt, shorts, and flip-flops. My boner is mostly concealed, but not completely.

"I don't want to hear it," I warn.

He raises both hands. "I'm not here to judge."

"You going for a run on the beach?" I ask.

"Yup."

"Give me ten and I'll join you."

"I'll meet you by the VIP beach entrance."

"Sounds good." I return to my room. There's a small puddle on the floor to the right of the bed. I'd be more concerned if I planned to sleep in here this week, but there's no reason to alert management about the issue for now. If they move me to another room, it might make it more of a challenge for me to sneak into Essie's.

I rub one out—it doesn't take long—change into running gear, and meet Flip on the beach.

"So Vegas wasn't a one-time thing, eh?" he asks as we fall into a light jog.

"Nope."

"You two dating now?"

I lift a shoulder. "Not really."

He's quiet for a few seconds. "She's a good person, Nate. And she has a big heart. Don't string her along."

"She said it was just about sex."

"Is it?"

"For her, yeah, I guess. She kicked me out this morning because she doesn't want Rix to find out and worry 'cause she's already stressed enough about the wedding." I sound pretty disgruntled about it.

"Rix is stressier than I expected, and Essie is hyper-cognizant of that, so I can see her wanting to avoid unnecessary drama. Are *you* worried about Rix and Tristan finding out?"

"Tristan wouldn't be very happy with me."

"Why do you think that?" Flip asks.

"Because my relationship track record isn't great."

"To be fair, Tristan didn't have a relationship track record until Rix, so he wouldn't have much of a leg to stand on if that's what he's upset about."

"She only wants dick from me anyway."

"But you want something else?"

"Yeah. No. I don't know."

"Sounds like maybe you do know and you're having a hard time admitting it."

I can't talk to Tristan about this, or my dad, or anyone else really. So I guess it's Flip. "I like her. Like in the bedroom, yeah, but also out of it. She's fun, and sweet, and thoughtful, and talented, and so smart." I should find her obsession with all things fairy tale and romance irritating, but now it's just... endearing. "She's a ray of sunshine. I like how I feel when I'm around her." Especially now that we're not fighting to stay away from each other. "And the sex is unreal."

"I knew it. I should have acted faster."

I punch him in the shoulder. "Fuck you."

"I'm kidding."

I give him a look.

"Mostly."

"Seriously, fuck you." I shove him, and he nearly loses his footing.

"Dude, I'm a guy with a dick, and she's ridiculously gorgeous, plus all the other things you so helpfully highlighted about her. I'm not ashamed to admit that I've thought about her in a Biblical way. But she's my sister's best friend, and I'm not ready for something real, which is what Essie deserves."

"Yeah, well, she doesn't want real with me," I grumble.

"I feel like you're not telling me something." We reach the end of the resort beach, and he stops, hands on his knees, sweat dripping from his brow.

I sigh and drag a hand through my sweaty hair.

"Spit it out, man. I won't tell Tris or Rix. Whatever you say stays here on this beach."

"I kissed her once at a party the summer before I went to university," I admit. "I've never told anyone. And as far as I know, she never has either."

"Interesting. What happened after the kiss?"

I scrub a hand over my face. "I was supposed to call her the next day."

"But you didn't."

I shake my head. "I didn't."

"Why not?"

I tip my head up. It's a clear, beautiful day. Not a cloud in the sky. "So many reasons. I was leaving for Kingston in a few weeks."

"And you didn't want to do the long-distance thing?"

"One of the guys I hung out with started giving me the gears. Told me about the friend of his Essie dated, how she was in love with him two weeks in, and I don't know... I guess I just freaked out?" I meet his gaze, expecting judgment, but all I get is Flip's impassive empathy, so I keep going. "I didn't think I could handle a relationship, especially not with someone who could fall in love with me. I just wanted to have fun, you know? I couldn't deal with serious then." Based on my track record, I don't know if I can handle it now. Ironic that for the first time since Lisa broke it off, it's something I'm considering. "So I ghosted her."

Flip nods. "Well, that explains the weird tension when you two were around each other until recently."

"What weird tension?"

"She's always fussing with herself, like she's self-conscious, and you're always in the worst of fucking moods. Probably because you feel like a guilty asshole."

"Basically, yeah."

"So you've explained why you ghosted her, then?" he asks.

"That's the thing…we haven't really addressed it." The times she's mentioned it, we haven't been in a place where I could issue the apology she deserves.

"But you're fucking." It's a statement, not a question.

Fucking sounds so…crude. Emotionless. "Yeah."

"You should at least be honest with her about the past. I'm hazarding a guess that she's okay with the current arrangement because she has ideas about why things went down the way they did back then. Telling her the truth could change that."

"I don't know if I want it to change."

His expression shifts, his smile a little sad. "It already has, Nate. It's written all over your face. Maybe the arrangement started as just sex, but you have feelings. Not sharing them with her doesn't stop them from existing." He's different than the Flip I moved in with almost a year ago. I'm not sure what inspired the change, but his insightfulness is surprising.

"What if she doesn't want what I want?" The twist in my stomach and the panic clogging my throat are more telling than I'd like.

"That's always the risk. You have to decide if she's worth it." He claps me on the shoulder. "You don't have to make a move now, or this week even. But weigh what you're willing to put out there. Maybe this is your second chance."

CHAPTER 21

ESSIE

I set my book on the table and stretch. I was right to kick Nate out early this morning. Rix came knocking on my door twenty minutes after he left, looking to grab coffee.

We followed it up with a group brunch—I sat at the other end of the table from Nate so I wouldn't accidentally flirt with him. We've been lounging by the pool since. "What time is it?"

"Just after noon. What's up?" Rix asks.

"I scheduled a private yoga session for us girls. We should get cleaned up and head over."

"I would have joined you for yoga," Flip says.

"Bond with the bros and do something competitive. We'll see you in a couple of hours." Rix, the girls, and I gather our stuff and stop by our rooms to freshen up.

I rinse off quickly in the shower, change into a pair of yoga shorts and a sports bra, and grab my bag and a gift I picked up for Rix on the way out of my room. I stop at Rix and Tristan's suite, crossing my fingers as I knock on her door.

"Who is it?" she calls.

"Your bestie!"

She opens the door dressed in yoga shorts and a crop top, looking relieved. "Thank God."

"Did Tristan follow you back and try to seduce you?"

"Yeah, but I put the safety latch on. There is no such thing as a quickie with him. It's always a marathon of orgasms."

"It's a hard life, being engaged to a hockey player who loves you to pieces." A pang of guilt hits me over the fact that I'm hiding things from her. But what's going on with me and Nate has an expiration date. We don't want the same things. I have my heart set on the fairy tale. I want someone who believes that love conquers all. I want a family and a cat named Teacup and a dog named Sparkles. I want romance and eventually babies and growing old and wrinkly together. I want someone who will love me even when the beauty fades.

Rix's face gets all dreamy for a moment. "Tristan is a really dedicated fiancé."

"He is. I'm so glad you fought for each other."

"Me too." She smiles. "Let's go do yoga with the girls."

We meet up with them and walk over to the studio.

"Thank you for setting this up for us." Hemi's arm is around Shilpa's shoulders. "I love that we're getting in some quality time that doesn't include a sports competition with the boys."

"Agreed! I love that the guys want to do things, but I can't be high octane every moment." Hammer rolls her head on her shoulders. "I could definitely use some yoga to stretch out all my tight muscles."

"Is that from the volleyball game earlier, or your alone time with Hollis?" Rix asks.

The guys spent about five minutes lounging before they became restless and decided beach volleyball was a good idea. They do nothing at a leisurely pace.

"Both." Hammer cringes and looks at Lexi. "I probably shouldn't admit these things in front of you."

Lexi shrugs. "Technically I know I'm your stepmom, which is all kinds of weird for both of us, but I view you as a friend. I will never repeat any of this to Roman, because it's better that he lives in the land of make-believe where you do none of the things the rest of us do with our partners behind closed doors."

Hammer hugs Lexi. "I appreciate you."

We enter the yoga studio, grab mats, and get comfortable as the instructor introduces herself. It's exactly what we all need—an hour of time with friends, without extreme cardio and testosterone. Shilpa falls asleep fifteen minutes in. The instructor covers her with a blanket and tucks a pillow under her head before the rest of us continue.

"Jeez, you're bendy," Dred says when I move into the advanced form of pigeon pose.

"I took gymnastics for a lot of years, and I was a cheerleader in high school and university." I often keep this kind of personal information to myself because people put me in a box labeled *too pretty to have a brain*, but I feel safe with these girls.

She nods. "That definitely explains the bendiness."

"And yes, I dated the quarterback." It was so cliché.

"Was he the hottest guy in the school?" Hammer asks.

"Tristan was the hottest back then, closely followed by Flip," I explain.

"But the quarterback ranked third overall," Rix chimes in. "What was his name again, Ess?"

"Jett Hudson." I gave him devil horns in my yearbook.

"Oh, that name screams hot jock," Dred replies.

"Right? He was such a bad choice." I roll my eyes.

"Did he know he was hot shit?" Hemi asks.

I nod. "Oh yeah, totally."

"But like, Essie was a legend in high school," Rix says.

"I was not," I mutter.

"She's lying. She was named the hottest girl in school every single year from grade nine through twelve," Rix explains.

"Was it in the yearbook?" Dred asks.

"Unfortunately, yes."

"Kind of sucks when people put you in a box based on one quality," Hemi says softly.

HELENA HUNTING

I nod. "Yeah, but Rix and I had each other, and that's what mattered."

"Always and forever my bestie." Rix reaches across the mat, and we link pinkies and smile.

High school was fun, and I was invited to every party, but no one expected me to make the honor roll or be the one with the answers. I was pretty and popular, fun to be around—the girl guys wanted to date but not get serious with. After a while, I started to believe that's who I was, too. I stopped fighting the stereotype. I thought I was beyond that, but the compliments from Nate about being math smart hit a soft part of me that longs to be seen completely.

After yoga, most of the girls head back to their rooms, and Rix and I stop in the lobby for a fruit shake. We find a table in the shade and drag our chairs close enough that our shoulders touch.

"I have something for you." I pull a small bag tied with ribbon out of my purse and set it on the table in front of her.

"You've already done so much, Ess. You don't need to buy me gifts."

"It's just little. No big thing, I promise."

Rix pulls the ribbon free and reaches inside, withdrawing the first small box. She throws her head back and laughs. "Oh my gosh, where in the world did you get this wrapping paper?"

"It's amazing, isn't it?"

"The most amazing." It's covered in a pattern of smiling cucumbers.

"I'll get you some for Tristan's birthday."

"That would be magical." She carefully opens the small box and hugs it to her chest. "Oh my gosh, are they all French mint?"

"Absolutely. You'll need to put them in the fridge when you get back to your room, so they don't turn into a chocolate puddle." I picked up a small box of her favorite chocolates.

"I will savor every single one." She tucks them into her bag and moves it into the shade. Next she opens the travel pack of her favorite lotion and shampoo. "How did you know I was almost out?"

"You mentioned you were running low in Vegas, and I wasn't sure you'd have time to pick up more before we came here. There's one more thing."

She unwraps the smallest box. Inside is a pair of custom-made smiling cucumber earrings.

She bursts out laughing and then bursts into tears.

I wrap my arms around her.

"These are joy tears. I'm so lucky to have you, Ess. I'm so glad you moved back to Toronto. Let's never be apart again, okay?"

"Never again," I agree. Although, Tristan's career could take them somewhere else in the future, depending on contracts. But for now, we're together. "I'm so happy that we're here in this beautiful place, and I get to celebrate this with you." I gently wipe her tears.

"How did I get so lucky, Ess? You're the *best* best friend in the world. My fiancé is incredible, and I have fabulous friends and a supportive family."

"You didn't get lucky, Rix. You attracted all these people to you by being who you are. People love you. People want you to succeed and be happy. Tristan knows how special you are. We all do. I'm so glad you've found your person. It brings me so much joy to see you in such a good place."

She squeezes my hand. "You'll find your person, too, Ess."

"I want what my parents have. I want what you have with Tristan." I shift and rest my chin on my knuckles. "But instead of Prince Charming, I always seem to pick the ones who are bad for me."

"Do you think it's because you're not ready for the one?" Rix asks softly.

"Maybe." I've thought about this a lot lately—the reasons for all these dead-end relationships. "In Vancouver, I kept dating all these pretty-boy B-list actors with connections." I swallow past the lump in my throat, because admitting this, even to my best friend, is hard. "But no one expected me to have input, or thoughts, or ideas. I was just the pretty makeup artist." And of course I could come to the next party as long as I could do their makeup.

I sigh. It was like this in high school, too. I was always the hot girl, and Rix was my smart, pretty best friend. She never worried about what other people thought the way I do.

Her eyes soften. "You're so much more than a pretty face, Ess. You're creative, smart, kind, thoughtful, and one of my favorite people in the world."

"And you're my favorite, forever and always."

"Are you happier back in Toronto?"

When I'm with Rix and the Babe Brigade, I'm just me, and they love and accept me as I am. So do my parents and my sister. "Yeah, the girls are amazing friends, and I won't fall back into the trap of dating actors."

"Has this job been better for you?"

"In Vancouver it was movie sets with a rotating cast and odd hours, but now it's stable, and my hours are normal. The people I work with are more down-to-earth. I have more time to spend with the people who matter to me. Like you."

"I'm so glad you're back. I loved that you were doing your thing, but I missed you so much."

I hug her arm. "I missed you, too. I'm really glad I get to be here with you and be part of your special day. And do your makeup! I feel like I've been training for it with all the girls' nights out over the past year."

"You're an artist with a makeup brush." She tips her head. "Have you ever thought about transitioning to wedding makeup?"

I scrunch my nose. "I helped out with a couple when I was training in school, and while it's cool that you get to be with people on what's supposed to be one of the happiest days of their lives, there is also the opportunity to really fuck it up for them."

Rix cringes. "Are you speaking from experience?"

"Personal? No. But I've heard the horror stories. Also, I'd always have to work on the weekend."

"True."

"I like working on a set where I can be creative, but I also know what's coming at me most of the time. The bridezilla factor is a real thing."

"Am I a bridezilla?" Rix looks suddenly worried.

"No." I laugh. "Not even a little. You want things to go smoothly. You want your special day to be good, not just for your sake, but for everyone and especially for Tristan. You know how much work it took to get where you are, so it makes sense that you want the day to be a good one."

She squeezes my hand. "I hope I can be half as helpful when it's your turn."

I smile, but there's a lump in my throat as I force any image of me in a wedding dress out of my head. "You will be the best matron of honor."

But I'm afraid I'll never be where she is. That I'll never be *the one* for someone.

The Nate I've come to know is softer and sweeter than anyone realizes, and it would be so easy to open my heart to that side of him. It would also be totally on brand for me to fall for another guy whose life vision doesn't align with mine. We can have fun this week, but when the wedding is over, so are we. It's the only way to keep my silly heart from being broken again.

CHAPTER 22
ESSIE

Towels and shirts are scattered over the lounge beds by the pool when we return, but the guys aren't there, which shouldn't be a surprise. They're probably doing something sporty because sitting still isn't any of their strong suits.

I scan the shoreline, which is full of people in swimwear, but I don't see the guys, so I look to the water instead. "There they are."

"Only they would play water Frisbee." Rix rolls her eyes. "No wonder Tristan is out cold the second his head hits the pillow."

"That's exactly what happened last—" I stop myself before I finish that sentence. Nate was out within seconds of turning off the bedside lamp last night, but I can't tell Rix that. "—time I dated a jock," I quickly amend.

"It always takes me a good half hour to fall asleep." Rix sighs.

"Same."

Nate misses a toss and swims out to retrieve it while the guys heckle him. He's on his way back when he starts thrashing. Tristan is the first to notice and quickly heads for his brother, the rest of the guys on his tail. Even from the beach we can hear Nate swearing a blue streak.

"What's going on out there?" I grab Rix's arm and drag her toward the water. My first thought is that Nate got bit by a freaking shark, but there's no blood swirling around him.

His face is contorted in pain though, so something happened. He brushes off his brother and Flip, heading directly for me and Rix.

"Are you okay? What happened?" Rix asks as he reaches the shore.

"I ran into a jellyfish. Or more than one. I don't know, but it really fucking hurts."

"Someone should pee on him!" Dallas shouts.

"I've got you, honey bear," Flip calls.

"Don't you dare! That's not what you're supposed to do anyway." He drops onto his ass and puts his head between his legs. "Fuck me, this is some pain."

Red welts line his back and side, traveling over his shoulder and down his right arm. More welts run down the inside of his left thigh. My throat constricts at how high up they might go.

I crouch beside him and put my hand on his unaffected left arm. "Hey, hi. I know you're hurting and it's probably hard to think around it, but can you walk? I'll take you to the medic and get you something to make you comfortable."

"I just need a sec. The burn is unreal, Ess," he grumbles.

"We can bring medical to you, if that's better." I wish I could do something to ease him, but then there will be questions.

"You'll come with me?" He turns his head, eyes glassy with agony as they meet mine. "You'll stay with me?"

My soft heart leaps at his pleading tone. "Yeah. Of course."

"Okay." He swallows. "Okay, let's go see the medic."

I help him to his feet and duck under his arm on the left side, careful to stay away from the welts.

Rix wrings her hands. "We should come with."

"I don't need an entourage. I just need Little Miss Sunshine and Rainbows," Nate barks.

"I've got him. He'll be fine. Just needs Benadryl and he'll be good to go." I point to the red cross symbol on the small white building just beyond the boardwalk. The clinic is literally a hundred feet away.

"Message as soon as you're done?" Rix presses.

"Absolutely." I kiss her on the cheek and lead Nate away.

He swears every three seconds until we enter the medical building. There's only one other person waiting, and they have a sunburn so bad on their feet that they've blistered.

The nurse takes one look at Nate and ushers him into an examination room. I help him up onto the table.

"We don't see many jellyfish stings this time of year," she says.

"Guess I'm just lucky," Nate mumbles.

She looks him over, pushing his shorts up to expose the stings on the inside of his thigh. "You must have run into a few of them. Maybe a mom and her babies. I'll give you a shot to help with the swelling and some cream to calm the itch once the burning settles down. You'll feel better inside the hour. Stay hydrated and avoid alcohol for the next twenty-four hours."

"I have a wedding in two days. Will I be okay by then?" Nate asks.

"You'll be much better by tomorrow," she assures him.

I hold Nate's hand while she gives him the shot.

"You'll want to take him back to your room right away," the nurse informs me. "This will make him groggy, and you don't want him passing out in a lounge chair by the pool. A sunburn will only exacerbate the problem."

"I'll do that right now."

She hands me a tube of cream. "You can rub this on the affected areas. It will help with the itching, but it'll be mostly managed by morning."

"Thank you for everything." I run my fingers through his hair. "Okay, Nate, we're going back to the room now."

"You're gonna stay with me, right? You're not gonna leave?" His eyes are glassy from the drugs instead of the pain now.

"No, I won't leave."

"Okay. Good." He lets me help him down from the exam table.

"Congratulations, by the way," the nurse says. "You're a beautiful couple."

"She's sunshine and a rainbow, and the dark eats the light," Nate says helpfully. His words are already slurring together.

"Looks like the antihistamines are hitting him hard. You'll want to get him into bed as soon as possible," the nurse says.

"That's his one and only stop." I'm grateful our block of rooms is close by, because Nate grows progressively less lucid as we go.

I manage to get him into my room, and he barely makes it to the bed, flopping down with a groan. "My back feels raw."

"Roll over and I'll put some cream on it."

He does as I ask and grabs my pillow and Catalina.

"Be careful with her."

He presses her to his face and inhales deeply. "She smells like you."

I sit beside him on the bed and gently rub cream over the angry, red welts.

"How bad is it? It feels bad. Not as bad as it did at first, but still not good," he says into my pillow.

"It looks uncomfortable."

He turns his head so he's looking at me. The furrow in his brow deepens. "Where'd the kitty go? I want it."

"You're holding it in your other hand."

"I wanna huff it," he mumbles.

I move Catalina so she's in front of his face again. "My pillow probably also smells like me and is in much better shape." He

171

likely won't remember any of this come morning, but I certainly will.

"But this is like...embezzled, embroidered, embroizeled, embedded with your scent. Do you snuggle it every night?"

"Pretty much, yeah." Again, he won't remember, so it's not like he'll be able to make fun of me for traveling with a stuffed cat.

"I would snuggle you every night. I wanna snuggle you right now." The slur in his words grows more pronounced. "Can we snuggle, Ess?"

"Yeah, Nate, we can snuggle." He'll be out like a light in five minutes.

"Snuggles." His big hand wraps around my waist, and he tries to pull me into him, grunting when my hand lands on his welts.

I stretch out beside him, pulling myself up higher on the bed. I grab my phone so I can message Rix once he's out. He wraps his arm around my waist and nuzzles in close, throwing his leg over mine.

"It's nice to feel like someone gives a shit about me who isn't my family or Flip."

My soft heart clenches, and I stroke his hair. "I wouldn't be here if I didn't give a shit, Nate."

He makes a contented sound. "I like this. I like you. You're beautiful. Everything about you. I just want to hold you. It's nice not to be alone all the time. We can have this week, right?"

My silly, sentimental heart is already bruising. "Yeah, Nate, we can have this week."

"Good. That's good. That's what I want. I'll make up for this when I'm not high."

I put my heart in a box and lock it away. Letting it get involved would be a huge mistake. He's not forever, he's for now, and I need to remember that. I can like him, and I can fuck him, but I can't fall for him. I promised I wouldn't do that again. Because when this week is over, I'll be Essie, and he'll be Nate.

But we'll never be Nate and Essie.

CHAPTER 23
NATE

The sun isn't even up when I crack a lid in the morning. The clock on the nightstand reads four forty-five, and my stomach feels like it's eating itself. Also, my skin is itchy. But I'm wrapped around Essie, which is nice.

"There's food on the table. Please make your stomach stop. It's been yelling louder than a grandpa without hearing aids for the past hour." Essie drags a pillow over her head.

I roll over and sit up, blinking into the murky darkness. My stomach gurgles embarrassingly.

"I can still hear your stomach, Nathan," Essie says from under the pillow.

I pad over to the table, eyes adjusting to the darkness. I pop the tops on three resealable containers and find an assortment of fresh fruit, pastries, and rolls with butter.

Essie lifts the pillow a few inches. "There are cold cuts, cheese, and condiments in the fridge if you want to make sand-wiches out of the buns."

My chest tightens in a weird, uncomfortable way. I'm not used to having someone do nice things for me. "Thanks."

I scavenge the fridge for the meat and cheese, grab a bottle of water, and plow through everything in less than fifteen minutes.

It takes the edge off, but now that I'm not hungry anymore, I'm really fucking itchy. I scratch my back, but it feels raw.

Essie tosses her pillow aside and rolls off the bed with a sigh. She disappears into the bathroom and closes the door. A minute later she reappears and flicks on one of the bedside lamps. She's wearing a nightshirt with a princess and her gaggle of smiling, hat wearing friends and the phrase *the original why choose*. Her hair tumbles over her shoulders in unruly waves. I want to drag her back to bed, curl myself around her, and bury my face in her hair.

"Sorry you're awake at stupid o'clock in the morning," I say as she crosses over to me.

"It's fine. I was in bed early, anyway." She taps the back of my hand. "Give me your hand, palm up."

I do as she asks, and she places a pill in the center. "Non-drowsy antihistamine. It'll help with the itching. You're supposed to stay out of the sun today. Sadly, you'll probably have to wear a shirt and rob me of the joy of checking out your fine-as-fuck body from behind the protective cover of my sunglasses."

I huff a laugh and take the pill. "Thank you for taking care of me last night. Sorry if it meant you didn't get time with Rix and the girls."

"Rix was busy boning your brother. Or being boned by your brother. As were the rest of the girls—except for Dred. She's on her fourth book already." Essie runs her hands through my hair. "How are you feeling?"

"Fine apart from really fucking itchy."

"I can apply more of the cream the nurse gave you."

"I can probably handle it." She's already done more than enough in the taking-care-of-me department.

"I don't mind. It's probably easier for me to get your back."

Her hands on me seems like a good way to start my day. "If you're sure."

She unscrews the lid and squeezes some onto her fingers,

175

moving to stand behind me as I sit in a chair. "It looks so much better this morning." She swipes gently over my skin.

I let my head fall forward and my eyes close, enjoying the contact. "That's good. It doesn't feel nearly as awful. Thanks for the food. That was nice of you."

"I figured you'd be hungry when you finally woke up, and my purse snacks, while good in a pinch, probably wouldn't have been enough."

"Purse snacks?"

"Yeah. I always keep snack items in my purse. Mostly it's a leftover habit from my university days with Rix," Essie explains.

"She does that, doesn't she? Always carries crackers and stuff."

"Mm-hmm." She settles one hand on my shoulder and skims my ribs with the other. I move my arm so it rests on the back of the chair, giving her better access to my side. "Fortune cookies, soup crackers, animal crackers, fruit leathers, mini bags of nuts —her purse is where airplane snacks live."

"We went to a maple farm once when we were kids, and Tris and Rix came along," I tell her as an old memory surfaces. "She wanted to buy one of those little bottles of maple syrup so badly."

"I remember her talking about it afterward. All she ever had growing up was the fakle stuff," Essie says.

"Fakle?" I parrot.

"Fake maple syrup. The kind made with corn syrup and food coloring."

I nod. "Oh yeah. I've never heard that term for it."

"It's what she always called it after she tried the real stuff."

"Makes sense. I didn't even know the fake stuff was different when I was a kid. I thought everyone had the real stuff until my dad explained that it's expensive and not everyone could afford it. Tristan went out and bought a big container for her family with his own money."

176

Essie's fingers stop moving for a second. "I thought it was your dad who did that. So did she."

"It was Tris. He's always had a soft spot for her. At least until our mom left. Then all his soft spots disappeared for a while." She moves around to my right, and I finger the hem of her nightshirt, less pleasant memories from all those years ago floating to the surface. "Tristan went from being fun to...angry. Lots of dents in the garage siding from pucks after she left." And broken sticks. Brody had always been quiet, but after Mom left, he turtled. I put all my energy into school.

"I'm so sorry, Nate." Essie caps the cream and sets it on the table, hands coming to rest on my shoulders again.

I want the affection. Crave it. Need it, even.

"I just wish she'd stay out of our lives. Everything was fine until she started calling again." I shake my head. "I don't know why I'm telling you this."

"Probably because our families arrive today, and I'm sure that's a weight for all of you." Her nails drag gently along the back of my neck.

"Yeah. Maybe." I settle my hand at the back of her thigh. Lately I find myself wanting to confide in her. "Most of my memories of her are shitty. She was always upset with one of us for something. Tristan's hockey equipment took up too much space, my projects were too messy, Brody was too quiet. And then she was just...gone."

I wish she would stay that way. I wish the calls would stop, along with everything else. They're needles under my skin, pricking at a wound that never heals. I wish she hadn't started calling again last year, acting like she could erase years of silence.

Essie cups my face in her palms. "You can talk to me, Nate. I can't even begin to imagine how hard that was for your family."

I pull her closer, needing the contact to ground me and keep me from falling back into a past that always hurts. "Talking about it makes me feel worse."

"I can understand that." She skims the edge of my jaw with her thumbs. "What do you need, Nathan?"

For you to stay. For this not to end after this week. I try to push that thought back down before it has a chance to dig its nails in, but it's too late. As I gaze into her soft, empathy-filled eyes, I realize that somewhere along the way this did stop being about just the sex. *What would she say if I wanted more than this week?*

She traces the contour of my bottom lip. "Do you need a distraction from all the stuff in your head?"

I lean into her touch. I don't know if I should take what she's offering, but I want her. Desperately. "Maybe."

Her expression is as gentle as her touch. "It's also okay if that's not what you need right now. You can be honest. It won't hurt my feelings."

"I just don't want to get lost in the past." I skim the curve of her ass, moving her to stand between my parted thighs. I wish I wasn't so closed off, that I wasn't so afraid of the feelings that prick at me.

"I can help with that, if you want me to." She runs her fingers down my forearm.

I run my hands along her bare thighs, her nightshirt riding up as I settle them at her hips. "Please."

"Okay." Essie lifts her nightshirt over her head and drops it on the floor, leaving her naked. The pink gems decorating her nipples glint in the dim room. She drags her nails down my chest and dips her fingers into the waistband of my shorts. "Should I take these off?"

"Yeah. Yes." I lift my hips and she tugs them down, freeing my erection.

She grips my length and strokes from base to tip. "How do you want me, Nate?" Her eyes are guileless, expression open.

And I'm suddenly terrified that she'll see the truth. I have feelings for her. Real ones. And I don't want to risk fucking things up. Not here. Not now. Not when I need her. So I grab her by the hips and spin her around, her back to my chest, and pull her into my lap.

There's a condom on the table. She tears it open and pushes the latex ring up, holding it out to me. I kiss the back of her neck as I roll it down my length.

I should take care of her first, make sure she comes. She stayed with me all night, took care of me, brought me food, and here I am, drowning out the shit in my head with her body. Hiding the feelings I'm not supposed to have. I'm half a second away from stopping, but Essie reaches between her legs, positions my cock at her entrance, and sinks down.

The relief is instantaneous and damning. I grip her hip with one hand and bar the other across her chest. Cupping one breast in my palm, I hold her tight and rest my forehead against the back of her neck, letting her warmth seep into me. Pleasure and need drown out the sadness and anger. Worry dissipates with primal hunger. "Fuck me."

"I'd like to, but it's hard to move like this." She shimmies her hips, her voice light.

I kiss her neck and slip a hand between her thighs. "Let me take care of you first."

"Don't worry, I'll come if you let me move."

I unbar my arm from across her chest, and she starts to lean forward.

"No." I pull her back against me. "Stay here. I want you like this."

"Whatever you need, Nathan." She rests her head on my shoulder as she rolls her hips, sliding her tight pussy up and down my cock.

"Just you. You're all I need." And I mean it, in ways she doesn't realize. Not yet. But I could tell her. After the wedding is over. When we're home.

Her lips brush the edge of my jaw as I move her over me.

"You feel so fucking good, Essie. You're perfect. Everything about you." I dip my fingers between her thighs and play with

179

her clit ring until she moans my name and spasms around me. I follow right behind her, holding her tightly.

I can hide how I feel for now. I have to.

But when we're back in Toronto, that could change.

Fear makes my throat tight but hope tugs at its fingers.

What if she could be mine?

CHAPTER 24

NATE

"How was the flight?" I hug my dad, and when his girlfriend steps forward, I awkwardly hug her too. "It's nice to see you again, Sophia."

I've only met her a couple of times. She's friends with Lavender, and only in her early thirties. I'm happy my dad is finally dating again, and she's nice, but it's weird to have her at my brother's wedding.

"This hotel is awesome!" My younger brother, Brody, is clearly pumped.

"We're gonna have the best time!" Chase Lovett, his best friend, is practically bouncing. He hugs his girlfriend to his side, who happens to be Essie's younger sister, Cammie. "Isn't that right, precious?"

She side-eyes him while he grins down, her expression impassive. "We will definitely have the best time, as long as you and Brody don't take excessive advantage of the free and plentiful booze."

"I'll keep them in line," I tell her.

Brody gives me a look. "You're not captain of the fun police."

"Oh fu—dgerdoodles. Save me from my sister." Cammie tries

to hide behind Chase. Which is fairly effective since Chase is well over six feet and Cammie is the size of my thumb.

Even so, Essie twirls in like a beautiful, pink storm. Essie's five seven, so average in terms of height, but she's much taller than Cammie.

"Cammie-Whammie!" Essie throws her arms around her.

Cammie looks less than enthused. "No. You do not get to call me Cammie-Whammie like we are still toddlers. It's mortifying."

"You love it." Essie kisses her on the cheek.

"I do not, and if you keep it up, I will flip you over my shoulder and everyone will see your underpants."

Apparently, Cammie has a black belt in karate and has done this to Chase.

"I'm less worried about my underwear and more concerned about potential bruises." Essie lets her go. "Where are Mom and Dad?"

"Still checking in, but they said they'd be down in a bit," Cammie replies.

"They're going to love it here." Essie turns to Brody. "Look at you! Wow! You're huge!" She squeezes my brother's biceps. "Are you bigger than Tristan?"

"I'm an inch shorter." He might as well have hearts for eyes with the way he's smiling at her. "But I might still grow a bit more."

"Well, you look great!" She pats him on the chest. "Very solid."

He beams like a fucking spotlight.

I want to toss him in the ocean.

Essie turns to my dad and his girlfriend. "Mr. Stiles, it's so lovely to see you." She hugs him briefly.

Dad arches a brow at me over her shoulder. I've mentioned that we've been tackling a lot of wedding related stuff together. And Brody has kindly brought up the fact that she was the hottest girl in high school once upon a time. I can only imagine the things that will come out of my brother's mouth, and all the ways I'll deflect them.

Essie turns her beautiful, megawatt smile on my dad's girl-friend. "And you must be Sophia. Lavender has told us all about you! If you'd like, I can introduce you to the girls while the boys get everything up to the rooms. But I also understand if you'd like to freshen up first."

"I wouldn't mind saying hi to everyone." Sophia turns to my dad. "If that's okay with you, Gideon."

"Of course. I'll get the boys settled and come find you in a bit." Dad kisses her on the cheek, and they share a look I would prefer to never see again.

Essie links arms with her sister and Sophia, like they've known each other for years and didn't just meet a few seconds ago. She always makes people feel included and important.

Chase bends to kiss Cammie before Essie guides them over to the girls, who shriek excitedly. Tally and Fee, along with Fee's little sister, Callie, have also joined the group, having just arrived today.

"How is it possible that Essie's gotten hotter?" Brody muses.

"You think Essie's hot?" Chase's brows pull together.

"Dude." Brody looks at him like he has two heads.

"Stop drooling," I mutter.

"She's a nice young lady," Dad says.

"She's a literal human rainbow." It comes out sounding irri-tated, mostly because there are enough people ogling Essie, and there's more to her than just her pretty face and smoking-hot body.

Chase grabs Brody's arm. "Holy crap! Is that Sam and Isaac? Hemi's brothers?"

Brody squints against the sun and follows Chase's finger. "It is."

"Let's go say hi!" Chase drags my brother off.

Dad settles a hand on my shoulder. "You doing okay, son?"

Freaking out about the wedding. Had sex with the maid of honor a few hours ago and couldn't look her in the eye because I was afraid she'd see my feelings for her all over my face. Have to keep those to myself for the rest of the week and make a plan. "Yup. All good here."

"Dad! You're here!" Tristan strides across the foyer, a wide smile on his face.

He and Dad hug and back slap each other.

"You ready to walk down the aisle?" Dad asks.

"Absolutely. I can't wait for tomorrow." I wouldn't be surprised if Tristan shot glitter out of his ass with how happy he is.

"I bet you can't." Dad may have some glitter in his cannon too.

Brody jogs over. "Sam and Isaac are going cliff jumping." He thumbs over his shoulder, then jams his hand in his pocket. "They have a boat to get there. Can Chase and I go with?"

Sam and Isaac head toward us. They're dressed in dark shorts and polo shirts with sunglasses and matching loafers. How they manage to look like they're ready for a round of golf and a mafia takedown at the same time is a mystery.

"Tristan, Nate! It's great to see you!" Sam says. We exchange a round of handshakes.

"You all right with us taking the boys to the cliffs?" Isaac asks. "There's more than enough room for the three of you to join as well, if you'd like."

"That sounds fun." Tristan looks to me and Dad. "You think you can swing it?"

"Sure, let me make sure Sophia is settled with the girls," Dad replies.

"We'll meet back here in twenty?" Sam suggests.

"Perfect," Tristan agrees.

Sophia has already been absorbed into the girl group out by the pool. She's sandwiched between Lavender and Essie, who's lost her beach cover-up. Today she's wearing a hot-pink ruffled bikini top and matching shorts. She looks relaxed and beautiful.

"Anyone want to come cliff jumping?" Sam asks as we approach.

Hemi pushes her sunglasses down her nose. "You're not serious."

"Of course we're serious." Isaac frowns at his sister.

Hemi sighs and shakes her head, like he's an idiot for even suggesting it. None of the girls are interested in cliff jumping.

"Please remember that not everyone lives their lives at Mach 10!" Hemi calls to her brothers as we head for the rooms to change.

"We'll be fine!" Sam calls over his shoulder.

We split off, Brody following Dad since his bag is currently in his room. He's staying with me, or at least he's staying in my room, but we'll bring his stuff over when we get back. Changing rooms now seems pointless. We can always push the bed to one side if it rains to avoid the leak.

I check my phone when I get to my room.

ESSIE

Do you have a roommate tonight? • •

NATE

Yeah, but Brody sleeps like the dead, so I should be able to sneak over.

ESSIE

I'll understand if you need bro time, tho.

NATE

You're much nicer to wake up next to.

ESSIE

And cuddle with. 😊 Have fun at the cliffs.

NATE

Have fun with the girls.

Essie hearts the message as a voicemail alert pops up from an unknown number. My stomach twists, but we're in a foreign country, and sometimes the carriers don't pick up familiar numbers.

I key in my passcode and hit play.

"Hi, Nate. It's your mom. I saw your brother's—"

Panic hits hard and fast. "No fucking way." I delete it without listening to the rest, then toss the phone on my bed. My skin prickles, and my chest tightens. I run my hands through my hair, gripping the strands tightly as I pace. I blocked my mom from my social media. As soon as she started calling, I set them all to private. But I'm sure she has a fake account set up, and Brody's accounts aren't set to private, so he probably doesn't realize she can see what he's posting.

I wish she'd just leave us alone.

My phone pings with new messages.

BRODY

Waiting on you.

I'd come get you, but you haven't sent me your room number yet.

Naaaaaaaate. Brooooooooo.

NATE

Be there in two.

I shove all my feelings about my mom and her fucking phone calls into a box. My dad and my brothers don't need to know she's still trying to reach us through me. I change into board shorts and a T-shirt and meet up with the rest of the guys.

"Took you long enough!" Brody rolls his eyes. "Did you need to iron your board shorts first?"

"Ha-ha." The ironing board is currently set up in the corner of my room because I like things neatly pressed, but I draw the line at swim- and underwear.

"Everything good?" Tristan asks.

I force a smile. "Great. Let's roll."

We follow Isaac and Sam to the pier and climb into a sweet speedboat with seating in the bow. Sam gets behind the wheel.

"This is lit!" Chase exclaims.

"It's awesome," Brody agrees and tucks his ball cap under his leg so he doesn't lose it in the water.

Isaac points to the rocky cliffs across the bay. "That's where we're going."

"This is freaking cool." Chase can hardly contain himself.

He's the extrovert to my younger brother's introvert.

"You all been having a good time?" Dad asks as we zip across the pale blue water.

Tristan nods. "It's been great. We had a hiccup in the beginning with the room situation, but Connor Grace pulled some strings and we ended up at Bea's dream resort, so it all worked out." He's in a buoyant fucking mood.

And why wouldn't he be? He's marrying the love of his life. He has no idea Mom is still trying to contact me. Or that I'm over here having an existential crisis because my views on love and relationships are suddenly shifting, and there's nothing I can do to stop it. But I can make a plan. I'm good at those.

"Sounds like everything is working out the way it should." Dad stretches an arm across the back of the seat.

"Aside from that and Nate here getting stung by jellyfish, it's been smooth sailing." He claps me on the shoulder.

"Jellyfish? Did someone have to pee on you?" Chase asks.

I roll my eyes. "That's not actually what you're supposed to do."

"You should probably send Essie a thank you for taking care of you last night," Tristan says.

"Yeah." I rub the back of my neck. "I owe her." For a lot more than just rubbing cream into my stings and making sure I had food when I woke up.

Brody perks up. "Essie took care of you?"

"I was high on antihistamines. There wasn't much to take care of."

"He passed out in her bed and snuggled with her stuffed cat," Tristan notes.

"I didn't snuggle with Catalina," I grumble.

"Yeah, you did. Bea stopped by to check on you and snapped a couple of photos."

Heat works its way into my cheeks. "That's some bullshit." I do vaguely remember trying to huff Catalina.

"Essie and Bea were talking about how cute you are when you've overindulged on antihistamines."

"I have never been cute a day in my life," I grouse.

He ignores me and turns to Dad. "How are things with Sophia?"

"Good." His smile softens. "Great, actually. She's a lot of fun. Smart, ambitious, patient."

And young. At least I think it and don't say it.

"She came to one of my university games last week," Brody says.

"She likes hockey?" Tristan asks.

"She went to a lot of Hockey Academy stuff out in Pearl Lake because her best friend is married to Maverick Waters," Brody explains. Maverick and Lavender are the kids of hockey legend Alex Waters.

"Nate and I will have to come to one so we can support you and get to know Sophia better," Tristan tells them. "Right, Nate?"

"Yeah, for sure." My stomach turns a little. I really hope this thing with my dad and Sophia doesn't go sideways, because Brody seems like he's getting attached.

I try to stay engaged while Brody and Chase talk about the awesome time they're having at the Hockey Academy this summer, but my mind drifts to Essie. I keep trying to pinpoint the moment it stopped being about just sex and became something else. It's been happening for a while, I decide. The woman I've gotten to know is still fairy-tale obsessed, but she's so much more than that. She loves with her whole heart. Even after I ghosted her all those years ago, she never stopped being nice to me. What if she could love me? What if I could love her? Would she be willing to try?

Sam pulls the boat into a slip at the pier. From across the bay, the cliffs don't look like much, but this close, the height makes me nauseous.

Isaac hops out of the boat and ties us off, and we all file onto the pier. Sam and Isaac are unreasonably excited about the prospect of jumping off a steep cliff into the churning waters below.

"That's quite the drop," Tristan observes.

"There are several levels," Sam informs us. "It's a bit of a climb to the top, but totally worth the rush."

Tristan rubs the back of his neck. "Not to pass on a good time, but Bea would be pretty pissed if I ended up with broken body parts the day before the wedding."

"Come on, Tris." Brody nudges him. "Bea won't mind."

"Pretty sure she would."

A guy jumps off the top and flails his way to a belly flop.

We cringe when he slaps the water, but Sam and Isaac clap and cheer.

"As the best man, it would be in my best interest to stay down here and watch you guys have a good time." I don't care if I get razzed. "I've already been stung by a family of jellyfish. I don't need to tick any more injury boxes."

"I'll stay back with these two." Dad pats me and Tristan on the shoulders.

"You two still in?" Isaac points at Brody and Chase.

"Absolutely!" Chase is all balls, zero brains, apparently.

Brody looks slightly unsure but still gives the guys a thumbs-up.

Chase snaps a selfie, sends it to someone—probably Cammie —and hands his phone to my dad. Brody does the same.

Sam slaps his palms together. "All right, let's do this."

He strides down the dock, Isaac beside him, while Brody and

Chase rush to keep up. They reach the zigzagging staircase leading to three jump points.

"They'll go all the way to the top," Tristan mutters.

"Yup, and I'm happy to watch that happen from down here." I heard about Dallas's day-long excursion with those two that nearly killed him when he started dating Hemi.

"Those two are intense," Dad observes.

"They're actually pretty laid-back today," Tristan replies.

"Huh. That's...something else," Dad muses.

"Yeah. Here's hoping Brodes and Chase make it out alive." Tristan doesn't seem all that worried as he points to a restaurant with a view of the cliffs. "Let's grab a beer and watch the adventure unfold."

CHAPTER 25
NATE

W e find a table and order a round of drinks. From where we're seated, Sam and Isaac are dots leading the way up the never-ending stairs to doom. Chase and Brody are already lagging.

"You seem level, Tristan," Dad notes after the server drops off our beers.

"Yeah. Getting Bea to take some time off before the wedding to relax has been great for both of us. I can't wait for tomorrow. I'm so ready to make Bea my wife and start this life with her." Tristan taps on the table. "I mean, I know we're already doing that since we live together, but getting married makes it feel… more permanent. Like we're making that commitment not just to each other, but to everyone we care about."

Dad smiles. "Rix is good for you. You're the happiest I've seen you since…well, in a long, long time."

We know what he means. Before Mom left we were different. Life with her wasn't easy, but neither was life without her. The way she left messed us all up. I thought I had relationships figured out with Lisa, but then she left, too.

"Aren't you afraid it could all just disappear?" The words are out before I think them through. "Shit. Sorry. Ignore me."

191

Tristan meets my gaze, empathy all over his face. "Fucking terrified, brother."

"But you still want to take that risk." I've shut down the conversation when he's brought this up before, but if I can learn his secret, maybe I can make it work with Essie. Maybe when we're back in Toronto I can ask her out on a real date and see where this goes. Maybe she's worth being scared for.

He nods. "My life is better when Bea is in it. I'm a better person with her. Don't get me wrong, it's scary as hell to fall in love. But once I stopped fighting all the feelings, falling was easy. The hard part was not sabotaging myself."

"How did you stop that from happening?" Even if Essie takes a chance on me, I could fuck it all up. I've done it before. I need to figure out how to keep it from happening again.

"The first couple of times I failed." Tristan's jaw tics. "But every time I shut down on Bea, I caused her pain. The worst part was, at the time, I didn't even realize what I was doing. I was so focused on myself and my own feelings that I couldn't take her's into account the way I needed to. I put up walls because I didn't know what to do with my feelings for her. They were too much, and I was overwhelmed."

"But you fixed it, right?" I'm desperate for some kind of magic recipe for relationship success.

"Yeah, with a lot of self-reflection and therapy."

"But then you have to talk about the bad stuff." Essie offered to listen, but I took her up on a distraction instead. Because talking about my mom hurts, and sex with Essie does not.

"Yup, and it absolutely sucked at the beginning. The first few sessions were rough, especially when I realized how tough I'd made things for Bea, and how I was damaging our relationship by avoiding the difficult things. I broke a few hockey sticks working out my feelings. But Bea and I made a lot of progress, and that made it easier to keep going." Tristan's voice is raw with emotion.

"So it's not as hard now?" I should stop digging at these wounds, his and mine and Dad's, but I want what Tristan has.

"Most of the time, yeah. Bea and I both have bad days, but we work through them."

He's so sure in his conviction that Bea's worth the pain. He believes in her, and she believes in him. Could I handle therapy if it meant someone as kind and full of love and light as Essie could be mine?

Dad's eyes bounce between us. "I should have made you boys talk to someone when you were younger."

"You did. I lasted one session. I told her to go fuck herself, and then I told you to do the same." Tristan takes a long pull of his beer.

"I should have made you try again," Dad presses.

"Don't be so hard on yourself, Dad." Tristan shakes his head. "I doubt I would have gotten much out of therapy as a teenager. I was too wrapped up in being angry."

"You might have been less angry." Dad looks down at the table, posture stiff. "I know I haven't been the best relationship role model."

"We were all just trying to survive," Tristan says, tone gentle. "You were raising three boys on your own."

"I had a lot of help," he says pointedly.

"That kept me out of trouble for the most part. Plus, look at how close we are." Tristan ruffles my hair. "My genius brother's my best man. My little bro is probably going to steal my spot on my team in a couple of years. It all worked out the way it was supposed to."

"I'm proud of you. Both of you." Dad motions to the cliff. "And the one out there making questionable decisions." He squints. "Where the heck are they?"

"They're at the top." They're impossible to miss. Sam and Isaac are both massive, and Brody and Chase, while still holding on to the narrowness of youth, are tall and muscular.

Chase approaches the edge and immediately steps back and puts his hands on his thighs. Brody runs his hand through his hair. Isaac and Sam do some knee bends. Sam steps up first, runs to the end of the diving board, and does some wild flip-twist-somersault as he flies through the air. He lands in the water with a graceful splash and pops up a few seconds later, fist pumping.

"Wow. That's…wow," Dad says.

"The guy goes on twenty-kilometer hikes for shits and giggles," Tristan explains.

Sam climbs out of the water on our side of the bay and shouts something that gets lost in the wind.

Chase is up next. He looks a lot more apprehensive. He walks to the end of the board, makes the sign of the cross, and jumps. He looks like a terrified dart as he plummets feet first into the water. When he pops out he's gasping for air. He coughs and sputters and slaps the waves, awkwardly swimming to Sam who cheers him on.

As soon as he's on the ladder, he vomits into the water.

Me, Dad, and Tristan exchange looks.

"I hope Brody fares better." But I have my doubts.

We all turn back and watch as our brother steps up. He's stoic, assessing the jump. Even from here I can sense his unease.

Tristan frowns. "He doesn't have to do it."

"He's gonna do it," I say.

"As long as he doesn't break anything." Dad raps anxiously on the table.

Brody jumps, tucking himself into a ball and protecting his head as he hits the water ass first.

Tristan is already out of his seat. "Oh man. Oh, that's not great."

I toss some money on the table, and we abandon our drinks, rushing down to where Sam and Chase are waiting for Brody. His face is green as he pulls himself out of the water and promptly drops to his knees, cupping his junk.

"Nothing hurts more than a water nut-slap," Sam says.

"Fuck, my balls…" Brody groans.

A mom ushers her preteen daughter away, firing a dirty look over her shoulder at Brody, who is far too busy cradling his bruised balls to notice.

I crouch beside him. "Everything feel like it's still intact?"

"I feel like they're in my throat." He gags. "I'm gonna—"

I move out of the way as he tosses his cookies.

"Guess you boys aren't up for a round two, huh?" Isaac pulls himself out of the water.

"We'll take a cab back," I suggest. Brody can't handle bouncing his balls across the ocean after this.

We leave Sam and Isaac to continue their adventure and cab it back to the resort. Chase disappears into his room, still looking green, and I grab Brody's bag from Dad's room and take him back to mine. He's in much better form, no longer choking on his balls.

"Look, the room situation isn't perfect."

"Why? What's going on?"

I hold my wrist to the door and let him in.

Brody frowns as he takes in the space. "Who did you piss off? Why do you have this room? Dad's is super nice. This is like… kinda shitty."

"It was the last room in the block. There's also a leak in the roof."

"Why didn't you ask to switch?"

My phone buzzes on the table.

Brody glances over. His eyes bug out as he grabs it and holds it in front of me, inadvertently unlocking it and opening to the first message. Which is from Essie. "Holy fuck. Holy *fuck*! Essie is sending you pictures?" His jaw drops. "Nate."

I pinch his nipple and pluck my phone out of his hand. "Those aren't for your eyes."

His mouth opens and closes. His eyes are saucers, and he

looks like his head is about to explode. "Essie is sending you mostly naked pictures. Bro!" He holds his hand up.

I stare at him.

"Dude." He grabs my hand and forces me to high-five him. "Are you two...like—" He motions to his junk.

"You can't tell anyone." I check her most recent message.

> **ESSIE**
>
> When are you back?
>
> You can stop by my room if you're interested in a little dessert before dinner.
>
> And help me pick a dress to go over this.

A picture of her in a pink lace bra and panty set follows. The messages were sent twenty minutes ago.

> **NATE**
>
> I can be there in two.

> **ESSIE**
>
> Better hurry up. We're running out of time.

"Dude! Are you sexting Essie?" He spins in a circle. "She is so hot."

"She's not just something to ogle, fuckhead."

"I know. She's like, super nice. But dude, she's like...wow."

"Look, you can't say anything. This information doesn't leave this room."

"I am a vault. I will say nothing." He makes a lips-zipped-and-throw-away-the-key motion. "She was a legend at our high school, Nate. Everyone talked about how hot she was. And still is. You are the man." He puts his hand on his chest, his smile sly. "I bow to you, you giant fucking nerd."

I frown.

"Seriously, though, how did you land her? Was it all your big books?" He smirks. "Did you wow her with your extensive use of words with lots of syllables?" He does jazz hands and a hip shimmy. "Was it science?"

"Fuck you. I'll be back in half an hour." I open the door.

"You're my hero," he calls after me as I leave him to deal with the shitstorm that is now *his* room.

Because Essie needs my help.

Once everyone's meals have been cleared at the rehearsal dinner, Tristan's dad stands and taps the edge of his pint glass, then brings two fingers to his lips and whistles shrilly to get everyone's attention. He and Sophia are seated at a table with my parents and Rix's. They're all smiling and laughing. My mom is tucked into my dad's side, and Howard's arm is draped across Muffy's chair. They're both couple goals. They have the kind of love I want for myself: limitless and enduring.

Gideon smiles and runs a hand over his tie, waiting for everyone to settle. "I wanted to take a moment to celebrate Tristan and Rix," he begins.

I set a packet of tissues on the table in front of Rix. She hugs my arm and kisses my cheek, then snuggles into Tristan's side.

Gideon turns toward the happy couple. "Tristan, I am so proud of you." He glances around the room, gaze stopping briefly at Brody and then Nate. "I'm proud of all my boys."

A round of applause follows, and he waits until the group settles before he continues. "Tristan, you have accomplished so much in your young life. You've always been determined, and when you set a goal, you work hard to achieve it. Your dedication to being the best you possibly can is not limited to your hockey career."

"You're a superstar!" Brody shouts.

"I'm pretty sure he's drunk," Rix whispers.

"Oh yeah, absolutely," Tristan agrees.

"Drink a glass of water, son," Gideon says.

Everyone chuckles.

Brody sinks into his chair. Chase passes him the pitcher of water.

Gideon turns back to Tristan. "You brought that dedication and determination to your relationship with Rix. You've both worked so hard to be the partner each other deserves. Watching you grow and learn together has been inspiring. I don't think either of you realizes how much you've taught me." He pauses and clears his throat. "We should all be so lucky to have the kind of love you share. To your future and everything it holds." He raises his glass in a toast.

Rix and Tristan push their chairs back and round the table. Tristan and his dad hug each other tightly, both clearly emotional. And then Gideon folds Rix into a hug. She's a weepy mess when he lets her go. Tristan tenderly curves his hand around the side of her neck, thumb sweeping across the edge of her jaw as he brushes his nose against hers.

I dab under my eyes with a tissue, my love for them too big to keep inside.

I glance to the left, where Nate sits two chairs down, hands folded in his lap. He glances my way for a second. I wish I knew what was happening in his head. Something has shifted. When he came to my room to help me pick my dress he was...sweet. And very focused on me and my needs. I need to keep reminding myself that he's not someone I can give my heart to. But it's hard when he cuddles me all night and tells me how sexy my spreadsheets are.

Rix and Tristan take their seats again. I hug Rix and free

another tissue from the pack, tipping her chin up so I can dab under her eyes.

She laughs and sniffles. "Am I melting?"

"No. You're perfect. I'm just fussing."

She hugs me. "I love you."

"I love you back."

Flip moves to the front of the room. He's dressed in khaki shorts and a short-sleeved white button-down. He sets his bottle of water on the podium and smiles at the crowd. "How's everyone doing tonight?"

"Feeling no pain!" Chase shouts.

"Seriously, slow down, you two." Flip motions between Chase and Brody.

Brody holds up his glass of water, face turning red.

The crowd chuckles.

"I just wanted to, uh, take a minute to express how much Tristan and Rix mean to me, to all of us here." Flip's eyes are already glassy. He blows out a breath. "Man, I've got a lot of feelings, and they're all right here." He taps his throat, then the corner of his eye. "And apparently here."

Tally hops up from her table near the podium and sets a travel packet of tissues next to him. She squeezes his arm and leans in to whisper something before she rushes back to her seat. She's sitting next to Fee, Dred on her other side. Callie, who is all of nine, is tucked into Connor's side, like he's her own personal, tattooed bean bag.

"Thanks, Talls." Flip plucks a tissue from the packet. "Okay, now I'm really ready."

Everyone laughs again.

Rix hooks her arms through mine and Tristan's, her expression soft.

"Tris, I'll start with you." Flip smiles at his best friend. "We've had a lot of years of friendship and some real ups and downs. We've seen each other through some tough times and some fan-freaking-tastic ones. Like winning the Cup."

"Five-star moment for sure," Tristan calls.

"I know it hasn't always been easy, but I love you, man. You've been a rock my entire life, and I am damn proud to call you my friend. You have worked so hard to be what Rix needs, and I'm forever grateful that the two of you believed in what you had and didn't let anyone stand in your way. Especially me, because we all know I have a hard time getting out of my own way most of the time." He laughs and shakes his head.

"I love you, buddy." Tristan taps his fingers over his heart.

They give each other a nod. It's an unspoken apology and forgiveness.

Flip's gaze shifts to Rix, and his smile softens. "Trixie Rixie, my beautiful baby sister. You are a force, and I am so thankful for you. The sacrifices you've made for me are too many to count."

Her smile is full of affection. "They weren't sacrifices, Phillip. I always knew you were destined for greatness."

He points at Rix. "This is what I'm talking about. You always put others ahead of yourself, forever the caretaker, just like our mom." He blows a kiss to Muffy before he turns back to Rix. "Even when we were kids, you tried to take care of me."

"Carrot chips and ranch dip," Muffy yells.

Rix throws her head back and laughs.

Flip addresses the crowd. "Exactly. Whether you were trying to get me to eat healthy, or manage my investments, or just making me own my shit." Flip clears his throat. "You are beyond remarkable, little sister. And the way you and Tristan take care of each other is a true inspiration."

"We had amazing role models." Rix blows a kiss to her parents.

"The best, right?" Flip nods to his parents, then turns back to Tristan and Rix. "There are so many great times ahead, so much to look forward to and celebrate, and I know when things get tough, you two will hold each other up. The commitment you're making to each other, to have someone's unconditional love, a person who will never leave, even when it gets tough—" he clears his throat. "Marriage is so special, and it's such an honor to be part of this with you. Your devotion to each other has made me want to be a better person for myself and the people I love. I adore you both. I'll always be in your corner, rooting for you. Thank you for sharing your hearts with all of us." He raises his glass. "To Tristan and Rix and a lifetime of love."

The crowd echoes Flip, and Tristan and Rix get up to hug him. Their parents join them, and they're a mass of love and laughter and happy tears.

Nate pushes his chair away from the table and ducks out the back of the tent. People leave their chairs and head for the bar while Muffy and Howard set up the slideshow. Everyone is occupied, so I follow Nate. He stops and leans against a palm tree, eyes on the ocean.

At the clip of my heels, his head swivels my way.

"Hey."

"Hey." He extends his hand as I near him.

I step out of my heels, leaving them on the boardwalk as I slip my fingers in his and move onto the grass with him. "You okay?"

"I just needed some air."

I don't comment on the fact that we've been sitting under an outdoor tent, breathing in the salty ocean breeze. All of this is a trigger for Nate, I've come to realize. The wedding, people being in love, families coming together to support and celebrate. He wants to be a good brother to Tristan, but it also hurts.

He tucks a lock of my hair behind my ear, his gaze shifting back to the ocean. He's so beautiful and brilliant and sad, and it makes my heart ache. I'm afraid to dig into his pain, but I don't want to leave him here hurting alone.

"It's okay if this is hard for you," I whisper.

He sighs, the sound heavy with hidden emotion. "I'm happy for them."

"You can be happy for someone else and still feel pain." I

give in to the desire to comfort him and gently skim his arm. "Is there anything I can do to help?"

"You're here. That helps."

I see the little boy who was left by someone who was supposed to love him unconditionally, and has become a man who fears the pain that love can bring when it's taken away. "Can I hug you?"

His eyes lift and he nods once.

I step forward and wrap my arms around his waist. He drops his head, pressing his face against my neck as he squeezes me tightly.

I run my hand up and down his back, soothing him. "It's okay that you're struggling, Nate."

"I wish I wasn't, though," he whispers. "I wish this didn't hurt. I wish I could just be happy and not afraid."

"We don't always get to choose the emotions we feel, but we do get to choose how we allow them to rule us."

He pulls back and strokes my cheek. "You're a beautiful person, Essie."

"Voted hottest in my class four years in a row," I joke and immediately hate how I've twisted his compliment to mirror my own fears and vulnerabilities.

That furrow I adore so much appears. "I don't need to tell you you're pretty on the outside." He taps gently over my heart. "This part of you is what makes you so incredible."

"Thanks." My heart stutters a beat.

"Thank you. For making a hard day manageable just by being you." He takes my hand and presses it to his chest. He opens his mouth to say something, but Muffy's voice comes over the mic.

"The slideshow is about to begin! You don't want to miss this."

"Did you want to say something else?" I ask.

"Nah, it can wait until later." He leans in and kisses my

cheek. "I'm just going to use the bathroom. I'll be right behind you."

I return to the tent and slide into my seat next to Rix. Tristan walks toward us, two drinks in his hands.

"Have you seen Nate?" Rix asks quietly.

"Yeah, he just went to the bathroom. He'll be right back."

"Is he okay?"

"Yeah, we were just talking. Everything's great." It's a little white lie, but she doesn't need to carry this with her.

Nate returns as the slideshow begins. Pictures of Tristan and Flip and me and Rix as kids flash across the screen. I see their family's story unfolding, the way Tristan and his dad were always together with his brothers. Little Brody already in love with hockey at the age of three. Nate more interested in the mechanics of skates than in shooting the puck.

A photo of Rix and Flip with Tristan's dad and brothers at the maple farm pops up. Rix is holding Brody's hand, and Nate is busy looking in a maple bucket, while Tristan and Flip grin cheesily. Tristan's smile stops appearing when he hits his teens, and anyone who knows their story can see the darkness that clouds his eyes.

The pictures of Tristan at Rix and Flip's house are endless. He was always there for dinner. They were forever playing hockey on the street, and birthday parties chronicle their friendship. There are just as many moments with Rix and me. Our lives play out on the screen: first days of school together, birthday celebrations, high school prom, our first year in university where we shared a room, our first apartment, cooking together, snuggling on the couch. Rix and I were inseparable all through university, until we graduated and I went to Vancouver to chase a dream that didn't quite fit my life goals.

Tristan and Flip's friendship spans two decades, from kids playing street hockey to making the pros, and then finally ending up on the same team.

And then Rix and Tristan appear together, their love so clear and beautiful on the screen. Tristan looks at her with such awe and adoration, and Rix's eyes are always so full of love for him. Someone managed to slip in a picture of Rix making cucumber salad. Her face goes red, and Tristan fights a grin while our friends laugh, and the parents and other friends look confused. It's perfect and amazing to see these two, who grew up in each other's orbit, find the truest kind of love in each other.

When the slideshow ends, so does the evening, and everyone heads back to their rooms. I hug Tristan and Rix good night and send them off with promises that I'll message first thing in the morning.

Once they're on their way, I turn to Nate. "I want to check in with the concierge to make sure everything is ready for our bridal breakfast, and double-check our hair appointments before I go to bed."

"I'll come with you," Nate offers.

"Okay."

He glances over his shoulder, making sure we're alone on the path before he links our pinkies. "Do you want your room to yourself tonight?"

I glance at him, but he's focused on some spot in the distance. "No." We don't have many days left here, and I want to make the most of them.

"It's okay if I stay with you?" His fingers press against my lower back as we maneuver around a drunk couple.

"I like Nate snuggles," I admit as we approach the concierge.

A small smile tugs the corner of his mouth. "Good. Me too."

As we reach reception, I notice a dark-haired woman arguing with one of the staff. "You can't be completely full! You must have something available."

"Ma'am, there's a wedding—"

"I'm aware! My son is the one getting married!" she snaps.

Nate freezes, the color draining from his face.

Time slows as she turns in our direction. The similarities are uncanny. The dark eyes and the slant of her brow are echoed on

Nate's face, as are his full lips. I see pieces of all the Stiles brothers. Tristan's cheekbones, Brody's nose.

Her eyes flare in recognition as they land on Nate, and he moves closer, his grip on my hand tightening.

"No. This isn't happening," he whispers.

She abandons the desk clerk and her luggage and heads straight for us. I step in front of Nate, a shield, a barrier, wishing I could protect him from this fresh, horrible pain.

"Nathan? Is that you?" Her eyes are wide with wonder as she takes in the man gripping my hand like a lifeline.

"What the fuck are you doing here?" Nate's voice is rough with fury and anguish. "Why would you come here?"

She takes a tentative step back, throat bobbing as she smiles uncertainly. "For the wedding." Her gaze shifts to me, assessing for a moment before she refocuses on her son without so much as an acknowledgement.

And the rage I felt a moment ago doubles. I'm so sick of being dismissed. I'm tired of being loved and hated for something I have no control over. Everything is easier and harder when all they see is a pretty face.

"You weren't invited," Nate grinds out.

"I'm your mother," she states, as if this somehow explains everything.

"The hell you are!" Nate gently moves me out of the way and steps forward, towering over her, but it's not anger infused into his posture and his tone, it's utter devastation. "I haven't seen you since I was eight. Until a few months ago, I hadn't heard your voice in more than a decade. You think because you gave birth to us that it gives you some kind of right to show up and blow our worlds apart all over again?"

"Nate, honey." She raises both her hands. "You don't understand. I was—"

"Fuck you." His voice cracks with emotion.

His mother recoils.

We're drawing attention, not just from the guests milling

around, but from the concierge. I'm terrified that Tristan or Brody will find a reason to follow us here and all of Rix's fears will come true.

Pain laces Nate's words as he continues to tear her down. "You lost the right to explain when you abandoned us. Do you have any idea the damage you did? You left all of us. Not just Dad. *All of us.* You left it up to Tristan to tell us you were gone. Do you know what that did to him? To us? You're not a mother, you're selfish and self-absorbed, and you have no right to insert yourself back into our lives after the hell you put us through."

Two security guards head for us at the same time Connor Grace comes striding across the lobby. He's wearing a button-down and black pants, tattoos covered, looking very much the part of hotel royalty, not a pro hockey player.

He meets my anxious gaze as he surveys the scene, eyes landing on Nate's mother. Understanding dawns, and cold, hard rage flashes for a moment. He holds up a hand, and the guards stop as he reaches us. His eyes narrow on the unwanted guest. "Nate, you need some help here?"

"This is a family discussion," Nate's mom snaps. "Nate, you need to calm down. You're causing a scene."

Connor levels her with a glare that makes my insides liquify. "You're not on the guest list."

"Excuse me?" Nate's mom looks stricken. "I am the mother of the groom."

"Biologically maybe." Connor crosses his arms. "But you gave that title up along with your right to be part of their lives when you abandoned your husband and your three sons."

She fidgets nervously with her purse strap. "You have no idea what you're talking about."

"Oh, I do. Tristan and I go way back. I know what you did to your family, and I know you don't belong here," Connor states flatly. "He does not deserve to have his wedding ruined by you."

Nate's mom rolls her shoulders back. "You can't make me leave."

"Haven't you done enough damage? What will it take to make you stop?" Nate's voice takes on a pleading edge. "Can't you do us all a favor and stay gone?"

"Everyone has a price," Connor says calmly. "What's yours?"

All three of our heads snap in his direction.

Nate's mom scoffs as if she's offended.

"Would a million do it? Maybe two?" Connor tilts his head.

"How dare—"

"Three? One for each of the kids whose lives you fucked up when you disappeared with no explanation? Would that be enough to keep you out of their lives for good?"

"You can't be serious." Nate's mom fingers the pendant at her throat.

My stomach sinks as I realize she's considering the proposal.

"Just think how much easier life will be when you don't have to worry about money," Connor continues. "I'll wire it to your account right after you sign a legal and binding document that states you will not contact your sons or their father again, and if you try, you'll have to pay it back." His expression darkens. "With interest."

She looks to Nate, expression uncertain.

"You should take the money," he says flatly. "None of us want to know you."

"But Brody—"

"He doesn't even remember you." His voice hardens. "You're dead to him. To all of us."

My stomach rolls as she turns back to Connor.

"Three million, and you never contact them again," he says.

"Never again," she agrees.

"You are a disgusting excuse for a human being." I thread my arm through Nate's. "I hope this decision haunts you for the rest of your miserable life."

"I've got this from here," Connor says, rage still simmering below the surface. This is the man who gets in fights on the ice, the one who doesn't mind being the villain.

Nate pales, like the truth of this is hitting him. "I can't pay you back, and I don't want Tristan to kn—"

"Consider it my wedding gift to Tristan and you and Brody." Connor motions for Nate's mother to follow him before he turns to me and murmurs, "Take care of him."

I nod. "I will, thank you."

Nate's mom glances over her shoulder once, but he isn't looking at her, he's looking at me, and he's utterly ruined.

I cup his cheek in my palm, wishing I could absorb the agony of it all. "She doesn't deserve any part of your heart."

CHAPTER 27
ESSIE

Nate is clearly in a state of shock as I guide him away from Connor and his mother.

"Where do you want to go right now?" I don't want to make assumptions, especially with how fragile he must be, but Brody is rooming with him. I worry about what could happen if Nate shows up there, looking destroyed.

"Back to your room." His voice is thready with anguish. "Unless you don't want me there. I'll understand if you don't."

I stop and turn to face him. "I'm here for you, however you need me to be, Nate, okay?"

He nods once, eyes sad and watery.

When we reach my room, I pass my wrist in front of the sensor and usher him inside.

His broad shoulders cave in as he crosses the threshold. His head drops and he runs his fingers through his hair, gripping tightly.

I flip the safety latch and move to stand in front of him, settling a palm on his chest. "I'm so sorry, Nate."

"Everything was going so good, and she had to ruin it," he whispers. "I fucking hate what she did to our family. She broke us all."

"I wish I could take away the hurt," I admit. "What can I do to help? What do you need?"

"You." He closes his eyes, covers my hand, and steps closer. When his gaze lifts to mine, longing and apology are reflected back at me. "I want to forget she was ever here. I need out of my head."

I wish I could get him to open up, to talk to me, let me in, but this is a deep, raw wound. Pushing could break him, so I move closer, sliding my hand up his chest to the back of his neck. "Show me how I can help you with that."

He lowers his head, and his soft, needy groan hums across my lips as he slants his mouth over mine. His hand tangles in my hair and the other winds around me, pulling me tight against him. He deepens the kiss, despair shifting to hunger. I want to siphon out his pain, kiss it all away, help him forget.

Eventually he stops to breathe, thumb brushing the edge of my jaw. "I need you, Ess. I'm sorry." He drops his forehead to mine. "I just need to feel you."

"It's okay. I'm here." I hold his face in my hands. "Let me make it disappear."

"Please."

I rid him of his shirt, and he peels me out of my dress, pushing my panties over my hips. I undress him the rest of the way, struggling to stay focused as his fingers whisper over my skin. When we're both naked, Nate leads me to the bed, pulls the sheets back, and lifts me onto the mattress before he stretches out beside me.

The walls between us are crumbling, and I see so clearly the man before me. His shattered heart is in my hands, and I desperately want to mend the broken parts of him.

His eyes never leave mine as he traces my curves with gentle fingers. "I want to see you come apart for me, Essie." He dips between my thighs.

"Whatever you need, Nate. I'll be that for you," I promise. *Even if it ruins me.*

His brow furrows. "Just be you. That's all I want, just you."

My heart stutters, and my body lights up at his earnestness and soft touch. His fingers move between my thighs, lips brushing over mine. His expression turns reverent as he finds the spot inside that makes me melt and moan for him.

His thumb circles my clit, and everything tightens. "That's it, Ess." He kisses me softly. "Let me see those pretty eyes when you're coming for me."

Heat funnels from my center as a rush of pleasure over-whelms me, spinning me out. And I have no chance to come down from the high, because Nate fits himself between my thighs, his erection sliding over sensitive skin.

I reach for the condoms on the nightstand.

He pushes up, fingers drifting over my cheek. "Can we...can I... I just want to feel you." His voice is rough with need.

He's seen my birth control pills on the bathroom counter. "You want to go bare?"

"I haven't... I'm safe. I don't want to pressure you, though." He kisses my chin and then my lips.

Sex with no barriers is different. It speaks of trust and inti-macy. Of more. And I want it, even though it terrifies me. "I don't feel pressured. And I'm safe, too." I shift my hips until the head nudges my entrance.

He exhales in a rush and frames my face with his wide palms. His brows pull together, and his mouth drops open as he fills me. Relief passes behind his eyes before it's usurped by euphoria. "God, Essie, you feel so good. You always make me feel so good."

I smile softly, hooking my feet at the small of his back. "So do you."

He rolls his hips, and we both moan. This is nothing like the escapism fuck from this morning. He doesn't hide from me, doesn't drop his head or close his eyes. His gaze stays fixed on my face, one hand at my cheek, the other bracing his weight as he moves over me.

That shift I felt this morning happens again, and the air between us becomes electric. We're not just two bodies joined by pleasure. He's not just inside me; I'm inside him, too. It's more than my arms winding around him, it's our souls twining—this connection we share is so much deeper, and it's not just sex anymore.

I'm losing my heart to him, to this broken man who moves above me with veneration. This doesn't feel like a distraction from his pain. This is me falling. Fallen. And I'm powerless to stop it.

"You are so beautiful," he whispers against my lips. "Every part of you."

"So are you." His heart is battered and bruised—I know now how badly—but I still want him.

Warmth spreads through me as I contract around him, and still I don't look away, don't break the connection as bliss pulls me into the undertow. He joins me, tipping over the edge, lips on mine. Even after we've floated back down to earth, he stays inside me, kisses soft and slow.

Eventually he pulls back and brushes my damp hair off my forehead. "Can I stay with you?"

"Of course." I'm relieved he doesn't want to leave, and that… Well, it speaks to how much it will hurt when this week ends.

"I'll be right back." He carefully pulls out and pads to the bathroom, returning a minute later with a damp cloth.

He cleans me up, then climbs back into bed, curling his body around mine. Nate holds me close, lips pressed to my shoulder. This has become something so much bigger. I'm not supposed to fall for the man who doesn't believe in love.

That's the last thought I have before I drift off into a fitful sleep.

And I wake the next morning alone.

CHAPTER 28

NATE

I wake up at five o'clock in the morning, wrapped around Essie. I have no desire to go anywhere, but the last thing we need is for Rix or Tristan to find us together on their wedding day. So I get dressed, kiss her on the forehead, and leave her sleeping.

The sun is peeking out across the water with the promise of another beautiful tropical day. Brody enjoyed the free booze last night, so I don't want to wake him too early. Hungover and tired isn't ideal for our brother's wedding.

I need to get my head on straight anyway, so I walk to the café, figuring coffee and a sunrise will help me reset.

I still can't believe my mother showed up last night. Seeing her unleashed a flood of terrible memories, and the price she put on us is another thing I'll have to deal with eventually. I don't want Brody to ever find out. He should never have to know our mother attached a dollar value to our place in her life.

And that brings me to this thing with Essie. The feelings I have for her are real—and bigger than I can handle right now. I feel raw with the gravity of it all. But I'm certain I want more than just this week, more than great sex and cuddling in bed. I want *her*. I want to date her. I want to be the person she can count on, just like she's been the person I could count on this entire time.

But that needs to wait until we're back in Toronto. Once we're off this island and our feet are on the ground of reality, I can ask her on a date. We can figure it out. Today my focus needs to be on my brother and his wedding.

The barista has just finished my order when I spot my dad crossing the lobby, heading my way with a questioning smile.

"You're up early." He pulls me in for a hug, then looks me over.

I'm still wearing the same clothes from last night.

"Everything okay?"

It's better for both of us if I don't hide the truth, at least not from him. Besides, he'll pick up on my edginess and just have more questions. "Mom showed up last night."

"What?" Dad's eyes flare. "When? Did your brothers see her?"

I shake my head. "We cut her off in the lobby. It was just me, Essie, and Connor Grace."

"Are you okay?" He rubs the back of his neck, expression pained. "Of course you're not. Do you want to tell me what happened? Is there anything I can do?" He motions to a table, then looks around. "Where is she now?"

I take the seat across from him. "She's gone." I explain what happened, how Connor intervened and paid her off.

His shock turns to concern. "She took three million dollars? Does Connor have that kind of money to throw around?"

"Pretty sure his family owns our hotel, so yeah, he's good for it."

"I cannot fucking believe I married that woman." Dad scrubs a hand over his face, his dismay matching mine. "I'm so sorry, son. I wish it had been me and not you."

I rub my chest to ease the ache, but it doesn't work. No wonder he never dated after she left. He probably worried he'd pick another woman just like her. Just like I worry I'll end up

215

with another Lisa. That I'm too messed up to deserve better. "At least she's gone for good this time." No more anxiety-invoking phone calls. No more worrying about her wreaking havoc on our lives.

Dad sighs. "I wish I could have protected you from this."

I swirl my coffee, watching the pattern dissolve. "You did for as long as you could. And I'm glad it was me and not Tristan or Brody."

"The things she's done are unforgivable, but this is beyond reprehensible."

"I used to wonder what we could have done differently," I tell him. "But then she took the money…" I shake my head. "The only person she was thinking about was herself. If she gave an actual shit about any of us, she wouldn't have shown up here like she had some kind of right."

Dad taps his coffee cup. "She was always very focused on herself. I wish I'd done things differently when you boys were younger. But I felt this responsibility to keep trying, thinking I could fix things, even though it wasn't good for any of us."

"We had you, and we had each other, and that was more than enough, Dad." It was hard after she left, and we all hurt, but it was better, too. The fighting stopped. No one yelled anymore. "And now we'll have Rix, and you have Sophia. She seems nice." She really does. She's gentle and patient like Rix. Like Essie, too.

"She is. She's kind, thoughtful. So is Rix," Dad agrees.

"So you learned, right? And so did Tristan. So there's hope for me and Brody yet." I'm reassuring myself as much as I am him.

He nods. "You protect the people you care about. The right person will come along and see all the good in you."

"Yeah."

Maybe I've already found her. Maybe she's been in my life all along, and I just couldn't see it because I was too afraid? What Essie said about the dark consuming the light continues to haunt me. I don't want to take without giving. I might share genetics with my mom, but I don't have to be like her. I can choose another path.

I'm drawn to Essie because of who she is at her core. She puts others' needs ahead of her own. Maybe to a fault. How many times did she step up for me during the planning stages of this wedding? How often has she quietly done the things I should have, but never made a big deal about it, and always played it off like we were in it together? Twice yesterday she was there when I needed her. Twice she put my needs in front of her own. But the second time, I didn't hide from my feelings. I tried to give as much as I took.

My phone buzzes. "Tristan is up and looking for us."

Dad nods. "Let's get him ready to walk down the aisle."

"Can I get something to drink? My mouth is so fucking dry. Why is my mouth so dry? Do you think I'm coming down with something?" Tristan paces the room.

"You're just nervous." I pass him a bottle of water.

"I want to be married." He says this like he's declaring war.

"I know, bro. But you can still be nervous." I can relate. I might know that my mother won't show up to ruin things, but it doesn't stop the churning in my gut.

He chugs the entire bottle in four long gulps.

The attendants arrive with the suits. Hemi is with them. I assume Essie sent her over to make sure everything is as it should be. Isaac and Sam trail her like lethal bodyguards. She surveys the room. "How is everyone doing?"

"Nate thinks I'm nervous." Tristan stops pacing and props his fists on his hips. "I need more water."

Hemi pulls a bottle out of her purse and hands it to him.

"You've got this, Tristan." She puts a hand on his shoulder. "I just came from the bridal suite, and your bride-to-be looks gorgeous."

"How's she doing?" he asks anxiously.

Hemi smiles. "She's so excited to walk down the aisle today, and I know you're right there with her."

"I just want her to be my wife," he agrees.

Hemi's eyes are warm. "She is ready to be yours forever, just like you're ready to be hers."

"I'm so ready."

"I know." She pats his chest. "Why don't you put your suit on?"

"Right. Yes. That's a great idea."

Hemi hands him the bag that says GROOM and ushers him into the changing room.

"Maybe don't go anywhere yet," I mutter.

"He's a nerves circus, huh?" Hemi's tone is all empathy.

"Yeah. I'm surprised he hasn't paced a hole in the floor."

Two minutes later, the door swings open. "I think there's a problem."

"Oh. Wow. Just…okay." Hemi's eyes flare. "Go Rix, I guess."

"Those can't be your pants." They're not only six inches too short, they're also way too tight.

"According to that bag they are. But I can't get married in these pants." Tristan points to his crotch. "Everyone can see my whole dick. You can see the fucking ridge."

"You're moose knuckling hard, bro," Brody says, unhelpfully.

I give him a look.

"Brody," Dad chastises.

"What? It's true." He points to Tristan's crotch, like it needs more attention. "He's all dick right now."

"It's not *that* bad," Flip lies.

"Rix is a lucky girl," Sam says without cracking a smile.

Flip frowns and busies himself with his phone.

"Why don't you try on my pants?" I suggest. The results may not be any better, since I am not shaped like someone who plays professional hockey. There's a reason Tristan and his teammates have all their clothes custom tailored, but at least we can try.

"You won't fit into these any better than I do," Tristan argues.

"I'm a size down from you, and I don't have the hockey butt or thighs, so it won't be as bad, and I'm not the one getting married." Will I enjoy having my balls crammed into a pair of too-tight pants? No. But better me than Tristan.

"You should definitely try on Nate's pants," Hemi agrees. "And I'll text Lavender. If anyone can help with last-minute alterations, she's our girl."

"That's right. She's a seamstress." Dad looks relieved.

I unzip my suit bag and pass Tristan my pants. He disappears into the changing room again, and we all cross our fingers.

"You should be proud," Sam says to my dad.

"Sam." Hemi side-eyes her brother.

"It's a compliment," Isaac explains.

"I'm pretty sure Essie's mom isn't complimenting Muffy on Rix's rack," Hemi points out.

The door to the dressing room swings open again. We all look at Tristan's crotch.

My pants have slightly more room behind the fly, but unfortunately they're still tight in the thighs and butt. We can see the outline of his junk, but it's not as glaringly obvious.

I go with honesty. "They're still a little snug."

"It's better, though," Hemi says. "And hopefully Lavender will be able to help."

"My ears are burning! How can I be of service?" Lavender appears, followed by her shadow/bodyguard/husband.

"I have a problem." Tristan motions to his crotch.

Lavender's gaze lands on Tristan. "Oooh. Those are a bit snug."

He props his fists on his hips. "Can you fix it?"

"I should be able to make you more comfortable," she assures him.

"Nate, you should try on the other pants so Lavender can make adjustments to those too," Tristan suggests as he glances at the clock. "If there's time."

"Good call." Hopefully there's time.

"What happened?" Kodiak asks.

"They must have laundered his suit and the pants shrunk. A lot," I explain. "The ones he's wearing are mine."

I disappear into the changing room and put on Tristan's pants. It looks like I'm smuggling baked potatoes in my boxers. I open the door a crack.

"Baby, uh, isn't there another way to do this?" Kodiak looks like his head is about to explode.

"No, sweetheart. I can't let out the crotch area of a pair of pants without touching the crotch area of a pair of pants while they are on the body they need to be adjusted for," she explains.

"Nate, how do those fit?" Hemi asks.

I throw the door open.

Everyone grimaces. Except Flip. He gives me two thumbs-up while smirking.

"Seriously, you guys have some good genetics," Sam offers.

"I'm just as blessed," Brody pipes up. Apparently he's in full extrovert mode with Sam and Isaac around. He's at risk of using all his words for the day before the ceremony even happens.

"Do you think you can help me too?" I ask Lavender.

She wrinkles her nose. "That's a big question mark."

"What size are those pants?" Isaac asks.

"The waist is like a thirty-four, but they were tailored to fit my hockey ass and thighs. Now it's anyone's guess." Tristan shrugs.

"Why don't you and I trade and see how that goes?" Isaac offers.

Isaac is broader across the shoulders, but he's narrower at the waist, which would be better than this.

Kodiak compulsively runs his hand through his hair. "Lavender, baby, can't you work on his pants when they're off his body?"

She shoots her husband a withering look, but continues to work on the seam on Tristan's right thigh. "Kodiak, sweetheart, this is my job. I do this all day, every single day. I put costumes on people, and then I alter them while they're wearing them. I'm at eye level with dick all day long. And sometimes vagina and boobs, and often asses. People's body parts are in my face constantly."

I cough to smother a laugh. Kodiak is huge, and one punch would feel like getting hit in the face with a truck. Also, I don't need a black eye or missing teeth to round out today.

"Kodiak, buddy, why don't we grab some refreshments for everyone?" Flip suggests.

"Oh! Yes, please! Sweetheart, can you grab me a lavender lemonade? Kiki at the café knows how I like them," Lavender says.

"Okay. Yeah. I can do that."

Flip and Kodiak leave the room.

"Will he be okay?" Tristan asks.

"He'll just need some snuggle time, and then he'll be fine," Lavender assures us.

Isaac and I trade pants while Kodiak and Flip get refreshments and Lavender works on Tristan's crotch.

Isaac's pants are a decent fit, which is a relief. Hopefully Tristan's pants will work for him, or he might have to resort to board shorts or linen pants. Isaac and I step out of the changing rooms at the same time. Lavender pauses her mission to make Tristan's crotch *not* the sole focus of the day.

Lavender glances between us. "Wow."

"Those are a decent fit on you." Isaac nods to my crotch.

"Yeah."

I can't say the same for him. The pants are capris on his long legs.

He props his fists on his hips and poses in front of the three-way mirror. "I think they work." He turns to Sam. "I can rock this look, right?"

"Oh yeah. Just lose the socks." Sam nods.

"Good call."

I'm unsure if they're serious or not until Isaac removes his socks and slips his feet back into his loafers.

"Better?" Isaac asks his brother.

Sam nods his approval.

"You comfortable with my pants?" Isaac gives me two thumbs-up.

"If you're sure you're good with mine, then yeah."

"Perfect. See you when you walk down the aisle, Tristan."

"All right, man." Tristan holds out his hand for a fist-bump.

Sam and Isaac step aside as Kodiak and Flip return with drinks. Then they leave the suite and head down the hall. Two women do a double take as they pass Isaac, and not in a shocked way, but more like they're considering pulling him into an empty room and banging his brains out.

"Only my brother could pull those off." Hemi rolls her eyes.

"All done!" Lavender stands. She doesn't even come close to reaching Tristan's shoulder.

"Thank God." Kodiak hands her the lavender lemonade. "We should go back to the room. I need a snack before the wedding." He ushers her out the door.

"Anyone feel like *snack* is a code word?" I ask.

"It means he's planning to eat her out. That's what Dallas does when he's anxious, too," Hemi announces, then bites her lips together.

"That's legit a solid strategy, though," Tristan muses. "And everyone wins."

Brody's ears are going red, but he also seems intrigued.

"Yup. Okay. Well." Hemi slaps her palms together. "I should check on the girls." She hustles out the door.

Dad clears his throat. "We should get ready, boys. We don't want to keep the bride waiting."

CHAPTER 29

ESSIE

"Do we have everything we need? What about tissues? Do I look okay? My curls aren't falling, are they? Is my hair frizzy?" Even glancing around wildly, Rix looks like a princess in her flowy island wedding dress.

"You are radiant, and we have everything we need." I dust her chin and forehead with setting powder.

She pulls me in for a tight hug. "I love you. Thank you for being here. Thank you for being my best friend for all these years."

"There's nowhere I would rather be, and no one I would rather price match with."

She smiles, but she still seems nervous, looking past me to the door.

"What is it, Trixie Rixie?"

"I just want today to be perfect," she whispers.

"Even if there are hiccups, it will be the best day because it's the start of your forever," I assure her.

"I don't want anything to mess this up."

"Is there anything that could keep you from marrying Tristan?" I ask gently.

She shakes her head. "Of course not."

"Can you imagine a world in which Tristan stops fighting for you, or you stop fighting for him?"

Her expression softens. "No, never."

"You have your person, Rix. He's so perfectly right for you, and you are perfectly right for him, and no matter what, you will always stand up for each other."

She nods and licks her lips. "You're right. I know you're right."

"Okay, so why do you still look worried?"

"I'm scared Tristan's mom will show up and ruin the wedding." She drops her voice. "There was a call from an unknown number twice this week. Tristan didn't answer, and no message was left, but it doesn't mean she can't figure out where we are. We've all been sharing pictures on our social media. It wouldn't be that hard to find us."

I'm keeping enough stuff from my best friend. I don't want to keep this from her too, especially not when I can put her mind at ease by telling her the truth. "She was here."

"What? When?" Her voice grows shrill. "Why didn't you say anything?"

"It was last night, after the rehearsal dinner. Only me, Nate, and Connor saw her. She's been handled, and she won't be coming back."

"Handled how?" The color drains from her face. "Please don't tell me Sam and Isaac got involved."

"No. Of course not." I squeeze her shoulders. "And I know you all think Sam is some kind of finisher, but I feel like he probably loves diamond paintings."

"I can see that." Rix barks out a laugh, but her expression sobers. "I wish I could say I can't believe she showed up, but all the phone calls recently…" She shakes her head. "How did Nate handle things? Is he okay?"

I consoled him with sex that felt a lot like making love is not a truth I'll share right now. "He was upset, but he's okay. He was glad it was him and not Tristan or Brody who had to deal with her. Neither of them knows anything about it."

She nods. "And you're sure she's gone?"

"Absolutely." I take her by the shoulders. "Deep breath, Trixie Rixie. I promise she's not coming back. And I can explain the full story later, and you can have feelings about it then, but she won't ruin today, or any other day in the future, and not because Sam fed her to the sharks." *Even if that's what she deserves.* "Connor Grace helped us out, and I'm pretty sure he has security on lock here, so you're safe to walk down the aisle with no one to interfere."

"Thank you." She hugs me.

"Anything for you, bestie. You know that."

"Everything okay in here?" Muffy pokes her head in the door.

"Mummy." Rix opens her arms, and her mom steps into them.

Muffy's eyes meet mine, questions there. I mouth *everything's good* to reassure her.

She releases Rix and takes her hands. "My baby girl, you look so perfect."

"Thank you for being my mom and for teaching me how to love right," Rix says softly.

I love their bond. Life was never easy for the Madden family, but they always stood beside each other.

"Oh my heart, you are the one who taught me how to love right. Every time you do something wonderful for the people you care about, you show me that love is the most important thing. Tristan loves you with his whole heart, and that's all I've ever wanted for you—to be happy and healthy and find the person who will weather all the ups and downs with you."

"Tristan is definitely that guy," Rix agrees.

They hug, and her mom whispers something that has me pulling out tissues so neither of them ruins their makeup, and then we're all laughing at how emotional we are and squeezing each other.

We untangle our limbs as Rix's dad knocks on the door. And then everyone is struggling to keep their emotions in check again over how beautiful Rix is.

Her dad takes her arm. "Should we walk you down the aisle?"

She smiles up at him. "I would love that, Daddy."

My heart is so full as we make our way to the beach, where the guests wait.

Tristan walks Muffy down the aisle to her seat. Flip and Brody hold white wicker baskets of rose petals that they toss—mostly at each other—as they walk down the aisle and take their seats with their families.

Nate and I fall into step beside each other at the end of the aisle. His expression is soft and warm as it moves over me. He's so handsome in his black suit and teal tie. My stomach twists and flips as he threads his arm through mine and bends to whisper, "Thank you for being you."

I smile up at him, at a loss for words, but then we're walking down the aisle, heading for Tristan waiting at the altar. He looks equal parts nervous and excited.

We take our places opposite each other, and I look around at all the people who are here to witness this special day. My parents are a couple of rows back, my dad's arm around Mom, their other hands clasped. The "Wedding March" begins, and I steady my breathing as Rix appears at the end of the aisle with her dad.

"Oh my God." Tristan tugs on his tie. "She's fucking beautiful."

I pull an extra packet of tissues from my pocket, make eye contact with Nate, and toss them to him underhand. He snatches them and passes one to Tristan who dabs at the corner of his eyes. He looks like he's half a second away from running down the aisle to get her. He takes a single step forward, and Nate puts a hand on his shoulder, leaning in to whisper something. Whatever he says settles his brother.

Tristan's love is written so plainly on his face, eyes shiny with adoration as Rix hugs her dad and turns toward him. Tristan holds out his hand, completely awestruck as she moves to stand beside him.

I step in to take Rix's bouquet. She squeezes my hand, and I tuck a tissue into it.

"I love you," she whispers.

"I love you, too." I step back, and Rix refocuses on Tristan.

He kisses the back of her hand, then presses it to his cheek.

"How you doin'?" she murmurs.

"So much better now that you're here with me." He kisses her palm. "You are just—" He shakes his head. "—stunning. I can't believe you're mine."

"And you're mine." She smiles. "Let's make it permanent."

I touch a tissue to the corner of my eyes as the officiant starts the ceremony. And even though I shouldn't, I can't help but picture Nate and me in their place.

I'm terrified that I'm following the same pattern I always do, that I've already done what I said I wouldn't, with the man I said I wouldn't get attached to.

He already hurt me once. It's my fault entirely if I let him do it again.

CHAPTER 30
NATE

Essie smells fantastic and looks like she stepped right out of a fairy tale. I rush to pull out her chair at the reception and offer my hand as we make our way to the podium for speeches.

Just like at the rehearsal dinner, we're separated by Tristan and Rix at the head table. That means I haven't touched her since photos this afternoon, and it feels like I'm going through withdrawal. Essie sets a packet of tissues and her glass of water on the podium and smiles out at the crowd of friends and family.

"Look at all you beautiful people." She claps, and everyone joins in.

Essie waits until the chatter subsides before she turns to the head table where Rix and Tristan are snuggled together, looking wildly, wonderfully happy. "And these two are a picture, aren't they? Just radiating pure joy."

Rix blows her a kiss, and Essie catches it and presses it to her cheek.

People *awww*, and I wish I'd gone first. I'm excellent at presenting facts, but I don't have a whole lot of experience wowing wedding crowds, and Essie is a natural.

"You meet this amazing person, and they just get you in a way no one else ever has before. They love everything about you, and you love everything about them, even the weird and quirky parts, especially those." She presses her hand to her heart and smiles fondly at Tristan and Rix. "And it's just so special, because you know in your heart that you're going to spend your lives together. You're going to love each other through thick and thin, and price match the old-school way until the end of time…" She turns her attention to the guests. "And that's how I feel about Rix."

The crowd laughs and claps.

"I feel the same way about you, Ess!" Rix calls.

Essie grabs a tissue, her eyes soft. "I met Rix on the first day of junior kindergarten. She had a green backpack, and all the other girls had pink, including me, and I immediately knew I wanted to be her friend. Fate gave us last names close to each other in the alphabet, so we ended up sitting next to each other, and from that day on, we were inseparable—except when they split us up in classes because we talked too much. Actually, it was me. I was always the one who was talking. Rix was very studious."

More chuckles follow.

"Trixie Rixie, we've been through so much together. We've seen each other through all the ups and downs of our teen years and the challenges of adulting. You have always had my back, every step of the way, and I'll adore you until the end of time. You are the most loyal, loving person I know, and seeing you and Tristan grow together has been so beautiful to watch. The way you protect each other's hearts and hold each other accountable every day is inspiring. You've both fought so hard to get where you are." She dabs away a tear. "And I know that no matter what life throws at you, you'll keep fighting for each other and the love you share. It is an honor to be your best friend, to be able to stand with you and celebrate your love and the beautiful life ahead of you. To Tristan and Rix!" She holds up her water and everyone clinks their glasses, shouting, "Kiss, kiss, kiss!"

Tristan helps Rix to her feet and places his hand at the side of her neck, brushing his nose against hers before he wraps his arm around her waist and lays one on her.

Everyone hoots and hollers. Rix is red faced and Tristan is smirking by the time they take their seats again.

Essie and I trade places. "I should have gone first," I say into the mic.

"You can do it, honey bear!" Flip shouts.

Essie plucks another tissue from the packet on the stand, but she leaves the rest beside the glass of water. She squeezes my arm and whispers, "You've got this."

I pat my pocket with the cue cards. If ever there was a time to speak from the heart, it's now. I adjust the mic. "It's an honor to be standing here today, celebrating my brother and his beautiful bride. Rix, you are stunning, and he is one hell of a lucky guy to have found you."

"Got that right!" Tristan kisses Rix on the temple.

"Growing up in a one-parent house wasn't easy. Everyone had to do their part to make things work. Tristan, you were always there when we needed you, not just because you had to be, but because you authentically wanted us to feel like we mattered and were loved. You always made time to shoot the puck around with Brody, and you always let me explain my newest ideas and designs, even though you probably didn't understand half of what I was saying."

"I didn't, but I love your huge, sexy brain, brother." Tristan's smile is soft and proud.

Brody nods his agreement. A few of the guys on the team shout and whistle, and Essie claps enthusiastically.

"I'm so grateful that I have you as a brother. Last year, when I switched gears and ended up back in Toronto, you and Rix opened your home to me while I figured out my living situation. And I witnessed firsthand the way you two love each other with your whole hearts. You taught me not to sweat the small stuff, but that it's the little gestures that have the biggest impact. The notes you'd leave on the fridge for Rix always made her smile, the treats that would show up when you were on an away series, the way Rix would always make your favorites when you came home, and of course the excessive PDA…"

Our friends snort, and someone coughs to cover a laugh.

Tristan just smirks, and Rix presses her face to his chest with a giggle.

"Despite some of the things I can't unsee or unhear, those little things you did for each other spoke volumes. You always put each other first, you stand up for and to each other, and I'm so thankful that I had the chance to watch you grow together, because it's given me hope I didn't know I needed until now." I clear my throat, exhaling the anxiety that comes with the honesty I'm about to share. "Being your best man, Tristan, and being able to be part of this journey with you has really restored my faith in love."

Tristan's eyes flare, and Essie lets out a little surprised sound beside me. She probably doesn't realize I'm talking about her, that she's the reason I want to believe in love.

I fight to keep my emotions in check and clear my throat before I continue. "Rix, I'm so happy that you're finally my sister. You've always been in our lives, and now you're truly a part of our family. It's funny now, when I think back to Thanksgiving when you and Flip came for dinner. My brother was awfully territorial when it came to you. It wasn't long after that I understood why he was so growly when I asked if you were single."

Rix's mouth drops open, and she elbows Tristan.

He shrugs. "He was trying to step on my toes."

"He was already head-over-heels for you, and seeing the way he loves you now is inspiring. I'm really looking forward to family holidays now that you'll be part of them."

"You're excited for pie!" Flip yells.

"This is true." I nod solemnly. "But aside from good food, I'm grateful for the light you bring to our family. Thank you for loving my brother. It's an honor to have you as a sister." I hold up Essie's water and toast the bride and groom.

Tristan and Rix meet us at the podium.

"Well done, brother." Tristan pulls me in for a tight hug.

"I'm glad you're my family, too," Rix whispers.

Essie and I return to our seats while Rix and Tristan thank everyone for being here to celebrate them. The two chairs that separate me from Essie feel like an ocean. All I want to do is slide over and hold her hand as she dabs at her eyes.

Once the speeches are over, Tristan and Rix share their first dance, and then we're called up to join them. I take Essie's hand and guide her to the dance floor. She lets me pull her into my arms, and I marvel at how perfectly we fit together.

All this time, she's been right in front of me, and I finally *see* her. She's the most devoted best friend. She has the kindest soul, the biggest heart. She's smart and fun and she brightens my world.

"That was a great speech." Her fingertips skim the side of my neck.

"So was yours, but I expected as much." I pull her closer. "I've been waiting all day to have you in my arms again."

"You're making me melt over here, Nathan," she whispers.

I think about what Flip said when we went for the run on the beach the other day. I need to own what I did all those years ago. It's time to fix what I broke. And then this week doesn't have to end when we leave the island. She could be mine, and I could be hers.

Essie loves love more than anyone else I know. This could be the beginning of something amazing.

So when the song comes to an end, I drop my mouth to her ear. "Can we talk?"

CHAPTER 31
ESSIE

He knows. My stomach feels like it's about to turn itself inside out. Somehow he's seen inside my head and has plucked out the fantasy where I've walked us down the aisle. That has to be the reason he looks serious and determined.

Just because he said he believes in love again, doesn't mean he wants it himself, or even believes in it with *me.*

I swallow down the bile made of anxiety and the fear of heartache. "Sure, we can talk."

The song changes, and people flood the dance floor, making it an easy escape. Nate keeps his hand on my lower back as he leads me away from the wedding festivities. His jaw is tight, and his brow is furrowed. I've grown accustomed to his softness over the past few days, to the warm smiles and casual affection. To falling asleep in his arms. I'm sure it's about to come to a screeching halt, and I'm not ready.

He leads me to an empty gazebo by the beach. The moon reflects off the water, and the sky is a wash of twinkling stars. The waves lap the sand like a soft heartbeat. It's perfectly romantic. Straight out of a fairy tale.

Nate tucks a hand in his pocket and turns to face me. "I need to apologize."

My throat is tight, and tears prick behind my eyes. How stupid that I let my heart out of its cage last night and forgot to put it back in when the sex was over. "For what?"

He rubs a hand over his chin. "For being a dick."

I frown. "I don't understand."

"For ghosting you before I left for university."

"Oh." My stomach fills with lead. I shoved that hurt into the closet with all the other boys who did the same, used it to fuel my belief that I could keep my feelings out of the equation with Nate.

"That kiss…" He shakes his head.

"You don—"

"It was the best kiss of my life. But then one of my friends started running his mouth, and I was leaving for Kingston in a few weeks, and I…" He runs a hand through his hair. "I panicked."

Shame washes through me, and I have to avert my gaze. I can imagine what his friends said.

"I'm sorry I didn't call," he presses on. "I'm sorry I ghosted you, Ess. I didn't want to start something when I was leaving in a few weeks. You were staying in Toronto, and I was going to be three hours away. It never would have worked."

"It's okay. I get it." He wasn't the first or the last guy to kiss me and make promises he never delivered on.

I was a serial dater in high school, which would have been less of a problem if I'd dated guys who *didn't* go to my high school. But in grade eleven, I had a new boyfriend every other month, and four of them went to my school. Regardless, they all ended the same way: with me by myself again.

I was pretty and popular, and boys wanted a taste, but they didn't want *me*. They wanted the checkmark of approval from their friends that they'd dated me. And every time my heart got stomped on, I believed just a little bit more that this was all I was. Someone to play with and discard.

But I still held onto hope for the fairy tale ending. I had faith that someone would see what was underneath and want all of me. That the love of a lifetime would find me the way it had found my parents when they met in university. That one day, someone would think I was worth falling for. I would finally give my heart to the right person, and they would take care of it.

"It's not okay. I was a dick to you, and I kept being a dick when you moved back. You just seemed so…unaffected. And I thought maybe that kiss didn't mean to you what it meant to me. It was a constant reminder of what I'd done all those years ago, and it made me feel like shit, so I took it out on you with my bad moods. You didn't deserve it. Not then and not now." His gaze meets mine, and he looks so *pained*. "Essie, I…I like you." He shakes his head. "No. That's not true."

The knife to the heart almost takes me to my knees.

"I don't just like you." His voice drops to a whisper, like he's sharing a forbidden secret. "I want a life with you."

For a moment, time stands still. This is the opposite of what I expected, and I'm reeling. His eyes are wild, the energy around him frenetic. Before I can even respond he starts again.

"It could work this time. You and me. You've been here all along. You've never left. I was just too scared to take the risk." He motions to our surroundings. "Being here together just proves how good everything will be. I can see our whole future playing out like a slideshow, Ess. I can see it with you." He barely takes a breath before he says, "I think we can do this. I love you."

Understanding pushes its way in, stomping on his declaration. He's mistaking wedding magic for feelings. His mother showing up, my taking care of him, his brother marrying the love of his life—all of it is swirling together, heightening his fragile state, making him believe what he's saying is true. But when we're back in Toronto and reality settles in, he'll realize none of what he thinks he's feeling is real.

I fell into bed with Nate knowing he was the king of wrong guys. He'd already rejected me once, and it made him safe to have some fun with. I want fairy-tale romance, and he thinks it's what he's offering, but I know if I reach out and take it, it will slip through my fingers and disappear.

"You don't, though," I say softly, my heart already breaking at his confused expression.

"What?"

"You think you're in love, Nate, but you're not." I motion to the twinkle lights and all the people dancing, laughing, and having a great time in the distance. "No one goes from hating the idea of commitment, to saying I love you nearly overnight. All of this is clouding your vision. You think you feel this way because we're surrounded by people who *are* in love. You want this to be real. Trust me, I get it. It's this beautiful beacon of hope, and I understand that you're searching for something to hold on to—that you're scared, especially with everything that's happened, Nate. Your mom—"

"This doesn't have anything to do with her," he snaps.

"But it does." My throat is tight, eyes filling with tears. "How could it not? She literally took the money and ran. You haven't even had time to process it. You won't talk to me about it. How can you believe you want a life together when you won't share your pain with me?" My heart feels like it's crumbling to dust. And right now, in this perfectly awful moment, I recognize I'm the one who's fallen. "You're mistaking fear and lust for love, Nate."

His brow furrows. "But you took care of me." He motions between us. "You keep taking care of me. I like how I feel when I'm with you."

"I'm sure that's true, but I've been a fun little distraction from all the things you want to avoid." I say it, I see the truth in it. Of course he's been seeking an escape from the pain of it all. And I gave him one. Willingly. "Everyone else's happiness is influencing you right now. You're not serious about me and you don't want a future with me. In a week you'll wake up and realize you professed your love to me out of fear, and then you'll panic because it's not what you want. You've told me—you've told everyone—love isn't real for years. This is just the wedding vibes and hot sex talking."

I would know. This has happened to me before, too many times to count. I've mistaken lust for something more, too. It's what I've been doing this whole time. Whatever these feelings are that he thinks he has, they'll fizzle out when we're back in Toronto. "Until this week you didn't even have faith Rix and Tristan could last, let alone you and someone."

With that, his walls come up, and he shuts down. It's what I've been waiting for, but it still shreds my heart.

"Right." He takes a step back. "We were only ever just fucking."

"Nate." I reach for him, but he shifts away.

"You were very clear, and I didn't listen. I get the message now." He spins around and walks away.

And I just…let him.

Because when he's had a chance to really think about it, he'll realize I'm the one who's right, even if I wish I weren't. I don't want to be the idea he clings to, the refuge he seeks to escape his pain. I want it to be real for him like it is for me.

"Essie?"

I look up to find Dred coming up the steps to the gazebo from the beach. "Hey."

She glances around, maybe searching for the other half of my conversation. "You out here talking to your fairy godmother?"

I laugh. "I wish I had one."

"Can't promise any magic, but I'm good at listening, if you want to tell me what's going on."

"It's Nate."

She nods and rests her hip against the railing. "There's been a vibe."

"You're good at catching the vibes, aren't you?" She was in the know on the Lexi-Roman situation before the rest of us had a clue.

She nods. "I am."

I word-vomit the entire story, starting with the kiss in high school and ending with me sabotaging Nate's declaration—but I leave out the part about his mother showing up.

She sighs. "Ah, well it all makes good sense now."

"He can't be falling for me." I need someone else to confirm this, to tell me I'm right. I have to be, it's the only thing that makes sense.

Her smile is soft and understanding. "Love makes us vulnerable in a way nothing else can, and Nate doesn't really seem like the type of guy who makes himself vulnerable on a whim. Love opens us up for wonderful and painful things. Look at Rix and Tristan. She was devastated that she'd fallen for him, and he was terrified of loving her. They both had to face their own feelings and fears. Maybe Nate's just had his epiphany. And maybe now it's your turn."

"I love people who will never love me back," I admit.

"That's not entirely true, though, is it? You love Rix, and she loves you back just as fiercely."

"Yeah, but it's different. She's my best friend. She'll never leave me, and I'll never leave her."

"Your relationship with Rix is so special, Ess. And you're right that platonic love is different, but it's still love, and it still makes us vulnerable. We should all be so lucky to have the kind of friendship you and Rix do."

"You have that with Lexi and Flip," I say.

"You're right, I do. Lexi is very much like a sister to me. We understand each other in a way not everyone can because we share common trauma. And I've had a lot of brothers and sisters over the years, but Flip is the truest family I've ever had. They both might as well be blood with how much space they take up in my heart."

"Flip really is your best friend, isn't he?"

"He is. One day, when he gets his head out of his ass and

realizes his soul mate is waiting for him to finally fucking see *her*, I'll be the one to help him through all those feelings."

I arch a brow. "Are you talking about who I think you're talking about?"

"I think her harmless teenage crush has shifted in the last year."

"It'll be messy when it happens, won't it?"

"Yeah. But she needs to live a little more, and he's not there yet, which isn't a bad thing, so that's a bridge for another day. Back to you and love. You're surrounded by people who adore you and see you, Essie. All of you. Anyone lucky to be in your orbit knows that you're wickedly smart, and kind, and generous, and the space in your heart is limitless. Take some of the faith you have in other people's love and share it with yourself. Nate might be your person, but how will you know if you don't give your hearts a chance outside of this bubble?"

CHAPTER 32

NATE

I should have kept my stupid mouth shut. I had a plan, and I deviated from it, and now it's shot all to shit. I won't get tonight with Essie. I won't get to hold her, or kiss her, or be with her.

But maybe she's right. Maybe this gaping hole in my chest has nothing to do with loving her. Maybe it is all the shit I've been keeping locked inside trying to gnaw its way out.

I can't go back to the wedding. Not when everyone is happy and my heart has been punted into the ocean and chewed on by sharks. I don't want Tristan or my dad to see me and ask questions. No one needs my rain cloud tonight but me.

I leave the boardwalk and take to the beach to avoid running into people. My shoes fill with sand, but I don't stop to take them off, even though it's uncomfortable and slows me down. I'm so up in my head that I almost trip over Connor. He's drinking straight from a bottle of expensive champagne.

"Shit, sorry." I stumble back and lose my footing, landing on my ass beside him.

"What are you doing out here?" His eyes narrow. "Your mother didn't try to crash the wedding, did she? Security is supposed to be on the lookout."

"She's not here. I'm just trying not to spread my bad mood around to people who don't deserve it."

"Ah. I get that." He passes me the bottle of champagne. "Feel free to stick around for as long as you like. We can be morose as fuck together."

"Why are you morose as fuck?" I'm happy to take my mind off my own problems and listen to someone else's. I tip the bottle back and let the bubbles coat my tongue.

"Because I'm me, and my family hates me. And because Meems is getting old, and all the fucking money in the world can't keep her here forever."

I pass the champagne back. "I'm really sorry." My mother might suck a bag of dicks, but my dad and my brothers more than make up for it. And now we have Rix. And my dad has Sophia. "For what it's worth, I think you're a good guy. I appreciate you helping us out with my mother. I owe you."

"I'm not a good guy, and you don't owe me anything." He takes a long swig from the bottle and wipes his mouth with the back of his hand. "I just know what it's like to have shitty parents. I'm glad I could save Tristan and Rix from the stress of that, but I'm sorry for whatever trash that's dug up for you."

We pass the bottle back and forth.

I keep trying to bury the memories of my mother, but they always work their way back to the surface. "I should probably go to therapy."

He nods slowly. "Tristan seems to be a fan."

"Yeah."

"Is that why you're morose as fuck?"

I shake my head. "Mostly no."

"Does it have anything to do with the maid of honor?"

I frown. "Why would you think that?"

"Just a sense I get. Lot of sexual tension there." He takes another swig from his champagne. "So what's going on?"

"Nothing anymore."

"Your decision or hers?"

"Hers."

"Did you help make it for her?"

"Probably." She would know when love is real and when it isn't better than me. "I hurt her a long time ago. Maybe this is karma's way of getting me back." She set the parameters from the beginning. She was clear about what this should be. About what we could be.

He passes me the bottle again, but I decline. "I'm going to take my black cloud back to my room."

"Sometimes things look different in the morning," he says.

"Yeah. Maybe. Thanks for everything this week. I know you've been pulling strings."

"Anything I can do to make my friends' lives better and piss off my parents is a win in my book."

"I'm sorry they're assholes."

"Me too. But I'm glad I could be helpful. I hope tomorrow brings fresh perspective."

"I hope so, too." Although I don't see how. "'Night, Connor."

I leave him on the beach and return to my room. It looks like a Brody bomb went off in here. Clothes are draped over every surface, and six pairs of shoes lie in a heap in the corner. I don't have the energy to tidy up, so I leave it all where it is.

I change into shorts and a T-shirt and grab all the mini bottles of booze from the fridge. I can't get the look on Essie's face out of my head, or the conviction in her tone when she told me I was wrong. That I couldn't possibly love her. I'm too broken. Too messed up. Too closed off and guarded.

Essie calls, but I can't handle more rejection, or worse, her checking on me to make sure I'm okay. So I polish off the little bottles of liquor, hoping I can get drunk enough to shut off my brain.

Brody stumbles into the room a long while later. "Bro!" He weaves over to the bed and flops down beside me. "What are you doing in here?"

"Bed was calling. This is my room."

He rolls onto his back. "Everyone's boning tonight."

If I'd kept my stupid fucking mouth shut, I'd be with Ess right now. "Yup."

"But not you."

"Not tonight. Why aren't you out there?" I ask.

"I was done being social. Some girl was chatting me up."

"Someone named Tally?"

Brody snorts a laugh. "Dude, you know as well as I do that Tally is all about someone else."

I crack a half smile. "You think so too, huh?"

"Oh yeah, the way she looks at him?" He blows out a breath. "Besides, I'm all about someone else, too."

"You want to talk about that?" Anything to keep my mind off Essie.

Brody folds his arm behind his head. "I just have so many fucking regrets, you know? Like, I fucked up so hard in high school, and now we're at the same university, but I've already blown my chance with Enid."

"You don't think it's fixable?" I'm the last person who should be giving him relationship advice.

"Would you get over it if the girl you crushed on fucked around with one of your best friends?"

Essie is too amazing to stay single for long. Will I have to see her happy with someone else? Someone better suited for her? "Maybe you just need to give it a bit more time. People change and grow." I thought I had. But turns out maybe I was wrong about that.

"Yeah." He sighs. "You know what the worst part is?"

"What's that?"

"I didn't even like her friend. She just kept pushing and pushing. I wish I could take it back."

I turn to my brother, giving him my full attention. My stomach twists as emotions pass over his face. "What do you mean she kept pushing?"

"She was pushy, like I said." He scrubs a hand across his face. "So I got her off."

"Did this girl force herself on you?" I press.

"We didn't have sex." His jaw works, and he clenches his fists. "I just wish I could forget it ever happened. I don't know why I'm talking about this. It's not like I can undo it, anyway."

"Okay, we can drop it." But I definitely want to come back to this when he's sober. It sounds like something happened that shouldn't have.

He presses the heels of his hands to his eyes.

"You okay?"

"Yeah. Just...my head's messy."

"About Enid?"

"Yeah. No. I don't know." He drops his hands. "It's stupid."

"What's stupid?" I'm having trouble following his train of thought.

He sighs. "I thought maybe Mom would show up for Tristan's wedding. I don't want to see her, but I do, you know? Maybe she did come, and I didn't even recognize her."

My chest tightens. She'll never upend his life again, but that choice was made for him, not by him. "Tristan didn't want her here," I remind him.

"I know. I just thought... I don't know. I don't remember much about her, but I remember missing her when she was gone, and not understanding what we did that was so wrong that she left."

"We weren't the problem," I assure him. "She was."

"Yeah. I still wish I understood why, though. Like, what happened to make us all too much for her to love?" He picks at a loose string on his sleeve. "But Tristan has made it okay. Rix is like, amazing and such a good person, and he's so in love with her, and she's so in love with him, so maybe there's still hope for us, too, right?"

"Yeah, Brodes, there's still hope," I lie.

His eyes slide closed, and thirty seconds later he's out cold. I

245

lie there for a long while, head spinning. I'm almost on the edge of sleep when there's a knock on my door.

I drag myself out of bed and open it a crack.

Essie's beautiful, anxious face greets me. She's still wearing her dress, but her hair is falling out of its updo. She's so beautiful it hurts. But she's not mine. She'll never be mine.

She wrings her hands. "Can we talk?"

I step outside and let the door fall closed behind me.

"I was wrong. I should have heard you out. I—"

"You were right. What I thought I was feeling isn't real." I can't trust my own emotions, and she knows more about love than I do.

Her face crumples like crushed tissue paper. "But I—"

"My own mother doesn't even want me. She put a price tag on my value as a human being and her son." Besides, she's probably right. I just got swept up in the wedding buzz. Everything would fall apart when we got home. I'd make sure of that. Better to end it all now than give either of us hope just to take it away again.

She reaches out, but I step back. I can't handle affection in the form of comfort.

"I can't love anyone, Essie." Not the way she deserves. "Especially not you."

CHAPTER 33

ESSIE

"Okay! All my single ladies line up! It's time for the bouquet toss since I totally forgot last night!" Rix hops out of her chair.

"That's you, honey." Mom nudges me with her arm.

I have not said a word about last night, but she knows something is going on. She's been super attentive and gentle with me. So has Dad. All it does is make me want to cry.

I slept like trash for obvious reasons. I cried myself to sleep after Nate took back everything he'd said. Erased his words and turned them into acid-dipped knives. He slid into brunch at the last minute this morning. He's been quiet ever since and looks about as well rested as me. I want to pull him aside, but there hasn't been an opportunity.

Dred gives my arm a squeeze as she joins me and all the other singles. "How you doing?"

"I've been better." I spent twenty minutes trying to tame my swollen eyelids. I gave up and put on sunglasses, and I refuse to take them off. Thankfully, brunch is an outdoor event.

"You two stop colluding!" Cammie pokes me in the side.

Rix counts down to one and tosses the bouquet over her

shoulder, but instead of coming toward us, it boomerangs in Nate's direction. He's not expecting it and gets beaned in the face.

"Yes!" Isaac jumps to his feet. "Fuck yeah! You and Essie next year, man! I better get an invite!" According to Hammer and Dred, Isaac spent the entire wedding fending off advances from hotel guests.

Nate's face turns a remarkable shade of red. I'm frozen to the spot as everyone bursts into surprised chatter.

"What the hell are you talking about?" Dallas snorts a laugh.

Hemi rolls her eyes. "Are you still drunk?"

Isaac glances around, expression expectant. Except for Dred and Flip, everyone else looks confused. "What do you mean what am I talking about?" He motions to us with both arms. "It's so freaking obvious these two have a huge heart-on for each other."

As more eyebrows rise, Isaac steps forward. "After everyone goes to bed, Nate sneaks into Essie's room and doesn't leave until five or six in the morning."

"You're high," Hemi snaps. "You need to stop."

"I watched it happen from my balcony!" He points to the second floor opposite my room. It would give him a perfect view. "Essie has been carrying around Benadryl all week for him. Also, Nate's shirts have matched Essie's clothes—maybe subconsciously, maybe not."

Even now they do.

Cammie grabs my arm. "Can I just say how much I love you with the hot nerd? It's like we're twins but opposite. My hot sister with the smart hot nerd, and I'm the nerd with the hot jock hockey player. Except you're also smart, and so is Chase, but you're both exceptionally hot and everyone wants to date you."

I'm pretty sure she's been going hard on the mimosas.

"How did I miss this?" Hammer muses.

Sam, also an observant guy, it seems, steps in to take over

where his brother left off. "And didn't anyone notice the way they shared Essie's glass of water during the speeches?"

I can't even look at Nate. I'm horrified and embarrassed.

Not to be upstaged by Sam, Isaac adds, "They also disappeared right after the first dance and didn't come back for the rest of the night. Maybe because they were celebrating with a horizontal tango of their own!"

"There are grandparents here!" Hemi smacks her brothers' arms. "I'm going to murder both of you. Why are you ruining my friends' lives?"

I glance at Nate, whose expression is frighteningly blank.

Rix and Tristan are wearing matching expressions of disbelief, eyes bouncing between us. I'm sure my guilt is written all over my horrified face.

"Is this for fucking real?" Tristan looks like he's ready to spit nails.

I wish someone would throw water on me so I'd melt into a puddle.

Nate crosses his arms.

"Have you learned nothing from me?" He shakes his head, and his disappointment makes me want to shrink into myself. "We don't keep secrets like this."

If only he knew what other secrets we're keeping.

Rix looks to me, hurt all over her beautiful face. I put that there. *Thanks so much, Isaac.*

"Okay." I raise my hand before anyone else can jump in with more unhelpful comments. Like hell am I going to make this about me and Nate. "We're all adults here, and we're all capable of making adult decisions. This brunch is a celebration for Rix and Tristan, so let's keep the focus there." I grab the bouquet and toss it directly at Hammer.

She catches it.

I burst into applause and start hooting and hollering and thank fucking God for my friends, because they join in too.

I look to Rix, who gets up from the table and heads for me, face etched with worry. "I think we need to talk."

I nod my agreement. "Let's go for a walk."

"When? Why? How? I thought you were on a dick hiatus," she says once we're away from our families and friends.

"Obviously I failed at the dick hiatus. We were planning a lot of things together for the wedding." I rest my head against her shoulder and hug her arm. "But it really started the summer before university."

She stops and turns to face me. "That was six years ago."

"It hasn't been going on for that long, but that was the catalyst." We sit in the sand and let the water lap at our toes as I explain what happened—how we kissed at a party, that he ghosted me and moved to Kingston, and I didn't hear from him again. Then we both moved back to Toronto, the engagement happened, and we were together a lot. "It was just supposed to be sex and nothing else."

"Don't we already know how this story ends?" She points to herself.

"You were hate fucking each other. We were having who-can-get-the-other-off-first competitions."

"Not that different." She squeezes me. "I'm not mad at you, but we are definitely going to talk when I get home."

"Yeah. I didn't keep it from you to hurt you." I exhale my relief. "I just didn't want to add to your worries, and it would have. No one was supposed to have feelings."

"But you do have feelings?"

"It's complicated. His mom showing up really hit him hard. I think he's been trying to protect Tristan and Brody, but in the process he's taken it all on himself, and I just need space to breathe." And not be under a microscope.

"I didn't realize it had gotten that bad. Between the phone calls and her showing up, he must be in a fragile place."

"Yeah. It would be hard on anyone." But hardest on a man who doesn't let his feelings out of the box.

"I haven't said anything to Tristan yet about that," Rix confides. "As much as I don't want to tell him, I need to tell him."

"It's a hard weight to carry." I squeeze her hand. "But you don't have to do it alone."

CHAPTER 34
NATE

I watch Essie link arms with Rix and walk away. Of all the ways for Tristan and Rix to find out, this was at the bottom of the fucking list.

Isaac pats me on the shoulder. "Sorry, man. I should have realized the sneaking out at six in the morning was you trying to keep it a secret, not going for a morning jog."

People are trying not to openly stare.

Brody seems too hungover to process much.

"Nate, we need to talk." Tristan pushes his chair back from the table.

My dad also stands.

I hold up a hand. "Give us a few minutes before you join us."

He nods and sits back down.

I follow Tristan away from the brunch. Which I've effectively ruined. Or Isaac ruined it for us. But either way, it's my fault.

Tristan spins around, eyes on fire. "What the hell were you thinking?"

I shrug. I don't know what to say.

"That's it?" He makes the same gesture back at me. He's livid. "You don't fuck around and keep secrets, Nathan!"

"You did," I grumble.

252

"And look how that almost turned out. I nearly lost Bea because of that. I did lose Bea because of it. And I almost blew up two decades of friendship because I couldn't be honest with anyone about my feelings for her, myself included. Essie is an incredible fucking person."

"I know."

"She doesn't deserve to be treated like your dirty little secret," he snaps. "This isn't a high-school victory lap where you got to bag the hottest girl in school, you asshole."

"That's not... I'm not—"

"She's my wife's best friend. She will be at birthday parties and family fucking events." Tristan clasps his hands behind his neck.

"You think I don't know that? She's the one who wanted it to only be about sex!"

His eyes narrow. "And was it? Just about sex? Were you just screwing the maid of honor behind everyone's back?"

"I told her I'm falling for her, and she told me my feelings aren't real and that it's just the wedding magic or some shit." I pace the gazebo.

He crosses his arms. "Is she right?"

"I don't know." I rub my chest. Should it really hurt this much if she is right?

Tristan grabs me by the shoulders. "Are you in love with Essie?"

"I don't fucking know, man. I thought I was, but then she said I couldn't be, that it was other people's happiness affecting my feelings. That I couldn't be serious about her. Essie knows what love looks like. She would know, wouldn't she? Maybe I'm too fucked up to love anyone. I thought I had it all figured out with Lisa, and look at how that turned out. Everyone just keeps leaving." I'm on the verge of a complete breakdown.

Tristan's expression softens, and he pulls me in for a tight hug. "Ah, man. Come on, bro." He steps back, hands still on my shoulders. "You fucked up, but you're not too fucked up to love."

"She's such a good person, Tris. I felt like it could be something good. I wanted it to be more, and I thought she'd want the same. I should have stuck with the plan and waited until we were back home, but I didn't, and now it's all a mess."

He pulls back, his expression serious. "Honestly, Nate, you shouldn't get into a relationship without getting help."

"I just need to sort my head out."

He squeezes my shoulder. "That's true, but brother to brother, please see someone. You need to talk this stuff out."

I nod. He's right, but everything already hurts. How much worse will it be when I'm digging around in all that old pain?

"You boys okay?" Dad asks.

"Yeah, just working through things," I tell him.

Dad and I exchange a meaningful look. I shake my head.

"What's going on?" Tristan motions between us. "What's that about?"

"I can tell him," I say.

"I think you have enough going on, son. This one should be mine."

Tristan's eyes go wide, head whipping back and forth. "What the fuck is going on?"

Dad positions himself between us and settles one hand on each of our shoulders. I wish it made me feel grounded, but it doesn't.

"Your mom was here."

"What? When? Brody didn't see her, did he?"

"No," I assure him. "It was just me, Essie, and Connor." At least the focus isn't on me and my fuck up anymore. Not that this hurts any less.

"How can we be sure she's gone? What if she's still here? Where's Brody right now?"

"He went back to his room to sleep off his hangover," Dad says.

"And Connor helped take care of the situation." I swallow the pain. It's too fresh. I'm too raw. Everything hurts.

Dad takes over, explaining what happened.

Tristan's expression shifts from disbelief, to rage, to the deepest, most telling empathy. "Nate, man—"

"It was better me than you or Brody. I'm fine," I grind out.

"You're not fucking fine." He curves his hand around the back of my neck, and I see it, his despair, like he's reliving what it was like when she left us.

"I couldn't have her ruin your wedding. I couldn't let that happen." I can feel his pain as deeply as my own.

Tristan's face clouds with anguish. "I'm sorry, man. I'm so sorry."

"She's never going to fuck with us again," I assure him, and maybe myself. "She can't get to Brody anymore."

"I wish I could have saved both of you from all of this," Dad says brokenly.

"We can't tell Brody." Tristan turns his pleading gaze on Dad. "He can't know she took money to stay out of our lives. We can't make that his."

"It stays between us," Dad agrees.

"Rix knows she was here," I tell Tristan.

"What? When did she find out?"

"Essie told her before the wedding. She was planning to tell you eventually, but she didn't want it to taint the day." It's astounding how much pain one person can cause.

"I didn't have the slightest clue."

"That's how she wanted it." Everyone has been carrying the weight of this secret to protect each other.

His phone buzzes in his pocket. It's Rix, based on the chime. "Bea's looking for us."

"You two head back." I thumb over my shoulder. "I need a little breather."

"You sure you're okay, son?"

I nod. "Yes. I'll be fine."

"I'll check on you in a bit," Dad says.

They both hug me before they head back up to find Rix.

All of this feels impossibly heavy, and the exhaustion is overwhelming.

We're still keeping secrets, protecting Brody from more pain.

But I realize, as I head back to my room—alone, again—that if I don't want history to keep repeating itself, I have to fix the problem. I have to fix myself.

CHAPTER 35

ESSIE

I'm bookended between my mom and Cammie as we board the plane, with Chase and my dad behind us. My stomach is in knots. We took a private transfer to the airport, but we're on the same flight as Nate and his family. There's security in being with my parents, and even my little sister, but it doesn't stop the churning in my stomach or the sharp ache in my chest as we shuffle through first class. Gideon and Sophia are on the right, three rows back, and Nate and Brody are across the aisle on the left.

Sophia and Gideon wear matching empathetic smiles as we pass, and Brody waves at me, but all I get is the top of Nate's head. His focus is on the phone in his hand. Brody elbows him, and he glances at his brother as we pass through into economy.

I changed my ticket so I could sit with my parents on the trip home. Tears prick behind my eyes, threatening to embarrass me in front of a plane full of mostly strangers.

I didn't see Nate again after Isaac outed us yesterday. I kept it together when I talked to Rix, but as soon as I was alone, I lost it. I spent the rest of the day locked in my room, crying my heart out. My mom ended up staying with me overnight, leaving dad on his own for his last night in Aruba.

Mom takes the window seat, I take the middle, and Cammie starts to slide into the seat next to mine.

"You can sit with Chase," I croak.

"We just spent the week together. He can handle sitting beside Dad for the next five hours."

Tears start to fall again. Cammie drops into her seat, and she and my mom engulf me in a hug from both sides.

"It'll be okay, honey," Mom says softly.

That just makes me cry harder.

"I'm sorry you're hurting," Cammie mumbles into my hair.

"He can't even look at me," I sob.

Mom kisses my temple. "He has a lot going on right now. Give him some time to process it all."

I swore her to secrecy before I told her what happened with Tristan's mother, followed by Nate's subsequent declaration and my insistence that he couldn't possibly be falling for me. "What if when he processes it all, he still thinks I'm right? I don't want to be right."

"Brody told Chase that Nate hasn't eaten anything since yesterday at brunch," Cammie whispers. "And he wouldn't leave his room at all yesterday."

"I should have kept my stupid mouth shut." I hiccup.

The flight attendant stops at our row and asks if everything is okay.

My dad assures them we're fine from across the aisle. But he asks for more tissues and a bottle of water when they have the chance.

"First of all, your mouth isn't stupid, honey, and I know right now every feeling you have is on fire, but when we're hurting, it's important to be especially kind to ourselves." Mom tucks my hair behind my ear. "You are incredibly perceptive and empathetic. Your concerns are valid, and voicing them was the right thing to do, even though it was hard and the results aren't the ones you hoped for. He's hurting right now, too, for a lot of reasons, and he needs time to sort through his feelings, just like

258

you do. You can't control his actions or reactions to what you say, but you can give yourself some grace."

"I just want my own happily ever after," I whisper. "What if it never happens?"

"If a weirdo like me can find my perfect match, so can you," Cammie assures me.

"Everyone is weird," I sniffle.

"So true, but I'm extra weird, and I own that. Remember when you told me it's better to live life scared than not live it at all?" Cammie says. "Maybe that's where Nate is. Maybe he's scared and hiding and he just needs time to figure it all out."

"What if he doesn't figure it out, though?" It's all been rolling around in my head for the past twenty-four hours. If I'd just accepted his words, where would I be now? Would I be smiling and happy? Would I be bleary-eyed because we'd stayed up half the night making love, instead of red-eyed because I've been crying? Would our last day in Aruba have been a fairy tale instead of sad?

How long would it have taken once we got home for the bottom to fall out? How quickly would he have realized he doesn't love me? That he never did. That it was wedding magic clouding his vision. Would it have been worth it?

Mom smiles softly. "If he doesn't figure it out, then he isn't the right guy for you."

"I have all these feelings for him, and I can't even tell him now," I whisper.

"Just give it time, honey. You might still get the chance," Mom says.

"What if I never find someone who sees all of me and deems me worthy of their love?" Despite what I said, I thought Nate liked the real me, the whole me.

Mom squeezes my hand. "You already have that, honey. Not just in me and your dad and Cammie, but also in your friends."

She's right, and after a moment I nod. "I want it with a partner, though. I want to find my one true love." I lean my head against her shoulder. "Why can't I have the fairy tale?"

"Remember that in every fairy tale, the prince and princess have to fight for their love, and there are always things that get in the way. Sometimes it's other people, and other times it's something inside themselves." She taps over her heart. "The deepest, truest love comes to us when we've learned how to fight for it. When we know each other's imperfections and our own, and can love ourselves and our partner wholly. Leave that space for Nate in your heart open, honey, and if he's deserving of it, he'll do the same for you."

CHAPTER 36
NATE

"Okay. This has got to end." Flip makes a circle motion around his face and plants his fists on his hips. "You're making me depressed. I know exactly what you need."

"I have exactly what I need." I hold up the box of After Eights, which are Essie's favorite. It's basically all I've eaten for the past ten days.

"If you eat any more of those, you're going to turn into one. Go shower and put on some clean clothes." He points to the bathroom.

"I don't want to go anywhere."

"I know, which is exactly why you need to go somewhere. There is a you-shaped groove in the fucking couch, dude. Your brother can't come back from his honeymoon and find you still in an espresso-depresso state. Either you get off your ass and into the shower, honey bear, or I will make you. I'm stronger than you, I'm tougher than you, and I have no problem getting naked with you."

He's right about all of it, and he's also fucking relentless when he puts his mind to something, so I toss the box of After Eights on the table and drag my ass off the couch.

"And do not put that shirt back on. It's really starting to stink!" he yells after me.

I fire the bird over my shoulder. I've changed into this shirt every day when I get home from work since we got home from Aruba. Essie slept in it one night, and it smelled like her, and I refuse to wash it, even though it smells more like my BO than her at this point.

Twenty minutes later, I'm wearing dress pants and a polo. Flip is dressed similarly.

"Where are you taking me, anyway?"

"To see some of my favorite ladies."

"I'm not in the mood for a strip club, Flip."

"I'm not in the mood for your bad attitude, honey bear. We are going out, and we're going to have fun, and that's the end of the fucking story."

Ten minutes later we're driving down a residential street, and there isn't one strip club in sight. Flip turns right into Sunny Acres Retirement Village.

"Are we going to see your grandma or something?"

"We're going to see someone's grandma, but not mine."

I perk up for half a second. "Essie's?"

He gives me a look. "You are such a fucking idiot. You know that, right?"

I frown.

He shakes his head. "You should have seen your face at the prospect of seeing Essie's grandma. If you miss her that much, why aren't you doing anything about it?"

I cross my arms and keep my mouth shut. I don't know what to think or feel. My chest aches these days in a way that's become familiar and really unpleasant.

Flip parks in the visitors' area and pops the trunk. Inside are two baskets of roses.

"What are these for?"

"You."

My eyebrows try to meet each other.

He shakes his head. "For a smart guy, you can be exceptionally clueless. They're for all the single old ladies. And the nursing staff. And some of the old men, too. Anyone who looks like they might need a rose gets a rose." He thrusts a basket at me.

I follow him up the walkway and into the home. It smells like old people, mints, cleaning supplies, and meatloaf.

"Flip!" someone exclaims.

"He's here!"

"Oh! He brought a friend!"

We're immediately bombarded by a gaggle of elderly ladies, all of whom are dressed like they're ready for Sunday night Mass. Flip accepts hugs and doesn't even flinch when a couple of the ladies pat his ass. They have stars in their eyes.

"Henny, Freida, Gretchen, Honey, and Jillian, this is my roommate, Nate. He's joining us for bingo."

"Is he a hockey player?"

"Is he your boyfriend?"

"He wishes he was my boyfriend, isn't that right, honey bear?" Flip winks at me.

I would flip him off if we weren't surrounded by octogenarians. I shake my head. "He's too high maintenance, and I like women."

"You're the high-maintenance one."

"You can sit with me, Nate. I'll take good care of you." A tiny lady who barely reaches my elbow takes my arm, the creases in her face deepening as she smiles up at me.

We're herded down the hall, our group growing as we get closer to the dining room. Flip and I hand a rose to pretty much anyone we talk to.

"How often do you do this?" I ask.

"Off season? Every week. During the season, whenever I don't have a game and we're not on the road."

"Does Hemi ever come and do photos?"

"Nah. I do this for me." The ladies usher us to one of the long tables and make sure no one takes our seats while we help them into theirs.

We spend the next hour playing bingo. It's definitely preferable to sitting on the couch feeling sorry for myself. And the stories these ladies tell are something else. At the end, Flip and I help the staff put everything away—and he flirts with all the nurses.

A husband and wife are some of the last to leave. She's in a wheelchair, and he has a cane, so the nurses help pull her away from the table and get her turned around. He tucks his cane into the corner and fusses over her, making sure she's comfortable before he hobbles around behind her and pushes her toward the doors.

"They've been married for sixty-five years," Flip says.

"That's a long time."

"It could be you if you get your head out of your ass," he says pointedly.

"Is this why you brought me here? So I can see what I'll look like in sixty years?"

"I brought you here because despite your black cloud of doom, you're a good-looking guy, and these ladies enjoy eye candy. And because I've had enough of the moping. But yeah, basically that's the reason. For a guy who says he doesn't believe in love, you seem pretty lovesick to me these days."

I sigh.

"You telling me you don't want that to be your future?" He motions to the couple who are almost at the doors.

I tuck my hand in my pocket.

"Because honestly, I don't have a problem stepping in and making it my future if you decide you can't or won't."

I frown. "You don't want Essie."

"You don't know that."

I know someone aside from me who would be absolutely gutted if he ended up with Essie. And me? I don't know if I'd ever get over it. How would I deal with family Christmas if they become Madden-and-Stiles fests? I'd be the biggest grinch in town.

"Come on." He claps me on the shoulder. "Let's go home."

We say good night to the staff and head out into the balmy August night.

"All right, buddy," Flip says once we're on the road. "You have to spit it out. You've got all the feelings, and you're holding everything inside. It's eating you alive and making you miserable."

I cross my arms. "You waited until we're in the car and I can't escape to start pushing, huh?"

"I know how much your mom leaving fucked Tristan up, and I'm pretty sure it fucked up you and Brody just as much, so let's get your cards on the table so you can start figuring your shit out."

"How am I supposed to have faith in love when one of the people who was supposed to love me unconditionally fucking bailed? All we got was a fucking Christmas card addressed to the three of us, sent to my fucking dad's house since I was a kid. And then she tries to come back into our lives after more than a decade and a half? What am I supposed to do with that?"

"Well, right now you're angry. How do you want to feel about it?" Flip asks.

"I don't want to care. I don't want it to hurt, but it fucking does. It hurts all the damn time. And then I think I have relationships figured out with Lisa, and she cheats on me with some guy who's more emotionally available! Nothing lasts!"

"Some things last," he argues. "Look at my parents. Look at Essie's parents."

"Nothing lasts for me. I told Essie I was falling for her, and she told me I wasn't, that I couldn't be." I don't tell Flip the rest of that story. About how I was already reeling because of my mother. Or that I kept defaulting to sex with Essie so I wouldn't have to deal with the fucking feelings.

"Is she right?" Flip asks.

"I don't know. I don't think so. This hurts way more than it did when Lisa and I ended. My heart feels like it's been put in a meat grinder. My chest physically aches."

"Is this how you want to live for the rest of your life?"

"What kind of question is that?"

"Look, man, I know this stuff is hard, but if you don't want to keep running into the same wall, you have to deal with it. It won't get better if you don't."

"You mean therapy."

"Yeah, I mean therapy."

"It's gonna suck."

"At first, yeah. But don't you think you deserve a better life, where the wounds your mom left behind aren't constantly bleeding?"

I rub my bottom lip. "I didn't really think about it that way."

"Essie's a great person. She deserves someone who can give her the fairy tale she's always dreamed about. You can be that guy, Nate, but you have to do the work. Show her she's worth it."

"What if I do the work and she still doesn't want me?"

"Wouldn't you rather try and know for sure than spend the rest of your life wondering what could have been?"

CHAPTER 37
ESSIE

"Oh my gosh, your hair!" Dred exclaims.

"Is it too drastic? It's too drastic, isn't it?" I run my fingers through it self-consciously.

"No. I love the pink streaks. It's very you." She glances at the box sitting close to the door. "What's going on here? And what the heck are you eating?"

Dred and I are going to the Watering Hole to grab a bite to eat. We've been home from Aruba for two weeks, and I've completed my Breakup Checklist. I watched all my favorite princess movies, took out my aggression and sadness on my dartboard, got a magic wand tattoo on my hip, and scrapbooked the heck out of the wedding photos I took. It's time to move forward.

"It's homemade chocolate icing." Another item from my Breakup Checklist.

"And you're eating it straight up?"

"Yup, while I watched all my favorite princess movies." I use the spoon to point to the box. "And I cleaned out my lingerie drawer. Everything that I wore for Nate had to go."

She nods slowly. "You guys had a lot of sex, huh?"

"We did." I wish I'd been able to keep my heart out of it, but

I've never been very good at that. I set the icing on the counter and grab my purse.

"You talk to him at all?" Dred asks as we step out into the hall.

I shake my head and make sure my apartment door is locked before we walk to the elevators. "He needs to figure himself out, and I need to give him the space to do that, even though it hurts." The elevator arrives, and we climb aboard. It's empty apart from us.

"Flip took him to retirement-village bingo the other night," Dred notes.

I laugh at the prospect of grumpy, gorgeous Nate surrounded by grandmas. And then I almost burst into tears.

Dred puts her arm around me. "Sorry. We don't have to talk about him."

"I'm fine. Just residual feelings leaking out." I pluck a tissue from my purse and dab at the corners of my eyes. "I guess that means he's past the brokenhearted phase."

The elevator doors slide open, and we step out into the warm August night.

"Eh, I don't know about that. I think it's more that Flip was tired of all the moping and felt like he needed to do something other than sit around the apartment and be sad."

It's a short walk to the Watering Hole. The familiar scent of wings, pizza, and beer greets me as we enter the pub. This is what I need—a dose of normalcy. I'm no stranger to shaking off heartbreak, but it feels harder this time.

We grab a table and order margaritas and some apps to share.

"Rix and Tristan look like they're having the best time on their honeymoon," Dred says.

"She's in her glory, for sure." Rix has been sending daily updates in our Babe chat. "And she really, really needed this vacation before she goes back to school in the fall."

"She definitely deserves the break," Dred agrees.

We talk and eat, and even though my heart still hurts, it feels good to be out with a friend.

My phone buzzes with a new message, and I glance at the screen. My stomach lurches and my heart rate spikes.

"Is he finally reaching out?" Dred asks. She doesn't seem that surprised.

I bite my lip. "Should I check it? I should check it."

"Do you want to check it?"

"Yes. No. Yes. It's been two weeks. It feels like an eternity." I open the message.

NATE

Hey. I'm so sorry for the silence. I've been working through my stuff. I don't know if you're up for it, but I'd really like to see you.

"He wants to meet up," I whisper.

"What do you want?" Dred asks.

For my heart to stop hurting. To be able to trust my gut. To give my soft parts to the right person. "To hear what he has to say."

"Then that's what you should do."

ESSIE

Okay.

NATE

Are you free tonight?

ESSIE

I'm with Dred right now.

NATE

Will you be available later? I could come to you.

My apartment is not ready for Nate, and I'm not ready for Nate to be in my apartment. Neutral territory would be better.

ESSIE

How about the Pancake House?

NATE

Just tell me what time, and I'll meet you there.

ESSIE

Nine?

NATE

I'll see you then.

Thank you.

"I'm meeting him in less than two hours," I tell Dred. "Should I go home and change?"

"If you feel like you need to, but he's woken up beside you plenty of times, hasn't he?"

"He has."

"So you don't need to show him what he's missing. He already knows."

Nate is at the Pancake House when I arrive. He looks gorgeous, and nervous, and I have no idea what's about to happen. I want to hear him out, but I don't want to open myself up for another shot of heartache.

He stands and runs his hands over his thighs. "Hey."

"Hey." I slip into the booth before he can make a move to touch me. We're not in a place where I can handle physical contact.

He takes his seat.

Rainbow, the server, comes over with coffee and water. "You need a few minutes with the menu?"

"I'll have the cookies and cream milkshake, please." I've been eating my feelings all day, why stop now?

"I'll have the same," Nate says.

"Sure thing!" Rainbow flounces off.

"How are you?" Nate asks. "You look good. You look great. I love the hair."

"Thanks." I finger one of the pink streaks. "I'm okay. How are you?"

"Okay. Getting better. The last couple of weeks have been rough," he admits.

I nod. "Yeah. They haven't been my favorite."

He swallows. "I wanted to message before today, but I wasn't ready."

"But you're ready now?" Everything feels so strained.

He nods.

"What are you ready for?"

"To talk things out." He fidgets with the napkin. "You were right, Ess. I didn't want you to be, but you were."

My stomach sinks and knots. I look down at my hands and fight the tears. I don't know if I'm ready to hear this.

"Not about me falling for you," he rushes on. "I'm definitely in love with you."

My heart drops from my throat back into my chest.

"But you were right that I was reacting to all the things happening around us. My mom showing up, taking the money…" He pauses to clear his throat. "I couldn't see anything clearly. And it wasn't until I got home and had some time to process that I realized every time you stepped in to take care of me and offer me support, I diverted all my feelings into sex."

Rainbow sets our shakes on the table and quietly rushes away, red faced.

"I started therapy today," Nate says softly.

"You did?" The hope blossoming in my chest scares the hell out of me.

He nods.

"How was it?"

"Pretty fucking awful, to be honest." The pain in his voice and behind his eyes affirms this truth.

"Will you go again?" It's one thing to start therapy; it's another to stick with it.

"Yeah. Twice a week until I can sort through the hardest shit. Then we'll adjust. I have some pretty deep-seated mommy issues, Ess."

"I know." I reach across the table, covering his hand with mine. "I'm sorry she's such a disappointment."

"Me too." He sighs. "But I don't want to go through life not being able to love someone the way they deserve, and you really deserve to have someone's whole heart, Ess."

"So do you," I whisper.

"I want to be able to accept that, and believe it, but I think it's going to take some work to get there." He licks his lips. "I don't know how long, but maybe you can give me some time to prove I'm going to make the effort?"

My whole body feels cold. I'm terrified that I could be setting myself up all over again. But he's doing and saying all the right things. I care about him too much to just walk away.

So I nod. "I can give you time."

CHAPTER 38
NATE

"I get it now," I tell my brother.

He and Rix returned from Aruba yesterday and invited me and Flip over for fajita and margarita night. Dred and Essie are coming, too. I haven't seen Ess since we met up at the Pancake House, but we're texting.

"Therapy is work, and sometimes it really sucks, but it's worth it. Essie is worth it," I explain.

He smiles faintly. "It changes everything, doesn't it?"

"It really does. I see the mistakes I was making clearly now, and I'm going to do my best not to make them again."

Flip's hand goes to his chest. "I'm so fucking proud of you, honey bear." He means it, too.

"You won't be perfect, and some sessions will hurt more than others," Tristan cautions. "Some days you'll struggle not to fall back into old patterns, but now you know they exist."

I nod. "That's exactly it. I might not always catch myself in the moment, but I can reflect on it, and hopefully get better at it."

"You will. It's like everything—it takes time and practice." He claps me on the shoulder. "You let me know if you need to get out some of the feelings with workouts. We can hit the gym, the ice, whatever you need, brother."

"We've been doing that a lot." I motion to Flip.

"Good. Now that I'm back, I can join you."

The doorbell rings, and Rix comes rushing down the hall. "Nate! Big brother! I didn't know you were already here!" She skids right into Tristan and tips her chin up for a kiss. She gives me and Flip both a quick hug. "Be right back."

Her excited squeal echoes off the walls.

"Essie must be here," Tristan says wryly.

"Yeah." I run a hand over my chest and then through my hair.

"How are things going there?" Tristan asks.

"Trying not to fuck things up again and be the kind of guy we both deserve," I reply.

"You're already making progress," he assures me.

Dred, Essie, and Rix appear.

Essie looks incredible in a pink summer dress that matches the streaks in her hair.

"Essie! The hair is my favorite!" Flip throws his arms around her, picks her up, and spins her. When he sets her down, he takes her hand and twirls her. "I love this new look."

I want to punch him.

"It's my breakup makeover," she says.

And now I want to punch myself.

Dred gives me an empathetic smile.

Essie finally turns her attention to me. "Hi, Nate."

"Hey, Ess."

"Anyone want a drink?" Rix asks.

Everyone raises their hand.

"I'll help you!" Essie links arms with her. "And so will Dred." The three of them disappear into the kitchen.

Flip rocks back on his heels. "You're really showing her how you feel, eh?"

"What the hell am I supposed to do with all of you standing around watching us?"

"Tell her it's great to see her. That you miss her, that your life is shit without her. Did you even bring her a gift?" Flip folds his arms over his chest.

"Why would I bring a gift to fajita night?"

"Why would you bring a gift to fajita night?" Flip parrots.

I look to Tristan.

He shrugs. "Flip has a point."

I throw my hands in the air. "Where was this advice an hour ago when we weren't both already here?"

Flip is all fucking smiles. "I didn't realize you were this much of a relationship novice."

"I'm rusty!"

"You can say that again." Flip crosses his arms. "Nut up or shut up, dude. Don't be a crying little chicken bitch if she's the one for you."

"I was going to wait until later," I mutter.

"Well, there might not be a later if you keep letting me step all over your toes."

"Why do the three of you look so serious? You can't be serious on fajita night!" Rix demands as she reappears.

The girls traipse in with margaritas.

Flip beelines it for Essie. "What are you doing after fajita night? Want to watch a movie with me?"

"I gotta go for a walk." I head for the door.

"Nate! Buddy, where you goin'?" Flip calls after me.

"Is he okay?" Dred asks.

It takes me five minutes to walk to the closest flower shop. I buy two dozen pink roses, a box of Essie's favorite chocolates, and a pink heart pillow to add to her collection before I return to Tristan's.

Everyone is sitting in the living room, drinking their cocktails and eating tortilla chips with salsa, queso, and Rix's famous street corn dip.

Flip grins when he sees me. "Honey bear! You shouldn't have!"

"I didn't." I cross over to Essie. "I got you…stuff."

"Smooth…" Flip coughs.

I shoot him a dirty look. "Can you fuck off? You're not helping."

Flip's eyes go comically wide. "Did I not do my part by getting your sorry ass off the couch? Was it not me who opened your eyes to the possibility of what you might be missing out on if you kept going the way you were? Did I not hook you up with a kickass therapist?"

I poke at my cheek with my tongue. "You did all those things, but I need you to not make this any harder or more awkward than it already is." I turn back to Essie. "Can we go talk in the kitchen for a minute and leave the heckler here?"

"Sure." Essie leaves her drink on the table. I would help her up if my arms weren't laden with things. We leave our friends and Flip's motor mouth and disappear into the kitchen.

"I got you flowers." I hold them out.

"They're really pretty." She takes them from me. "Thank you."

"And I got you a heart pillow and chocolate." I thrust them at her. "They're your favorite. The chocolate, I mean. And we both know you love heart pillows."

"I do love chocolate and heart pillows."

I shove my hands in my pockets. Pull them out. Run one through my hair.

"Did you go out and buy all this stuff for a reason?" she asks softly.

"Tristan and Flip were razzing me. I was nervous about seeing you today, and I'm pretty sure I'm fucking all of this up. Can I hug you, please?" My eyes close. *Yeah, I'm really fucking this up.* I crack a lid.

Essie looks up at me with soft eyes as she steps forward and wraps her arms around my waist. I fold my arms over her, soaking up the contact like a balm. "I've missed you so much, Ess. So fucking much."

"I've missed you too," she whispers. Eventually she pulls away. "How's therapy?"

"Hard. It sucks a lot right now, but it'll get easier with time." I want to reassure her that I'm not going to stop going. "I know it's important that I do the work so I can have the kind of relationships I deserve, and so I can be a good partner."

She smiles softly. "I'm really happy to hear that."

"Do you think maybe you'd want to go on a date with me?"

Her lips pull to the side, and her eyes drop to the floor for a moment before they meet mine. "Can I think about it?"

My stomach sinks, but I nod anyway. "Of course. Take all the time you need."

CHAPTER 39

ESSIE

On Sunday afternoon, my phone pings.

NATE

How's the thinking going?

ESSIE

As well as can be expected.

NATE

Is there anything I can do to help?

ESSIE

Send a selfie.

A picture of Nate with my favorite furrowed brow appears.

ESSIE

Amending: send a shirtless selfie.

Another picture comes through. This time Nate's hair is mussed, and he's standing in front of a full-length mirror in a pair of dress pants.

NATE

Is this helpful?

> **ESSIE**
> Very.
>
> Send a shirtless selfie of you ironing your shirt.

NATE
???

> **ESSIE**
> It helps me think.

It takes a few minutes, but the selfie pops up.

NATE
Is there anything else you need?

Assistance picking an outfit, perhaps?

I'm here to support however I can.

> **ESSIE**
> Thanks. I'll let you know if I think of something.

Monday evening, my phone pings again.

NATE
How's the thinking going today?

> **ESSIE**
> Decent.

NATE
This seems like an upgrade. How are the roses holding up?

> **ESSIE**
> Quite well.

I snap a photo of the overflowing vase and send it to him.

NATE
Is that your bedroom? O_o

> Where did you put the pillow?

I snap a close-up of the pillow and send it along.

NATE

> Catalina!

> Tell her I miss her.

> I miss you.

My phone rings, and I don't hesitate to answer. "Hi."

"Hi. It's good to hear your voice." He sighs.

"It's good to hear yours too." I flop down on my bed and hug Catalina to my chest. "How's work?"

"Good. It's good. It's been keeping me busy, which I need right now. Flip and Tristan are testing out the prototype with me tomorrow, so that's exciting."

"That's great! This could be your engineering skate-design breakout, and right at the beginning of your career. You should be so proud of yourself, Nate. I know I am."

"Thanks, Essie. Really the prototype is just step one, and it'll take a while to get it where it needs to be, but it's affirming to have a team that supports me. How's your work?"

"I'm on a fantasy set right now, and one of the senior artists has taken me under her wing. It's been a challenge, and I love it."

"That's great, Ess. I saw one of your posts, but I didn't comment because I wanted to respect your space. I didn't want to be a creeper."

I want to crawl through the phone and hug him. "You're not a creeper unless you start liking my stuff from five years ago and commenting on all of it."

"I was only planning to go back three years," he jokes.

"Totally reasonable and safely outside of creeper territory." I trade Catalina for the heart pillow he bought me and hug it to my chest. It's soft and fuzzy and my new favorite. "How's therapy?"

He exhales a long breath.

"That good, eh?" I laugh, but I'm nervous.

"Half the time it's as if she can read my mind. Like, how dare she know me so well already, you know? What is she, a witch?" He chuckles. "Mostly it's good, though, even though it's hard."

"What do you talk about?" This is what I want most from him, for him to open up to me, too. To share the parts of himself he's afraid to share with anyone else.

"The obvious stuff—my mom, what it was like growing up before she left, what it was like after, what my relationships have been like." His voice drops to a whisper. "I talk about you a lot, too."

"Oh?" My heart stutters.

"I told her all the reasons I'm in love with you."

"Do you want to tell me about those?" My heart beats faster. He's showing me he's trying in all the ways that count, that he thinks I'm worth the effort.

"You have the most amazing, open heart."

"Sometimes it gets me into trouble," I counter.

"I think that's probably true for all of us," he replies. "You're truly sunshine and rainbows. You make people happy just by being you. Talking to you right now is the highlight of my day."

My heart squeezes. I've missed him so much—the banter, planning things with him, spending time with him. So many times he's affirmed me without even knowing, and maybe this time it's intentional, but it's softening my already marshmallow soft heart. "It's the highlight of mine, too."

"You're smart and fun to be around. You're a caretaker, and you always show up for people when it matters the most." He clears his throat. "You have such beautiful faith in the power of love. I was so jaded that I couldn't understand why you'd welcome the potential for pain. It scared the hell out of me."

"Does it still scare you?" My heart hammers in my chest. He's trying so hard, sharing his vulnerability with me.

"Absolutely. But it's worth it if it means I get to have a life that's full and it includes people like you."

"I'm done thinking," I blurt. "I'll go on a date with you."

CHAPTER 40
NATE

"Looking good, my man." Flip stops eating his giant bowl of KD long enough to give me an approving thumbs-up and a nod. "Where are you taking Essie for dinner?"

"We're going to Scaramouche, and then I'm taking her to see *Wicked* the musical."

Tonight is our first official date. The past few weeks have been hard, but I'm making strides in therapy and learning how to let my walls down so I can love the people in my life the way they deserve.

"Nice. She'll love that." Flip nods his approval.

"I think so, too." I check for my phone, wallet, and keys before I grab the bouquet of hot pink flowers and the box of chocolates from the counter. "You have plans tonight?"

Flip glances at his phone. "A couple of the guys are talking about going to the Watering Hole. I might join them."

"Say hi to everyone, if you do."

"I will. Have fun and play safe, honey bear." He winks.

I have no expectations for tonight, other than spending time with Essie. Would I love to end up curled around her and wake up the next morning with her hair in my face? Absolutely. But one step at a time.

I leave Flip to his neon noodles and drive the short distance to Essie's apartment. We all live in the same area, close to the arena and the business sector of downtown. Essie buzzes me in, and my heart rate jacks up as the elevator climbs to her floor.

Her door opens before I can even knock.

"Hi." Seeing her for the first time in days is like seeing a rainbow after a storm. She's wearing a long, gauzy pink dress, and her dark hair with matching pink streaks falls in loose waves over her shoulders. Her makeup is light, eyes rimmed in liner to make them pop, and her lips are glossy. "You look incredible."

The smile that lights up her face is better than a tropical sunrise. "And you look like a seven-course meal, including my favorite dessert."

"I'm glad you approve." I hold out the flowers. "I brought you something pretty."

"They're beautiful." She brings them to her nose, eyes fluttering closed as she inhales.

"Just like you." I hold out the chocolates. "And I brought you something sweet, also just like you."

"You are so thoughtful." She motions for me to follow her. "Come in for a minute. I want to put these in water."

I haven't been here since I dropped off the box of sashes for the girls, and tonight I see it with fresh eyes. The space really is an homage to Essie's personality. Everything is bright and soft and pretty, just like her.

She retrieves a vase and fills it with water and the flower food before she carefully arranges the flowers. "They really are gorgeous, Nate." She turns and wraps her arms around my waist, setting her cheek against my chest on a soft sigh. "I missed you."

I fold her in my arms and kiss the top of her head, absorbing the warmth, appreciating the way I instantly settle when I have her close like this. "I missed you, too."

We stand there for a long time, just holding each other.

Finally, she steps back, smiles up at me, and pats me on the chest. "I could happily stand here all night, but you have this great date planned, so we should probably go on it."

"Seems like a good idea," I agree.

She slips her feet into a pair of strappy sandals, grabs her heart-shaped, hot pink, jewel-encrusted purse, and links her arm with mine. We leave her apartment and take the elevator to the lobby. I help her into the passenger seat before I round the hood and take my place behind the wheel.

Essie angles her body toward me. "How was your day?"

"Good, but long. I couldn't wait to see you. How about yours?"

"The same." She skims the shell of my ear. "But the fantasy show I'm working on has been so much fun."

"Tell me more about that." I love the way she grows animated when she's excited about something.

"It's all princes and princesses, which is obviously right up my alley. And today I worked on one of the elves. It really pushes me to grow my skill set," she explains.

"I'd love to see you in action one day."

Her eyes light up. "I could practice on you."

Her hands on my face, transforming me into something else? Being turned into her art? "Sure. Yeah. I'd be game."

She shimmies in her seat. "Halloween could be so fun this year."

"Yeah. It could." Her enthusiasm gives me hope that she can see a future with me the way I can with her.

I pull into the restaurant parking lot.

"Oh wow. This is fancy."

"It's our first official date. I wanted it to be special." I take her hand and press my lips to her knuckles. "Stay right here, please."

"Okay."

I unbuckle my seat belt and hop out of the car, coming around to open her door.

She takes my hand and carefully steps out.

It's a beautiful night. Though the evenings are starting to cool with the promise of fall. Heads turn as we enter the restaurant. That's always the way it is with Essie. She's so beautiful that she stops traffic and earns endless double takes. But for me, it's about so much more than how she looks. She brings the most wonderful energy into a room, and I love that I get to stand beside her and soak it all in.

The host is a couple years younger than we are. His eyes flare as he looks at Essie, and he strobe-blinks several times before his attention moves to me.

"I have a reservation for two under Stiles." I absolutely used my brother's connections.

"Stiles. Yes. Thank you so much for joining us."

"It's our first date." Essie's smile nearly knocks the guy unconscious.

"Well, Mr. Stiles must think very highly of you," the host croaks.

"Is that right, Mr. Stiles?" She aims her radiant smile at me.

"Absolutely." I squeeze her gently.

"I'll just show you to your table." The host leads us to a private terrace.

"This is so nice, Nate." Essie reaches across the table, and I take her hand.

"Good. I'm glad I chose right."

"Honestly, you could have taken me to East Side, and I would have loved it."

"Even with the screaming children?"

She smiles. "The music here is more of a mood setter, but we would have made the best of it."

"Tristan and Rix still go there once a month with Flip," I muse.

"I've gone with them a couple of times. The unlimited salad and bread are tough to beat."

"This is true." I run my thumb back and forth over her hand.

We order appetizers and drinks and talk about work and our friends, holding hands across the table. It feels so good to be with her again, to have the closeness that seems to come so easily in her presence.

"What's going on in your head?" Essie asks.

"I'm just so grateful that you're here and willing to give me another chance," I admit. "I've never been great at talking about my feelings, or expressing them in other healthy ways, but with you, I want to be."

"I know you're putting all the work in, Nate. I see the difference, and I know it can't be easy." She squeezes my hand.

"When I was younger and my mom was still with us, I learned it was better to stay quiet."

"To avoid fighting?"

"Sort of. But it was mostly one-sided. We were just trying to keep the peace. But I can see now why my relationship with Lisa ended the way it did. I'm not excusing her for cheating on me. She could have and should have ended things before it ever came to that, but I played a part by not being open with my feelings. I'm working on being better at that. You are such an incredible light, Essie, and you give your heart so completely to the people you care about. I want to honor that and give you the same kind of love back, because it's what we both deserve."

Her eyes turn glassy, and her chin wobbles.

My throat tightens. "Ess?"

"It's good emotion." She raises our hands and kisses the back of mine. "I love that you're doing this, not just for us, but for you and the people you care about. I see all that love inside you, and I'm so thankful that I get to be one of the people you share it with. I'll be here to love you and listen whenever you need to talk things through, especially when it's hard."

"You're amazing," I whisper.

"So are you," she whispers back.

"I'm really glad your best friend married my brother."

"Me too."

The server delivers our appetizers, and we take a quick spin through the menu so we can order our mains.

Then Essie shifts gears as she pops a bite of beet salad into her mouth. "Talk to me about the prototype and how things are going."

"We made some tweaks, so we're moving into round two of testing."

"That's so exciting. What does that entail? Tell me all about it." She smiles expectantly. "Give me all the science-y details."

"So, comfort and support are key to a good skate, but there are other elements to consider. The thickness of the blade, the shape and curve, and the weight of the player all need to be factored in. The best skates on the market most accurately take in force as it relates to the conversion of the ice into water, which allows for better speed. We use specific formulas to determine the ideal combination for frictional heat production, which is related to the thermal conductivity of metals. Oh, and skates have two working edges with a hollow curve in the center to allow for this."

Essie has stopped eating her salad.

"Sorry. I'm probably boring you."

"Not even a little." She licks her lips and leans in, whispering, "A lot of this is over my head, but my panties are damp, so please keep sciencing me."

I fight a grin. "Sciencing is not a verb."

"I know, but it makes your brow furrow, which also makes my panties damp, so it's my new favorite word. Please, keep explaining force and friction."

So I do, and Essie asks all kinds of questions, hanging on my every word, making me feel like everything I say matters, like I'm the center of her universe.

This is what love is supposed to be like. This feeling is the reason I'm willing to do the work and talk through all the hard things.

After dinner, we cross the street and walk down the block.

"Oh my gosh." She grabs my arm as I guide her to the box office. "You're taking me to the theater?"

"I am."

She gazes up at me, eyes soft and warm. "Best first date ever, Nathan."

We have great seats, and Essie hugs my arm through the entire performance. I've never been one for live theater, but Essie is almost as entertaining as the musical numbers. She smiles and laughs, eyes lit up with delight, and I spend half of it watching her instead of the people on the stage. I couldn't tell you what the musical was about, but I definitely enjoyed the experience.

Afterward, I guide her back to the car and head for her place.

"Thank you for such a wonderful first date." She links her pinkie with mine.

"I'm sorry it took six years for it to happen."

"Totally worth the wait." She tips her head. "I don't really want it to end yet, though."

I glance at her. "Do you want to go to the Pancake House or something?"

"You could come up to my place," she suggests.

"Yeah?"

"Yeah."

I park in a visitor's spot, and we hold hands while we wait for the elevator. It's empty apart from us, so when the doors close, she links her fingers behind my neck, her body flush against mine. "Will you stay the night?"

"Do you want me to?"

"I've missed waking up with you wrapped around me."

"Me too." I trace the edge of her jaw with my finger. "I'm a huge fan of all-night snuggles."

"Same," she agrees.

The elevator dings, signaling our arrival at her floor. Essie exits, and I follow her down the hall. The tension between us has been growing all evening. I don't want to make assumptions about where this will go—apart from all-night snuggles—but I get my answer as soon as we're inside her apartment.

"Thank you for taking care of your heart so we can be good at taking care of each other's." Essie drags my mouth to hers.

We both groan as our tongues brush.

"Wait." I pull back, and Essie frowns.

I cup her face in my hands. "I have to ask you something before this goes any further."

"Okay." Essie gazes up at me with uncertain, but hopeful eyes.

"I know we just had our first date, but will you be my girl-friend? Officially."

"Yes. Absolutely. Nothing would make me happier." She tips her head. "Well, that and getting you into my bedroom."

"I can make that happen." I lift her off the floor and carry her down the hall.

When we cross the threshold I set her down and break the kiss. "Wow."

Essie looks nervous. "I warned you. It's very princessy."

The walls aren't quite white but tinged with a hint of pink. A four-poster bed takes up one wall. The nightstands bracketing her bed are white, and gauzy curtains are pulled back to reveal the exceptional number of throw pillows, all in various shades of pink. Catalina, ratty and well loved, is perched on her night-stand. "It's perfectly you."

"You don't hate it?" She wrings her hands.

I take them in mine. "No. Not at all." Would this be a choice I would make for myself? No. But it's a reflection of the woman I'm in love with, and therefore, I also love this room. "I feel like the forbidden prince who's come to steal you away."

An impish smile curves Essie's pretty lips. "You definitely could be."

I arch a brow.

She slips my tie around her hand, and her voice drops to a

sultry whisper. "Would you like to be my forbidden prince, Nate?"

I nod slowly. "Yeah, I think I would. Do you want to be the sweet princess I plan to steal from the castle and keep for my own?"

Excitement flashes in her eyes. "So, so much." She pushes on my chest.

I frown.

"Give me a minute. I need to get ready for my prince."

I still don't move.

"Unless you're opposed to naughty princess lingerie?"

It takes a moment for that to click. "Not even remotely opposed." I step out and head for the living room. "I'll be out here, waiting."

Essie closes the door. I've never engaged in role play before, but based on what's happening in my pants, I'm here for it. I loosen my tie and open the first few buttons on my shirt. I also run to the bathroom to swish with mouthwash and mess up my hair, going for the roguish, rumpled, forbidden-prince look, before I return to my place outside her door.

"Oh my prince, where are you?" she calls.

I take it as a sign that she's ready and crack the bedroom door. The only illumination comes from the lamp beside her bed. It takes a moment for my eyes to adjust. Movement comes from behind the gauzy curtain. "Oh my prince, my forbidden love, when will you save me from this wretched existence?" Essie murmurs.

I smile and close the door with a quiet snick. I cross to the bed, carefully pulling the curtain back and hooking it on the post. My breath leaves me on a whoosh.

The pillows have been swept to the floor, the covers pulled back. Essie lies on the pale pink sheets, hair fanned across the pillow, eyes closed. One hand lies palm up on the mattress, the other rests low on her stomach. Her sheer pink negligee, trimmed in lace, dips low in the front and barely skims the top of her thighs. The heart shields decorating her nipples glint enticingly.

She is the most stunning woman in the world, and she's agreed to be mine. I reach out and skim her cheek, channeling my inner forbidden prince—but I don't have much experience there. I do have experience lusting after this woman and wanting to find a way to hold her perfect, soft heart.

She sighs and chases the touch, my fingers dancing over her cheek.

"My sweet princess." I capture her hand in mine and bring it to my lips. "I've come to steal you away."

Her eyes flutter open on a gasp. "Is it really you?" She sits up in a rush, eyes wide. "Please don't let this be a dream."

I place her hand against my chest. "Do I feel like a dream, my love?"

"You're truly here!" She giggles, cups my face in her hands, and kisses me, but she pulls back a moment later, eyes wide with pretend panic. "How ever did you get past the guards?"

I search for a plausible way to have tricked the fictional guards. "I pretended I was but a mere servant and dosed their mead with fairy dust. They will slumber for hours." I may or may not have spent a lot of time watching princess movies over the past few weeks just to feel close to Essie.

She runs her hands down my chest, bottom lip sliding through her teeth. "We have hours?"

"That's right, my love." I brush over her nipple with my thumb. "Hours for me to kiss every inch of you." I skim her hip and dip between her thighs. "To bring you limitless pleasure." I kiss the edge of her jaw. "To worship you." I take her face in my hands. "To make you mine."

"That's all I want," she whispers against my lips.

We kiss while she undresses me and pulls me onto the bed. I stretch out over her, settling in the cradle of her hips. "I would slay a thousand dragons to be with you."

She runs her fingers through my hair. "Claim me, Nathan. Take me. Make me yours."

"Always mine." I kiss my way down her body, obsessed with the soft sounds she makes and the way her nails press into my shoulders as I make her come with my mouth, and then again with my fingers.

I pepper every inch of her with kisses as I work my way back to her lips. "Can this stay on?"

She grins. "You like my princess lingerie?"

"I love your princess lingerie." I suck a nipple through the sheer fabric. "You are unbearably sexy."

"So are you." She hooks her leg over my hip. "Please make love to me."

I settle between her thighs, and my erection slides over slick, hot skin. I hold her gaze as I sink into her, joining us.

"I love you," I whisper against her lips.

Her expression softens, eyes glassy with desire. "I love you, too."

"With my whole heart," I promise.

We move together, limbs entwined, eyes fixed on each other. My heart is safe with her, protected, cared for. I feel it in the gentle way she invites me inside her, mind, body, and soul.

She's everything I've ever wanted, and I'll spend the rest of my life making sure her heart is cared for in the same tender way she cares for mine.

My sunshine-and-rainbows other half.

The love of my life.

The woman of my dreams.

"Where the heck is it?" I plant my hands on my hips, close my eyes, inhale through my nose, and exhale through my mouth. "Please be there when I open my eyes."

I crack a lid, but my most favorite dress of all is still not where I expect it to be. To be fair, *nothing* I own is where I expect it to be anymore.

"Do not murder your very smart, very thoughtful, exceptionally organized, well-endowed, hot-as-hell boyfriend who embraces you and your slightly manic love of all things pink and romance because you cannot find your dress. Or literally anything you own," I mutter.

"Who you talking to, sweetness?" Nate appears out of nowhere.

I shriek and slap a hand to my heart.

He hugs me and kisses the top of my head, and I melt a little at the feel of his arms around me and the smell of his cologne. "I didn't mean to scare you." He pulls back, and that delightful furrow in his brow makes traitorous parts of my body excited.

I try to remember that I'm slightly annoyed with him for not being able to telepathically communicate where he's moved all my things. "Do you know where my pink, cap-sleeved, A-line, knee-length dress with the heart-patterned, hot pink belt is?"

He blinks at me. "I don't know what half of those descriptors mean."

"My favorite pink dress. The one that really highlights my cleavage." It might be modest, but I know how to work it. Also, Nate is highly obsessed with my piercings and never passes up a chance to play with them. "Do you have any idea where it might be?"

"Oh! Yes." He steps inside the tiny walk-in closet with me. I move to the doorway so he can turn around because the closet only qualifies as a walk-in when you're under five-seven and not as broad as the doorway. "It's right here." He magically produces it. "I reorganized the closet, and since it's technically autumn as of yesterday, I rotated these dresses to the back and brought your fall clothes to the front. I don't know what your fall favorites are yet, but when I do, I'll cycle them to the front so they're easy for you to find."

He smiles down at me, proud as punch and completely oblivious to the upheaval his organizational skills are creating in my life. But he's so handsome when he smiles like that. And he's just trying to be helpful.

"Can you also help me find the shoes that go with the dress?" I ask, as sweetly as I can.

"Absolutely. Again, I cycled your summer shoes to the back of the closet, because of seasonal changes. Your sandals are all here, arranged according to style, height of heel, and color. If you'd prefer closed toes because it gets cooler at night, and I know you're not a fan of cold toes, your hot pink kitten heels are right here." He helpfully pulls down both pairs.

I bat my lashes. "Can you also help me find my matching bra and panty set?"

"Of course." He leads the way out of the closet, carefully setting the shoeboxes and my dress on the bed before he crosses to the dresser.

Since I've become Nate's girlfriend officially, he's started spending more nights here, which I love, a lot. But it means making room for his things in my tiny apartment, like his suits and changes of clothes. I've freed up a couple of drawers in my dresser for boxers, socks, T-shirts, and loungewear. Nate took it upon himself to reorganize the kitchen cupboards to make room for his snacks and his collection of Star Wars glassware. I should not be surprised that C-3PO is his favorite.

I love Nate. I love his big brain and his thoughtfulness and snuggling with him when he sleeps over. I love the days that start and end with his beautiful face the most. But it has become woefully apparent that my apartment will not be big enough for the two of us long term, even with Nate's remarkable ability to make space where there is none.

He tugs on the knob, revealing brand-new dividers so every single pair of underpants I own now lives in its own little square of space. "All your everyday bras and underwear are in the top drawer." He closes it and opens the next one down. "This is where you'll find your pajamas and sleep sets. I can move these down, if you'd prefer, but they're more-frequent-use items, so I figured it made the most sense." He moves on to the next drawer. "All your athletic wear is in here." He crouches to get to the bottom. "And this is where your special lingerie is." He pulls out my pale pink lace and satin set. "Is this the one you were looking for?"

"That's the one."

He passes me the bra and panties.

I shrug out of my robe. I'm naked underneath.

His nostrils flare. He glances at the clock on the nightstand, then back at me. "Can I make you come before we go?"

Despite the orgasm turning into two and me climbing into his lap to ride his big, beautiful cock, we still manage to make it to the restaurant with two minutes to spare. Double dating with Tristan and Rix is another new favorite thing.

When we arrive, Rix hops up and hugs me, and I squeeze her

back. We settle in the seats across from them, and Nate stretches his arm across the back of my chair at the same time Tristan does this with Rix. Like mirrors of each other, Rix and I lean into our men, both smiling and happy to have the connection.

"Not long now before the official start of the season," I note. "How are you feeling with it being Ryker's time to step up?"

Roman Forrest-Hammer, formerly Hammerstein, the Terror's long-time goalie, hung up his skates at the end of last season, and Kellan Ryker, the backup goalie, is stepping into his shoes.

"Good. Ryker is excited to be in net. He has the skill set, and we have a great defensive line," Tristan replies.

"I'm so glad the Terror picked up Quinn Romero in the trades. It was a good move," Rix says.

"I agree." Tristan nods. "I know it's his first year in the pros, but he's still a seasoned player, and he'll be good for the offensive line with Hollis off the ice, too."

"I love that Roman and Hollis are coaching at the Hockey Academy together." They're already proving to be quite the coaching duo for the boys' team.

"Right? Brody had such a great summer with them." Tristan smiles. "I have a feeling they'll be instrumental in feeding the Terror the best up-and-comers in future seasons."

There's a collective buzz at the table as all of our phones chime with a new message. And then chime again. And again.

"Maybe Shilpa finally had the baby!" Rix and I rush to dig our phones out of our bags.

I pull up the group chat message. "I still can't believe this is really happening."

"Is it about Dred and Connor?" Nate asks.

Rix and I both hold our phones up so the boys can see the engagement party invitation. Last week Dred and Connor announced their engagement. It came out of left field, and there are obviously things none of us know, but Dred has asked us to support her, so that's what we're doing. Or at least trying.

"I still don't understand what's going on there," Tristan mutters.

"I don't think any of us do," I reply. "Maybe they hooked up at your wedding in secret and that got the ball rolling?" We were all exceptionally preoccupied with other things.

"I mean...I guess it's possible," Rix muses.

We've had countless hypothetical conversations about this. None of them quite seem plausible. "How's Flip handling this?"

Nate fingers an errant pink curl. "I mean, obviously he's not the happiest about it—especially since Dred won't tell him why she's doing this—but he's trying to be a good friend."

"Do you think it would help if Flip knew all the things Connor did behind the scenes at your wedding?" I ask softly.

"Connor made it clear he didn't want anyone to know he was directly involved," Tristan replies. "And I want to honor that, because he saved us more than once."

We leave the Dred and Connor situation alone and Tristan talks about how excited he is to test out Nate's most recent prototype. Nate thinks this could be the one. It feels amazing to be able to spend time with my best friend and my boyfriend.

Rix and Tristan go over to see Flip after dinner, and Nate and I head back to my place.

"This season might be a tough one," Nate says as we enter the apartment, toeing off our shoes at the door.

"It might." I wrap my arms around his waist. "But we'll all be here to support them, however they need us."

"It's a pretty incredible family we've inherited with this group of friends, isn't it?" Nate lifts me onto the counter and steps between my legs.

"It really is."

"I wonder how soon the wedding will be," he muses.

"That's a good question. It's been all of a week, and the engagement party is already happening."

He pulls down the zipper on my dress. "I wonder who will end up together at the next wedding?"

"I already have some ideas." I wrap my arms and legs around him. "Take me to bed and make me yours."

"Your wish is my command."

EPILOGUE
NATE

O ne week later

"You look handsome." Essie presses her palms to my chest and smiles up at me. She's wearing a pale pink wrap dress and a hot pink wrap, accented with a silver purse and matching shoes. Her long, dark hair hangs over her shoulders in artful waves. Her makeup is subtle, but her dark eyes pop, and her lips are glossy and tempting, as usual.

"You're beautiful." I take her hand and kiss her knuckles.

"What's that look?"

"What look?" I bite back a smile.

"You're wearing your devious face." Her eyes light up. "Like you have a secret you're dying to tell."

I lean in, brushing my lips across her cheek until I reach her ear. "I bought you something special for tonight."

While Essie and Rix were getting their hair done this morning, I ran out to pick up a few last-minute items for Dred and Connor's engagement party. And I made a stop at Essie's favorite lingerie store, as well as the jeweler.

Last week my skate was put into production for a short run, and the Terror will be using them during practice. It's pretty freaking unreal to be at this point so soon, and definitely something to celebrate.

Essie quirks an eyebrow. "What kind of something special?"

"It's pretty, and lacy, and princessy," I hint.

"Oh my gosh!" She claps. "Did you get me the sleep set I sent you a picture of last week?"

One of Essie's favorite new pastimes is sending me pictures of princess-inspired lingerie, followed by detailed scenes we could act out while wearing it. Sex with Essie is always an adventure, and I'm more than happy to play out these fantasies with her.

"You'll have to wait until we're home to find out."

"Can't I have a little peek before we leave?"

Our phones buzz.

"Rix and Tristan are waiting for us."

Essie's bottom lip juts out.

I suck on it. "Don't worry, sweetness. I'll make up for it when I steal you away later tonight."

She sighs. "Fine. I guess I can wait." She grabs her purse, and I tuck Dred and Connor's gift under my arm. We leave the apartment and head down to the lobby.

I smile as I discreetly pat the inside pocket of my suit jacket. Essie's engagement ring is currently nestled against my heart. We're still in the early days yet, but she's it for me, and I want to be ready when the time is right. Which will probably be sooner than later.

All our friends are either getting engaged, planning weddings, or having babies. I want it all with Essie—the celebrations, walking down the aisle with her, a family. Essie's heart is the most beautiful thing about her, and together, with the support of our families and friends, we'll have a lifetime full of love.

We're looking at getting an apartment together in Flip's building so we're not tripping over each other. It's a two-bedroom, with a walk-in closet that will fit all her clothes. Plus, there's a second, small bedroom that we can turn into an office.

We pile into the back of Rix's SUV with Flip, who looks put together, but not all that enthused. "Let's get this over with," he grumbles.

"Where's your gift?" Rix asks.

He pats his breast pocket. "In here."

Rix narrows her eyes at him. "What is it?"

"A gift certificate for an excellent divorce attorney."

Tristan frowns. "Please tell me you're not serious."

"He specializes in getting around prenups." Flip looks terribly serious.

Rix shoots him a look. "Don't be a dick!"

"I'm kidding. Mostly." Flip rolls his eyes. "I got them a one-night stay at a winery in Niagara. Dred is obsessed with the place, and they have this suite with a library."

"Oh." Rix's eyebrows rise. "That was nice of you."

"I might not like Grace, and I might not like that he's engaged to one of my best friends, but I care about Dred, and I want her to be happy. If this dickbag makes her happy, I'll support her."

"Can you avoid referring to him as a dickbag for the rest of the day?" Essie asks.

"I guess. Yeah."

"I'm kind of excited to see his parents' house," Rix says.

They have a home in one of the most affluent neighborhoods in Toronto. Apparently, they also have homes in several states, as well as a summer home in Bala. It's no secret Connor comes from a very wealthy family. It's also no secret that he's not the biggest fan of his family, and that his family aren't the biggest fans of him—other than his grandmother.

"I'm fascinated to meet his family," Essie says. "The guy comes from old money, yet he's covered in tattoos and plays professional hockey. He's such a contradiction."

"He better not fuck Dred over," Flip mutters.

Essie and I have done our fair share of brainstorming about the whole thing. We know Connor isn't all bad, but Flip hasn't seen that side of him. And I'm not about to spill his secrets, considering the way he saved me and my brothers from what would have been a nightmare situation at Tristan's wedding.

We arrive at the house at the same time as some of Tristan and Flip's teammates. Lavender and Kodiak flew in from New York to be here, and Quinn Romero, the newest addition to the Terror and their long-time family friend, is with them.

Essie's sister, Cammie, and her boyfriend, Chase, as well as her best friends, Fee and Tally, approach us. Flip does a double take as Tally rushes up and gives him a quick hug before moving on to Rix. Her long, blonde hair is pinned at the sides, revealing a ladder of hoops in her right ear. Her dress is deep blue, with a slit that reveals her dancer's legs. The girls form a circle and comment on how much they love each other's dresses.

Flip rubs the back of his neck. "I bet my sister helped Tally pick that dress."

"If she was looking to get noticed, it's working," I murmur.

"What's that supposed to mean?"

I pat him on the shoulder. "You'll figure it out eventually."

Dallas inserts himself between us. "This is going to be one hell of an engagement party."

I laugh as I take in his suit. As usual, he's wearing plaid, but his tie has a sexy-peach pattern on it. "You put the *ass* in classy, Bright."

"I know." He winks. "Let's do this."

Essie slips her arm through mine as we walk up the winding driveway to the massive, sprawling, modern mansion. We're greeted by a butler as we enter the foyer and are immediately handed glasses of champagne.

Everything is white, on white, on white.

"This is like a snow palace." Essie drops her voice to a whisper. "I wonder if they have a ballroom."

"I bet they do." It seems logical in a house this big.

Rix and the girls call for Essie to join them. They now have a very nervous-looking Dred with them. "I'll find you later." Essie kisses me on the cheek and flits off.

My brother calls me over to say hello to Connor and meet his grandmother. He's dressed in a teal suit, like he's representing his team, not hosting his engagement party. His grandmother is wearing a matching teal sequin dress and looks like the picture of old money.

She smiles up at Tristan. "You must be my grandson's teammate."

Tristan takes her tiny hand in his. "I am. It's nice to meet you. You must be excited about the engagement."

"I couldn't be more thrilled. Dred is smart as a whip. My grandson needs someone like her to keep him in line."

"You're quite the matchmaker, Meems," Connor says with a wry smile.

"Matchmaker?" Tristan asks.

"Connor hasn't told you the story?" She *tsks*. "Every week I go to the public library and take out two new books, and Dred always helps me pick them. But a while ago I wasn't feeling well and couldn't get to the library, so I sent Connor."

Connor stuffs his hand in his pocket. "I'd met Mildred plenty of times, though, Meems. We both attend Callie's hockey games."

"That may be true, but that trip to the library is what made her see the you *I* see." She pats his cheek, and then smiles at us. "Thank you for being here. I know Connor appreciates it." She wraps her arm around Connor, and he bends to give her his ear.

"Enjoy the party," he tells us. "Thanks for coming." He winks and guides her away.

I look at my brother. "That was interesting."

"Yeah, it was."

An hour into the party, Essie sidles up beside me. "Come with me."

"Everything okay?"

"Everything is great. I just need you for a minute." She guides me out of the room and down the hall, glancing over her shoulder before she pushes her way through an ornately carved set of double doors. "Check this out."

"Oh wow." We're standing in a stunning ballroom, but all I can see is the wonder on her face. "Imagine dancing in here."

"We don't have to imagine; we can do that right now." I pull my phone out, cue up our favorite song, and hold my hand out to her.

Her smile widens, and she slips her fingers into mine, letting me pull her close. We move around the room, lost in each other and the music. I can see our life together unfolding a little more every day. And here, in this room that speaks of fairy tales and romance, I can envision her dressed in a wedding gown—not white, but the palest blush pink, satin and lace, her dark hair coiled on top of her head, smiling at me exactly the way she is now. And I want that future, the one full of possibilities and the kind of love that erases all my fears and replaces them with hope.

I stroke her cheek and brush my lips over hers. "Thank you for sharing your light with me."

She presses her hand to my cheek, her smile soft and warm like sunshine. "Thank you for trusting me with your heart. I promise I'll always keep it safe."

One day, in the not-too-distant future, I'll ask her to be my wife, and we can start our own forever.

Need more Nate and Essie? Subscribe to my newsletter for instant access to an exclusive bonus scene:

IF YOU CLAIM ME
SNEAK PEEK
CONNOR

"I asked you a fucking question, Grace." Flip pushes into my personal space, his nose an inch from mine. "What are you doing with Dred?"

"That's my business, not yours." I goad him, poking the bear, and hope he takes a swing. I deserve a split lip and black eye for what I've just done to his best friend.

The door behind me opens.

"For fuck's sake." Mildred sighs and tries to push her way between us. She gives me a look that reeks of disappointment. "Let Connor go, Flip."

I arch a brow. "Yes, Flip, let me go."

"You're not helping," Mildred snaps.

"I'm not trying to."

Her nails scratch my skin as she pries his hand from my collar.

"What is this asshole doing in your apartment, Dred?" Flip's anger is usurped by another emotion—maybe betrayal, or hurt.

For a moment I regret pushing his buttons. Mildred's already stuck with me for the foreseeable future. Straining the relationships that are important to her, my fiancée, is not in my best interest. I need her happy and compliant, not angry and defensive.

Flip grabs her hand, eyes wide with shock and horror. "What the fuck?"

I wish I could revel in the glee of knocking him off-kilter, but he's touching what's mine and raising his voice, and I won't have it.

I settle a palm on Mildred's shoulder. I've recently discovered that it's startlingly soothing to touch her. "Stop yelling at my fiancée," I warn through gritted teeth.

"Just throw gasoline on the fire, why don't you?" Mildred mutters with an eye roll.

Preorder Dred and Connor's standalone marriage of convenience hockey romance:

ABOUT THE AUTHOR HELENA HUNTING

NYT and USA Today bestselling author, Helena Hunting lives on the outskirts of Toronto with her amazing family and her adorable kitty, who thinks the best place to sleep is her keyboard. Helena writes everything from emotional contemporary romance to romantic comedies that will have you laughing until you cry. If you're looking for a tearjerker, you can find her angsty side under H. Hunting.

OTHER TITLES BY HELENA HUNTING

ALL IN SERIES

A Lie for a Lie

A Favor for a Favor

A Secret for a Secret

A Kiss for a Kiss

LIES, HEARTS & TRUTHS SERIES

Little Lies

Bitter Sweet Heart

Shattered Truths

SHACKING UP SERIES

Shacking Up

Getting Down (Novella)

Hooking Up

I Flipping Love You

Making Up

Handle with Care

SPARK SISTERS SERIES

When Sparks Fly

Starry-Eyed Love

Make A Wish

LAKESIDE SERIES

Love Next Door

Love on the Lake

THE CLIPPED WINGS SERIES

Cupcakes and Ink

Clipped Wings

Between the Cracks

Inked Armor

Cracks in the Armor

Fractures in Ink

STANDALONE NOVELS

The Librarian Principle

Felony Ever After

Before You Ghost (with Debra Anastasia)

FOREVER ROMANCE STANDALONES

The Good Luck Charm

Meet Cute

Kiss my Cupcake

A Love Catastrophe